Waking the Tiger

Waking the Tiger

A Novel of Sri Lanka

Leonard Feinberg

This is a work of fiction. All characters and events portrayed in this book are either products of the author's imagination or are used fictitiously.

No part of this book may be reproduced in any form or by any electronic means, including information storage and retrieval systems, without the written permission from the copyright holders, except for brief passages quoted in reviews.

Waking the Tiger
A Novel of Sri Lanka
by
Leonard Feinberg

Many of the illustrations were taken from early twentieth century postcards in the publisher's collection.

Content © 2005 by Leonard Feinberg
Book Design © 2005 by Pilgrims Process, Inc.
ISBN:0-9749597-3-1
Library of Congress Control Number:
2005900727
Printed in the United States of America

0 9 8 7 6 5 4 3 2 1

Typeset in Tolkein (various sizes), Century Gothic (various sizes), and Adobe Jenson Pro (11 pt) using Adobe InDesign CS

To Elyn and Gary

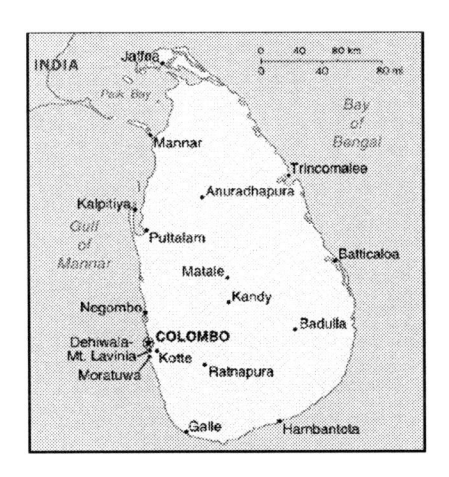

Preface

Professor Leonard Feinberg, who is now Distinguished Professor Emeritus at Iowa State University, was a Fulbright lecturer in American Literature at the University of Ceylon in 1957-58. This novel is loosely based on Feinberg's experiences during that academic year, a time when Ceylon's idyllic image was relatively intact—at least to outsiders.

Ceylon, also known as Serendip (the word from which "serendipity" was derived) by Arab traders, was once referred to as the "Pearl of the Orient." It is a tear-drop-shaped tropical island, rich in gems, rubber, spices, and tea, situated just below India in the Indian Ocean.

A number of ethnic groups have lived on the island for centuries, if not millennia. The Veddahs or Wanniya-laeto ('forest-dwellers'), as they call themselves, preserve a direct line of descent from the island's original Neolithic community dating from at least 16,000 BCE (Before Current Era). The Sinhalese probably came from northern India during the sixth century BCE. Buddhism arrived in the mid-third century BCE and spread rapidly. Classical Sinhalese civilization developed from 200 BCE – 1200 CE, complete with major cities, aristocracies, and large irrigation projects. Tamils from south India began arriving on the island perhaps as early as 1000 CE, and a Tamil kingdom was established in the north in the thirteenth or fourteenth century. Sometimes Tamil and Sinhalese kingdoms fought; at other times they lived peacefully together.

Too attractive to be left alone for long once it was discovered by European seagoing powers, Ceylon was colonized by the Portuguese, who introduced Catholicism, in 1505. The Dutch supplanted them in 1658. The British took over from the Dutch in 1796 and, in 1815, defeated the last native ruler, the king of Kandy, turning Ceylon into a Crown Colony. At that time, Ceylon's population included Sinhalese, Tamils, Burghers (Dutch descendents), and Moors, with their associated Buddhist, Hindu, Christian, and Muslim religions—as well as various castes and ethnicities. In 2004, the island had a population of approximately 19,000,000 people. Sinhalese represented 74%; Tamils 18%; Moors 7%; and Burghers, Malays, and Veddahs 1% of the population.

Ceylon negotiated its independence from Great Britain in 1947, and in 1948 it became an independent nation. Beginning that same year, several pieces of legislation essentially disenfranchised the Tamil minority, and cleavage along ethnic lines—including between Sri Lankan Tamils and Indian Tamils (brought in by the British in the nineteenth century)—became obvious.

The 1956 election was a turning point in a social revolution. The head of the winning party, S.W.R.D. Bandaranaike, who had been educated at Oxford, defended "beleaguered" Sinhalese culture and rejected Western and Christian elements, embraced Buddhism and adopted native garb. During his successful campaign, he announced that Sinhala would be the official language and that Tamil and English were cultural imports. The "Sinhala-only act" restricted many government jobs to Sinhala speakers and changed university admissions policies, greatly reducing the number of Tamils getting higher education. (The Sinhalese argued that Tamils had received preferential treatment under British rule and were disproportionately represented in civil service, medicine, and law.) In 1958 the island exploded in ethnic violence. The following year, a Buddhist extremist assassinated Prime Minister Bandaranaike.

The years that followed were characterized by economic challenges, political instability, social unrest, deteriorating Sinhalese/Tamil/Christian relationships, Maoist uprisings, and the formation in 1972 of the Tamil Tigers, a powerful guerilla organization. That same year, the country became a republic and changed its name to Sri Lanka. Buddhism was made the state's primary religion.

During 1977, communal rioting again engulfed the island, leading to ever-deeper divisions. Casualties were many. More communal riots followed in 1983. Violence has continued sporadically ever since, causing a heavy toll to the country's economy, tourism, and social stability. By 1985 there were as many as 50,000 displaced Tamil refugees in Sri Lanka and 100,000 Tamils who had fled or been exiled to India. A cease-fire was brokered by Norway in 2001 and renewed in 2002, but it has not always held. In 2003, the peace process appeared to have stalled, and there were fears it might collapse completely.

On December 26, 2004, parts of the island were devastated by the horrific tsunamis that swept across Southeast Asia in the aftermath of an underwater earthquake centered off the western coast of Sumatra. Some observers are hopeful that the cooperative humanitarian work being done by Tamils and Sinhalese may lead to a new era of peaceful coexistence.

—The Publisher

One

I met Anthony Moss by sheer chance at the foot of Adam's Peak. A large footprint is imbedded in stone on top of Adam's Peak, seven thousand feet above sea level. A billion people in the Orient think that this footprint is holy, and thousands of them make the climb every year. It was a hot July night and our party was just about to start the climb when Piodasa ran up to me, his wild black hair blowing and his widely spaced teeth gleaming with foolish amiability, and said, "Master, American man just come to make climb. Maybe you ask him join you?"

After consulting with my friends I agreed, and Piodasa ran off. He returned a few minutes later with Moss. In the light of the full moon the angles of Moss's narrow face and slim body were accentuated, and he seemed both older and taller than he actually was. There was a reticent dignity about him, and also a kind of eagerness that struck me as somewhat naïve for a man in his middle twenties. His brown hair was so thick that his crew cut seemed longer than the typical American haircut, and his gray eyes were friendly and forthright. I was surprised by the melodious quality of his voice, almost as if he were a professional singer trying to restrain his power, and I looked carefully at his broad nose, high cheekbones, and wide mouth.

I introduced him to my friends and he shook hands politely with five of them, and then paused momentarily when the swami, instead of putting out his hand, pressed his palms together in front of his chest in a gesture called *namaskar*. It must have been a little startling for Moss, even in the heart of Ceylon, to meet a turbaned, blond-bearded, barefoot Englishman in a white sarong. He recovered quickly, pressed his own palms in front of his chest, and thanked us for inviting him to join our party. We turned to the mountain.

After we had climbed a few hundred feet the road narrowed, people began walking two by two, and Moss became my companion, immediately behind the swami and Ramanathan. Piodasa walked alone behind us, carrying a large basket on his head. There were more than a thousand pilgrims on the road that night, old and young, men and women, all except the saffron-robed monks dressed in white, some carrying children, others bearing packages on their heads. A few of the men carried burning torches; George Burton had a flashlight. Except for the narrow footpath, everything around us was thick jungle, forest untouched by man for thousands of years. Ordinarily, I suppose, the jungle was quiet. But tonight the pilgrims were making noises that carried into the jungle, and as we walked I could identify the cry of the leopard, the call of the sambhur deer, the chattering of monkeys, and at long intervals the trumpeting of elephants. I heard the sounds and distinguished among them, but my attention was centered on avoiding the boulders and gnarled roots that blocked the road.

When the road cleared a little Moss asked what I was doing in Ceylon. I told him I was teaching philosophy at the university. He nodded, then said quietly, "Who is the swami?"

It wasn't an easy question to answer. I remembered my own speculations when, months before, I had met the tall Englishman with the massive head, the carefully trimmed beard, the small brown mole on his left temple. I remembered that his nose had seemed incongruously thin for so wide a face, and that his pale blue eyes never showed the slightest emotion. "The swami calls himself Shantinaha," I told Moss. "He was an officer in the British army during the war, stationed in Ceylon. After the war he left the service and became a swami. He has a hermitage somewhere in the jungle, I'm told. I've never seen it."

"Isn't it unusual for a Westerner to live like that?" Moss asked.

"Unusual," I said, "but not unique. There is a German swami who has lived in Ceylon for twenty-five years. Near him lives a young nobleman who has renounced one of the oldest and wealthiest titles in England. Another former military man, a captain in British intelligence, lived as a Buddhist monk here for fifteen years. He died last month."

We walked quietly for a while, and then Moss said, "And Mr. Ramanathan, the elderly man in Indian attire? I liked him immediately."

"Your instinct was right," I said. "Ramanathan is one of the most respected men on the island. He has held high posts in the government. He's a Hindu, a Tamil, you know—Ramanathan is a typical Tamil name. The Tamils are a minority in Ceylon, though there are thirty million of them in India. His family is quite distinguished too. They've endowed schools and temples all over Ceylon, and his father was an organizer of Ceylon's independence movement. Ramanathan's son had been a very promising young lawyer before he died."

At that moment Ramanathan turned to smile pleasantly at us, and Moss stared at his round brown face, the halo of white hair around his bald pate, the sad black eyes, and the reassuringly serene expression. When he had turned back, Moss said, "How about the American couple?"

I said something noncommittal about George Burton. I didn't really feel that I knew him well, although I had seen a good deal of him during the past year. He was the Ceylon representative of a large American electronics firm, and he seemed in most ways a bright young business executive, always neatly groomed, fashionably dressed, and courteous to his business associates. But there was a moodiness about his hawk-like face and a tenseness in his tall, thin body. He often borrowed poetry and philosophy from my library, and I sometimes caught him staring out into space, oblivious to everyone around him. During the year I had known him I noticed that he often became very enthusiastic over people when he first met them, then quickly lost interest and made scathing remarks about them.

I thought I understood his wife better. Marian was a chubby little woman, always friendly and cordial. She was past thirty, two or three years older than George, and she had given up her job as editor of an American women's magazine to get married and come out to the Orient with him. She was very sensitive to his moods and tried continually, sometimes desperately, to please him. Her thick lips had parted sensually when George greeted Moss warmly, and she beamed when Moss shook her hand. "You must come see us in Colombo," she said.

"And the other couple?" Moss asked.

The Gunesenas, good Buddhists and polite, had greeted Moss in both Oriental and Western fashion. First they pressed their palms together in front of their chests, and then they shook hands. "Lakshman is one of the kindest people I know," I told Moss. "He not only professes Buddhism, he lives it. His family is quite influential, and he manages their department store in Kandy. Chitra and he are my best friends."

"Chitra's a lovely little thing, isn't she?" Moss said.

I agreed. Everyone who met Chitra was captivated by this doll-like creature with olive skin and delicate features. Tonight she was wearing an expensive but simple-looking white sari, emerald earrings, a blue sapphire ring, and thick gold bracelets. When Moss had been introduced to her she chirped merrily and agreed with everything he said. I knew that didn't mean much because Chitra tended to agree with whatever anyone around her said. She disliked controversy, and she liked cheerfulness and pretty clothes and good food and parties. Her parents were wealthy; there had been many suitors for her hand; and she had always had more freedom than most Ceylonese women enjoyed. Yet she helped Lakshman enthusiastically and efficiently in his work with the orphans of Kandy. Usually they wore Western clothes, but tonight, like everyone except the Americans in our group, they were barefoot, and Lakshman wore a white sarong.

A little after midnight we reached a plateau from which we could see the cone-shaped peak, the top of the mountain we were climbing. Shantinaha dropped back and accompanied us. He pointed to the side of the road. "There is a famous pool here. Sita, the beautiful wife of Rama, is supposed to have bathed here."

"I've just been in Ceylon a few days," Moss said, "and I know very little about the mountain. What was Sita doing here?"

He asked the question seriously and Shantinaha, after a quick glance, answered courteously. "The Ramayana is the great epic of ancient India. According to it, King Ravanna of Ceylon kidnapped the wife of the god Rama in India and brought her here in a flying machine, anticipating the actual invention of the airplane by several thousand years. Then Rama, aided by an army of monkeys and bears, came to save Sita. The monkeys built a bridge from India to Ceylon—the islands under water now are supposed to be the remains of that bridge. Rama flew here from India and landed on top of this mountain. Hindus believe that the footprint in the rock is Rama's. Don't you, Ramanathan?"

Ramanathan turned his head. "Yes," he said pleasantly. "We do. We don't find it any harder to believe that than Christians do who believe in the miracles of the Old Testament—and the New."

Shantinaha smiled. The moonlight dramatized his turban, beard, and features, and he seemed massive. "Of course. So for Hindus the mountain is holy on account of Rama. The bears helped him fight Ravanna's soldiers and rescue Sita."

There was a rumble from behind us. "Lots leeches here," Piodasa said. "Master be careful."

Shantinaha nodded. "He is right. It's quite damp here near the pool, and there are many leeches. If you aren't careful they'll attach themselves to your flesh and suck blood. Rather a nuisance."

"I have limes," Piodasa said proudly. "I squeeze lime, leech go away."

Shantinaha nodded again. "Yes. That's a good way to make leeches let go. The only other way, for most people, is to burn them off."

Moss looked at him quizzically. "For most people, you say. Does that mean you know other ways?"

Shantinaha smiled. "We who live in the jungle learn a few tricks. But we were talking about the footprint. Muslims believe it is Adam's. When Adam had committed his well-publicized indiscretions in the Garden of Eden, God let him choose any place on earth to live. Naturally, he chose Ceylon. But first he had to atone for his sin by standing on one foot for a thousand years. This is the mountaintop he stood on, the Muslims say, and that's how the footprint was made. After that he went to the Middle East, where Eve had been keeping house in the interim, and brought her back here to live."

"I can understand his choice," Moss said. "This country is so beautiful, I can see why of all the places in the world one might prefer Ceylon."

Ramanathan looked back. "There is no lovelier place in the world than this country," he said earnestly.

We walked on, then Shantinaha said, "Even the Chinese have a theory about this footprint. One of their professors wrote a book claiming that this is the footprint of the first man in the world. But the Chinese call him Pawn-Koo, not Adam. Some anthropologists think Ceylon is the first land where men lived."

As we climbed, the air grew cooler. We came to a gorge and Shantinaha carefully led us along the path, hugging the mountainside. "This is a dangerous place," he said. "There is a legend that many years ago a girl fell here, and her spirit now lives down below. If a man shouts here, the echo is supposed to come back in her voice, not his. But tonight would hardly be an appropriate time to test that legend."

The climb became more difficult now, the road steeper and overgrown in places with underbrush. When we were more at ease on the slope, Shantinaha resumed his commentary. "Christians also wanted to get in on the act. Some Eastern Christians believe the footprint is St. Thomas the Doubter's. St. Thomas is popular in India."

We had grown accustomed to the chattering of monkeys but suddenly a leopard cried and everyone was still. Then an elephant trumpeted, far away, and the leopard was quiet, and we walked on.

"They out there," Piodasa said softly.

"The elephants?" Moss asked.

Piodasa grumbled. "The Old Ones. The Gray Ones. They out there."

Shantinaha explained that Piodasa was avoiding a direct reference to the elephants because, like many natives, he was afraid to name animals that could be particularly dangerous. Piodasa agreed and wiped his forehead with his sleeve. "Lord Buddha make footprint," he said. "When he make third visit to Ceylon, just before he go to Nirvana. Lord Buddha fly here to meet King of Nagas, and he land on this mountaintop."

Everyone paused to rest a while. We Americans took off our shoes and socks and shook them out. Then we put them back on and resumed the climb. Two hours later, just before dawn, we reached the top. We took off our shoes and waited.

When the sun came up we marveled at the view. In a general way, from what I had read and people had told me, I knew what to expect. And yet I was genuinely awed by what I saw. Marian said that for the first time she felt Ceylon was not just beautiful but sublime. It really looked, from the tiny summit of the mountain, as if we had reached the end of the world. The land around us fell away sharply and dissolved, and the sea fifty miles away seemed interminable and boundless. There was no land between the southern coast of Ceylon and the Antarctic, thousands of miles away. The feeling of minuteness, the sense of imminent danger, was more intense than in an airplane, for the summit seemed smaller than a plane, more like a scaffolding, and the mountain sloped so precipitously on the opposite side that it was hard to believe men had used that route.

But Shantinaha told us that they had, holding on to enormous iron chains built centuries ago into the mountain rock. Hundreds of people in the past, including entire families, had been caught by mountain winds and blown out into space, suspended over the gorge until their grasp weakened, and then tumbled thousands of feet to the crags and treetops below. Even now, Shantinaha said, some hermits make the climb by way of the rungs, for they achieve greater merit by that dangerous performance. "There is a legend," Shantinaha said dryly, "that the chains were installed by Alexander the Great. An impressive achievement, in view of the fact that Alexander never came to Ceylon."

An extraordinary phenomenon now took place—the Shadow of the Peak. We saw it, but we could not understand it. A giant cone of darkness reached into the sky, not resting upon the forest below as one's eyes expected, not resting on anything, but standing straight up and down, a slender column pointing toward the sky.

We stood for a long time without making a sound. Then Moss spoke softly. "I've seen the Alps," he said, "and the Himalayas and the Rockies. They are grander, more majestic. But this is different from anything I have ever experienced. It's not like being on top of the world. It's more like hanging out of a gondola above the world."

The ringing of a brass bell in the shrine on the summit broke the silence. Shantinaha explained. "Pilgrims who climb up here are permitted to ring the bell once for each climb." We stood in line, waiting to see the footprint and then to ring the bell. Most of the people rang it once, but one old man rang it twelve times, and another, a thin little woman, rang it nine times. She looked very tired.

The holy spot was a shallow indentation in the rock, roughly in the shape of a human footprint but almost five feet long. I looked at it and moved on. Moss stared raptly for a long time. Ramanathan, Piodasa, and the Gunesenas knelt, pressed their palms together high in front of their faces, and closed their eyes for a long moment. Then each of us rang the bell once and stepped aside for the pilgrims. Shantinaha and Lakshman rang the bell three times.

The forest grew almost up to the peak, and for many miles in the distance its thick rough growth covered the country in an impenetrable tangle. Moss was looking at it thoughtfully.

"Does anyone live out there?" he asked.

"Don't know," Piodasa said quickly. "Nobody know. This place mysterious. People say bad spirits live there. Nobody go there."

Moss was still looking. "There might be a whole civilization there," he said thoughtfully. "It's completely isolated from everyone."

Shantinaha shook his head. "No," he said. "Only Veddas live there, aborigines who were on the island long before the Sinhalese came three thousand years ago. There are only a few hundred Veddas left now. What you call 'civilization' has almost obliterated them."

As we stood talking, pilgrims kept arriving, looking at the footprint, ringing the bell, and starting the climb down. Moss looked at them admiringly. "Beautiful people," he said.

I looked at the men and women near us. Except for the old, their complexions were clear and smooth. They ranged from what might be called an attractive olive, through bronze, to black. Their features were sharp and delicate, thinner than were our Caucasian features. And they moved gracefully, easily, the women swinging their arms casually as they carried bundles on their heads.

"Beautiful people in a beautiful country," Moss said. I nodded. Shantinaha said nothing.

By now the summit was filling with pilgrims, all eager to see the footprint that Adam, or Buddha, or Rama, or somebody with a gigantic foot had made. We gathered our party together and reluctantly started down the mountainside. An eagle screamed suddenly overhead and dived into the treetops. Along the roadside begonias and pink orchids, ferns, hibiscus, and rhododendrons glorified the landscape. Thousands of brightly colored butterflies filled the air. Ramanathan pointed to them.

"They come here every year to die," he said. "Millions of them. Aren't they beautiful?" He looked at Moss and me and said softly, "They don't really die, you know. Nobody really dies."

When we reached a wide plateau along the roadside, we stopped to eat. Piodasa unloaded the basket he had been carrying and served us rice and curry on large plantain leaves.

"Did you bring the salt and pepper shakers?" I asked him.

Piodasa giggled and brought out the shakers. I told Moss that the first time I had told Piodasa to fill the peppershaker, he had spent a long afternoon trying to get the pepper in through the little holes on top. He explained that he didn't understand how American shakers were supposed to be filled, but my neighbors just laughed and added the incident to their collection of Piodasa's stupidities. They had a large collection.

Now Piodasa spilled some rice on George's trousers and George angrily shoved him away. Piodasa apologized and tried to wipe the spot with his hand, but he only made it worse, until Ramanathan wet his handkerchief in the pool and handed it to George.

"A beautiful view," Lakshman said. "This is the third time I've been here, and it's as impressive as ever."

Chitra nodded. She was eating rice and curry with her fingers, making little lumps of food between her thumb and forefinger and flipping them deftly into her mouth. Her sari was tucked neatly between her legs, and her feet were bruised. But she had never seemed so much at ease during the year I had known her. A dog came by, sniffing at the food, and Piodasa kicked it hard in the stomach. A minute later Ramanathan unobtrusively walked a few steps away and put some of his own rice on the ground for the dog to eat. Moss noticed it too and whispered, when Ramanathan returned, "That was kind."

Ramanathan's eyes were serene. "There is enough sadness in the world," he said softly.

As we ate we watched the pilgrims traveling along the road. Suddenly a man heading up the hill looked at us, stopped, and said something to his companions. Four people turned off the road and approached us, smiling and waving. The European couple was the most dapper of the persons on the mountain. The tall man was wearing a tie, a stiffly starched shirt with gold cuff links, and an elegant, broad-lapelled English suit. A handkerchief showed slightly from his breast pocket, and his wide reddish mustache was perfectly combed and smoothly waxed. The woman with him, almost a foot shorter than he was, also had a glazed look more suitable for London than a Ceylon mountainside. Like him she was in her middle thirties, but her exquisitely groomed ash-blond hair, her classical features and large slate gray eyes, her quiet turquoise dress made her seem, at first, considerably younger. There was a large white scar on her neck, just below and to the left of her chin. She walked demurely and said affectedly to Shantinaha, "Jack dear. How lovely to see you."

Shantinaha waved amiably, without rising. "How are you, Mavis? And you, Roger?" He turned to us. "This is Mr. And Mrs. Chilton. He's a Pooh-Bah for the British oil interests here. Aren't you, Roger?"

Chilton smiled glacially as he shook hands with us. His mannerisms were so reserved that he looked like a caricature of an Oxonian dandy. But although he remained aloof, his handshake was strong and his glance shrewd and observant. His wife murmured to him, then she introduced the young couple with them.

"This is Siri Banda," he said, putting his arm around the stocky, black-skinned young man in a shirt and white trousers. Banda nodded sullenly.

"And Ranjini Jayaratrie," Chilton said. The young woman was strikingly beautiful, and I heard Moss draw in his breath. She was tall for a Sinhalese, almost five feet six, and her long black hair fell luxuriantly on her shoulders. Her bronze skin, small and delicate nose, full red mouth and straight white teeth were perfect, and she sparkled with vivacity. As she shook hands with me I noticed that her meticulously manicured fingernails were extraordinarily long. She looked at Moss a long time, playfully provocative, as he held her hand almost touching the full bold breast bulging out of her silver-streaked sari. After he let her hand go, she crossed her arms gracefully across her chest.

As we stood talking, George pointed suddenly to the road. A dozen young women in white blouses and skirts were walking together down the mountain.

"Prostitutes," he said. "Professionals. But on this journey they'll have nothing to do with anyone. And no one will molest them. The mountain is holy."

I looked at the faces around me. Chilton and George were smiling appraisingly. Ramanathan and Lakshman looked sad. Chitra was pouting. Mrs. Chilton frowned. Ranjini stared avidly, unconsciously wetting her lips with her tongue. Moss was looking at Ranjini. And Marian Black showed no expression at all.

The young women disappeared around the mountain bend, and our visitors said goodbye and went back to the road. Banda helped Mrs. Chilton get over a boulder, then Chilton politely held Ranjini's hand as she stepped over. Soon they were swallowed up in the stream of white-robed pilgrims.

"No racial discrimination there," Lakshman said. "It's wonderful to see how well those two couples get along."

"Not really," George said, while Piodasa cleared up and we got ready to go. "Siri Banda's been sleeping with Mavis Chilton for months. Everybody in the foreign colony knows it."

Moss shook his head. "I could have sworn Mrs. Chilton has an American accent—southern American."

George lit a cigarette for Marian, then for himself. "She was born in Mississippi and brought up there. Chilton met her when he was in America on business ten years ago."

Moss absent-mindedly took a cigarette out of a gold case and lit it. "And is Ranjini—"

"No," George said. "There's nothing between her and Chilton as far as I know. She's just along on the trip for window-dressing."

We were walking down the road now, staying to the left side as local custom demanded. "What's Ranjini's background?" Moss asked after a while.

Marian Burton gave him a side-glance. "Among other things, she was the mistress of a previous prime minister. He had trouble getting rid of her, so he married her off to a bright young protégé of his. He gave them a large dowry, and he threw a lot of government business their way, and they both understood exactly what the arrangement was. After the next government was voted in, Ranjini and her husband separated, both rich and both satisfied. She enjoys life, Ranjini does."

Moss nodded thoughtfully. "She certainly looks as if she does."

We were now approaching the narrow place on the road near the gorge and again Shantinaha shepherded us close to the mountainside. Coming up the mountain towards us was a round-faced, beak-nosed Buddhist monk in a saffron robe. He walked slowly, apparently engrossed in his thoughts and totally impervious to the rock-strewn road beneath his feet. As he approached us he became aware of our presence and veered absent-mindedly along the path to give us more room. His foot slipped and suddenly, silently, he lost his balance and fell across the edge. Only his hands were there now, gripping tightly the hard dry earth.

We all stood petrified, except Ramanathan. He quickly jumped across the road, sprawled on his stomach, and grasped the fingers of the monk. The earth along the edge crumbed and only the powerful hands of Ramanathan now held the man. Ramanathan tensed his muscles agonizingly but his body began to slide slowly toward the edge. I grabbed his legs and held them while Lakshman and Moss crawled to the ledge and began pulling the monk up. With excruciating slowness they managed to raise the man high enough to shift his weight onto the road. Then he swung his legs over the edge and we all lay, exhausted and panting, on the dry rocky ground.

When I looked up I saw Shantinaha standing at the very edge of the road. He had taken no part in the rescue but his careless disregard of danger now suggested that detachment rather than fear had kept him inactive. George was standing with the women on the other side of the road, his back pressed against the mountainside. His face was slightly greenish.

By now a number of pilgrims had gathered around us, offering drinks and fruits, and chattering. The monk stood up and while one of the pilgrims carefully brushed off his robe, I looked carefully at the face, which a few months later would stare from newspapers all over the world. His cleanly shaven head was a little lighter than his round brown face, and his beaked nose protruded prominently. But it was the unwavering intensity of his bulging black eyes that was his striking feature. His lips were thin and pursed, and his ears had no lobes.

Ramanathan said something to him in Sinhalese and the monk spoke for the first time. His voice was high and thin, he said only a few words, then he pressed his palms in front of his chest and walked on up the mountain.

"What did he say?" Moss asked. He was still sitting on the ground resting.

"He said that the country is in trouble and he must pray at Buddha's footprint."

"He didn't even thank you for saving his life?"

Ramanathan smiled deprecatingly. "You mustn't misinterpret that. A devout Buddhist doesn't say 'thank you' to anyone. He believes that whatever good a man does rebounds to his own credit and helps him on the eternal climb to perfection. Why, then, should man be thanked for doing good, if virtue is literally its own reward? I am a Hindu, but I understand his attitude and I agree with it."

By this time we had all started moving down the mountain. Moss was walking with Ramanathan, just behind me, and I heard him say, "Your strength and speed amazed me. You're by far the oldest man here, and yet it was you who saved him."

"There is no great mystery about that," Ramanathan said. "I've practiced yoga every day of my life, and my body is in much better shape than yours."

The road widened and we walked more easily along the edge of the jungle. There were boulders and twisted roots to look out for, and the jungle was full of sounds. Birds chirped, cawed, and trilled; monkeys chattered incessantly; once in a while the deep trumpeting of the elephant sounded in the distance. But we saw none of these animals, for the jungle was much too thick to show anything except the ferns and rhododendrons, the orchids and begonias, and rich splashes of other flowers whose names I didn't know.

Soon we met a procession led by a tall, thin, gray-haired man wearing dark glasses. His brown face was intelligent and sensitive, and he walked slowly in his long white banian cloth. When he came abreast of us he paused and pressed his palms together, breast high. Lakshman, Ranjini, and Ramanathan stopped immediately, held their palms together in front of their faces, and bowed low. The man spoke to them, in smoothly oratorical English and with perfect Oxford inflection. After asking about their health, he said he had heard that a bikkhu had almost fallen off the mountain. Chitra excitedly told him what had happened, while he listened attentively and smiled at her benevolently.

"That was a brave deed, Sri Ramanathan," he said. "I will not forget it."

He pressed his palms together again and walked on, followed by an entourage of white-clad men. When they were out of sight, Moss said, "Who is he?"

"That's the prime minister," Lakshman said. "A wonderful man. He is one of the richest men in the country, yet he is helping the poor and redistributing the land so the country will prosper."

George snorted. "He's a smart politician. He knows that preaching socialism is the only way to power in the Orient."

Lakshman spoke slowly. "You don't know everything, George. The prime minister is a genuinely religious man."

"Hah," George said. "You mean he figured out that by getting the Buddhist clergy behind him, he could win the election. That's the extent of his religion."

Lakshman opened his mouth, then closed it, coming as close as I had ever seen him to showing irritation. We finished the walk in silence.

In the valley at the foot of the mountain where rows of parked cars waited, a boy in a dirty dhoti was badgering pilgrims, trying to sell them lottery tickets. When he saw us, he rushed over. "Very auspicious time for buy lottery ticket, masters," he said. He was a bright-eyed, black skinned boy, with an attractive smile. Chitra coaxed Lakshman into buying her a ticket, then George bought one.

"Why don't you get one too, Moss," he urged.

Moss laughed. "I wouldn't know what to do with it. I don't need it."

"Get one anyway," George said. "Maybe you'll improve my chances, since you don't care about winning."

Reluctantly Moss bought a lottery ticket, and the boy turned to Ramanathan. The old man smiled and bought five tickets. When the boy had gone Ramanathan tossed the tickets carelessly into his pouch. "I buy for the sake of the salesman," he said gently. "I don't need winning tickets either."

Moss turned to me. "Where is the university where you teach?"

I told him it was near Kandy. "And what are you doing in Ceylon?" I asked.

"I'm searching," he said. "In a week I plan to be in Kandy. May I visit you then?"

I assured him that he would be welcome, and he said good-bye to everyone and walked toward the black air-conditioned Mercedes-Benz that had pulled out of the parking area and stopped near us. The driver, a big Sikh with a white turban and a black beard, looked at us impassively. Moss got in, waved to us, and rode off. By the time Piodasa and I drove off in my Volkswagen all the other cars were out of sight. The valley was green and lovely, and dark men in loincloths worked in the rice fields, swinging their hoes together in the graceful and effortless rhythm of ballet dancers. I looked back once at the majestic mountain and thought about the footprint in the stone at the top of Adam's Peak.

Two

The following Friday when I came home from school at noon I saw the Mercedes-Benz parked in the driveway. The big Sikh chauffeur was sitting on the garage floor chatting with my houseboy, Vasumal. Moss was in the living room, drinking a glass of orange juice and telling Piodasa that he preferred not to eat the two-layer cake Piodasa had brought out. After I welcomed him, Moss explained that he had taken a room at Queens Hotel in Kandy, four miles away, and that he expected to stay there a couple of weeks.

"I want to see as much of central Ceylon as I can and I'll be very grateful for your help. But don't let me impose on you."

I assured him that having an American visitor, after a year away from the States, was delightful and that I would be glad to show him around. Then I called Piodasa.

"Mr. Moss will eat lunch and dinner here today," I told him.

"Yes, Master," he said, grinning broadly.

"Can you set another place in a hurry?"

"Yes, Master," he said happily and trotted back into the kitchen.

Moss looked after him and smiled. "He's eager enough, but he doesn't seem too bright."

I sighed and admitted that my cook wasn't too bright. A few minutes later Piodasa came in to tell us that lunch was ready and we followed him to the dining room. As we sat down, I asked, "Has the postman been here yet?"

Piodasa drew himself up proudly. "I no tell policeman nothing, Master," he said. After he had gone Moss looked at me, perplexed.

"I must have missed something in that dialogue," he said.

"No," I said wearily. "It's just another imperfection in Piodasa. He has one deaf ear."

Moss smiled. "That could lead to problems."

"It does," I admitted. "The most embarrassing one was at a big party I gave. Since many of my guests were teetotalers, I told Piodasa to put cherries in the ice mold. The Gunasenas came early and Chitra went into the kitchen to check on things. I heard a loud wail.

"'Oh, no,' she cried. 'Piodasa, what did you put in the fruit punch?'

"'Piodas's voice was complacent. 'Chilies, Lady, chilies. Like Master say.'"

Piodasa finally brought out rice and curry, and as we ate we watched, through the dining room windows, Lela being bathed in the waterfall just below my bungalow. Lela was a six-month-old elephant, which had been found abandoned in a jungle ditch and brought, barely alive, to the veterinary college. The veterinarians treated her wounds, fed her milk from a baby-bottle and pabulum by hand, and provided an affectionate young mahout whom she followed like a human infant. She was now three feet tall and weighed four hundred pounds, and her attitude toward the noon bath was childishly inconsistent. Sometimes she splashed around happily; at others she refused to go in and had to be pushed by the mahout and several volunteer bystanders. Today she seemed to be having a wonderful time, filling her little trunk with water and showering her mahout, trumpeting squeakily, and rolling around like a happy porpoise. Students walking to their dormitories for lunch stopped to watch and smile and admire her antics. At the other end of the waterfall a Ceylonese woman, spreading out her blue sari around her, and a little naked boy stepped into the water and washed themselves quietly.

"A lovely country," Moss said. "The more I see of it, the more I like it."

After we had eaten the rice and curry, Piodasa brought delicious mangoes to the table, a gift from Ramanathan in northern Ceylon where the best mangoes grow.

When we went back into the living room Piodasa followed us, an eager grin on his face. "I make good dessert for American master," he said. "What Master like?"

I turned to Moss. "What would you like for dessert tonight? Piodasa wants to make something special."

Moss hesitated. "Oh, I don't know. Lemon cream pie?"

"You know how to make lemon cream pie?" I asked Piodasa.

He beamed. "Very good pie. I start now." He bustled off into the kitchen, humming and hissing.

We looked out of the spacious windows at the campus. The university was set in a large rolling hollow, surrounded by mountains that grew steeper as one approached the center of the island but which at our location were just pleasant—not grand, not superb, just picturesque and nicely balanced. There were palm trees shading the campus road, and behind my house grew banana trees, a cashew-nut tree, and a jak fruit tree. The grass was lush and neatly mowed, and the pinkish stone of the university buildings gleamed pleasantly across the campus. A slight breeze circulated through the house, keeping it cool and restful.

"What brings you to Ceylon?" I said, finally.

Moss waved his hand at the valley below us. "Beauty like this, for one thing."

"There are other beautiful places in the world."

"Of course. Landscape's not enough." He turned to face me. "Please don't think I'm as naïve as this sounds, but I'm looking for a place where people are happy."

I lit a cigarette and inhaled deeply, then I stared out of the window. Moss looked at me anxiously. "You're wondering," he said quietly, "what you can reply to a remark like that without sounding either sarcastic or banal. But think of it this way, if you will. It's my hobby. I'm wealthy. Some men spend their money on call girls, or paintings, or racehorses. I spend mine on the search for a happy land. Is that so eccentric?"

"Everyone has a right to a hobby," I agreed. "But how on earth can an educated adult believe in utopia?"

"I'd begun to suspect there isn't any," he said, "until I came to Ceylon. Now I think perhaps I've found it."

"Well," I said, "let's take a closer look at it." I told Vasumal that we would be back for tea, and led Moss down the hill onto the campus. I had put on a cap and Moss had taken his sun helmet, and as we walked out into the tropical sunlight we were both glad of the covering. Students on their way from class held books up over their heads to shield them from the rays, and yellow-robed monks walked slowly across the campus, protecting their shaved heads with black umbrellas or large green palm leaves. Ceylonese natives never wore hats. In the distance a file of tea pickers, finished for the day, carried empty baskets down the hill.

As we walked Moss talked about himself. He was an only child. His mother had died in childbirth, and his father, a New York corporation lawyer, had left him a great deal of money. For a while after graduating from an Ivy League school Moss had lived in New York and San Francisco. But the last two years he had spent in constant travel.

"I never really enjoyed college," he said. "It was my own fault, I suppose. I lived in a good fraternity and did a lot of drinking and sleeping around. I had all the money I wanted and a Cadillac convertible, so women weren't hard to get. But I just couldn't get excited about parties and football games and campus activities. I majored in philosophy, but none of the philosophies seemed to answer my personal needs. I wanted—and still do—the concrete, the immediate, people who've had meaningful experiences. Not abstract theorizing about metaphysics. I had a growing feeling of emptiness, inadequacy—as if I were the only outsider wandering around among people who all belonged."

"Many people feel like outsiders," I said. "You learn to live with it."

"I haven't learned. I keep getting twinges of social consciousness, a feeling of personal responsibility to southern Negroes, bums on the Battery, lonely old people. It depressed me to see families living in tar-paper shacks in the middle of Hong Kong and children sleeping on sidewalks in Calcutta. I remember a young woman in an Indian village whose job all day consisted of patting cow-dung into patties so they could be dried in the sun and used for fuel."

"Few people really feel they're their brothers' keepers. They get over that notion when they grow up. It's called 'maturing.'"

Moss nodded. "I know that. I realize that many people actually enjoy competition, conflict, a chance to be aggressive. But I'm just not built like that. I want to avoid people's sufferings, yet I feel guilty about avoiding them."

"Not so guilty," I said, smiling, "that you give up air-conditioned automobiles."

He agreed. "Nor other pleasures the best hotels provide—swimming, good food, comfort, service. I like that."

We approached the cricket field and watched while a middle-aged man in Western clothes stopped the match and gave some instructions to the batsman.

"Is that the coach?" Moss asked.

I smiled. "I suppose you could call him that. This is the university's cricket team practicing, and he is coaching them now. But his full-time job is being professor of classical literature."

"Oh," Moss said. "Then cricket isn't very important in Ceylon."

"It's the most popular sport in the country, and the students get as excited as ours do over football."

Moss looked quizzical, so I explained, "The attitude of educators here is somewhat different. When I told my present colleagues that my university in America hired a coach and five assistants to do nothing but proselytize football players and coach them, they were sure I was lying. They can't understand why I should dream up as ridiculous a lie as that, and it bothers them a little, but not one of them would believe for a moment that a university—an institution of higher learning—could find any conceivable justification for subsidizing professional athletics. 'You have grown men doing this?' one of them asked, open-mouthed. I finally pretended I was just joking and haven't mentioned the matter since."

A group of students in Western clothes, sarongs, and saris, watching the practice. The batsman hit the ball over the fielder's head and a student near us murmured, "Good show."

"They're not too demonstrative, are they?" Moss remarked.

"It's the English tradition. I watched the Up-Country rugby team play the touring Australians the other day. In rugby, you know, only the captain is permitted to make encouraging remarks. The crowd was very excited during the match but the only cheer I heard came from an elderly tea planter I sat next to. Every once in a while he muttered quietly, "Go, Up-Country."

We were walking across the cricket field now and Moss stopped suddenly and jumped back. About five feet ahead of us a long dark shape slithered through the grass, paused for a moment, then glided on away from us.

"I'm afraid of snakes," Moss said.

"That was just a rat snake, one of the 90 varieties of snakes in Ceylon. It's harmless."

"I don't care. I don't like them."

We watched our footing until we came to the road.

"Is it true that cobras don't go after people who leave them alone?" Moss asked.

"That's what Piodasa tells me," I said. "He called me outside the other day to show me a giant cobra sunning itself on a rock behind our house. He refused to chase it away. 'Master no bother cobra, cobra no bother Master,' he explained."

I took Moss into the Arts Building and we strolled through the long central hall of the building. Moss was fascinated by the large masks hanging on the walls. "This is the best collection of authentic masks in the country," I told him. "What do you think of them?"

He spent a long time admiring the workmanship and the symbolism of the wooden masks. The ones representing the king and queen had each been carved out of a separate tree trunk and weighed more than fifty pounds apiece. Other masks represented horrible snarling demons, goddesses devouring human beings, birds swallowing snakes, and a fiend whose head was wrapped in cobras. "Strange that such a gentle people should create such hideous masks," Moss said.

We walked on, past the faculty club and along the Mahaweliganga, the largest river in Ceylon. The water was murky and the current ran sluggishly. Moss looked at the water as he spoke.

"I realize that to most people my search for a happy land seems absurd. And yet, in a sense, that's what almost everyone would like to do. It just happens that I can afford to do it in style. You'd be surprised how many people, in their different ways, are also looking."

The tea pickers whom we had seen on the hill now passed us and giggled. They were all Tamil women, dressed in cheap cotton saris, red and pink and orange, and they wore gold necklaces, gold bracelets, gold earrings, gold nose studs, and gold rings. They chattered gaily as they turned off the road.

Moss smiled. "I've seen more happy people here than anywhere in the world. A lot more than in the United States." He turned to me earnestly. "You know, intellectuals like to think that they're the only ones looking for the meaning of life. That's nonsense. Millions of people read *Peace of Mind* and *How to Stop Worrying* and 'inspirational' trash by superficial clergymen. How about the tremendous growth, among least-educated people, of fundamentalist churches? How about the hundreds of clubs and organizations in America that people join, hoping to find something that will give meaning to their lives? One sociologist calls it 'other-directed' drives, another calls it 'self-transcendent' urges. But no matter what you call it, it means dissatisfaction, emptiness. We have more entertainment gadgets than ever before, and we're lonelier than ever before."

Moss paused but I looked at the river and didn't say anything. After a while he went on.

"My minister was genuinely puzzled about me. He's a decent, liberal Episcopalian, and he's accustomed to adolescent and academic doubts. But the advantages of belief so far outweigh the intellectual pleasures of skepticism—and are so much more genteel—that he can't understand why I'm dissatisfied and why I keep searching. He honestly feels that I'm too nice a person to be offbeat so long."

I flipped my cigarette butt into the muddy river. "So you really think many Americans are dissatisfied?"

"I can speak only for those I know," Moss said. "Most of my friends have money, but very few of them are happy. They're all trying to prove something, but they're not sure what, or why, or to whom. The country club doesn't really satisfy them, or the suburb, or the garden. They're not doing things for the reasons they say they're doing them—and neither are the Bohemians and the beatniks and the parlor pinks.

"And it isn't just Americans who are looking for a meaning in life. I've seen Indians by the thousands walking to the Ganges. I've seen pilgrims on the way to Mecca and to Jerusalem. I've seen the seekers in Rome and I've seen them in Lourdes. Even at the Temple of the Dawn in Bangkok, full of tourists every day, they tell you that the higher you climb the more merit you gain. But in Nepal they don't work very hard for this merit. They just spin their prayer wheels, letting each spin pile up a credit for them in Heaven. And some Nepalese are so lazy that they just sit by the riverside and let the current spin their prayer wheels for them."

"I wouldn't do it in this river," I said. "There are crocodiles in the Mahaweliganga."

We looked at the river for a while. "That dirty water reminds me of the tea a priest in a Japanese temple once gave me," Moss said. "There were some Americans there—Zen Buddhism's popularity is another sign of what I'm telling you. People don't find the traditional answers satisfying and begin to look for offbeat ones. Everything is getting a try—existentialism, Bahai, Jehovah's Witnesses, Unitarianism." He paused. "And Zen Buddhism. After I drank that scummy tea, the priest gave me a souvenir—a comic book about Buddha, in English.

"So I've been traveling and looking. But I haven't found—until now—a place where people really seem to be happy. In most Oriental countries there is gracious living for a few and terrible poverty for many. In the Middle East there is religious fanaticism and brutal selfishness. In Scandinavia, economic security, physical comfort—and a spiritual vacuum. The United States has the old rat race—opportunity for all and insecurity for all. And everywhere even the successful people seemed to me unhappy, or uncertain, or bigoted. So I kept traveling. And now for the first time, here in Ceylon, I've found serenity and beauty and relaxation."

We turned away from the river and walked on. Soon we came to a bodhi tree, holy to all Buddhists because it was under a bodhi tree that Buddha, found the secret of life. There was a small wooden shrine at the base of the tree, with a crude clay figure of the sitting Buddha, and a few pieces of colored paper hanging from the widespread lower branches. At night I had seen entire families come here to pray to the Buddha leaving lighted candles in little clay saucers and hanging strips of paper from the holy tree as a sign of their devotion. A woman was now kneeling in front of the shrine, her head touching her hands on the ground. We walked by quietly.

"There is another God seeker," Moss said softly. "You have no idea how many people are looking. In two years I've learned to recognize the type. There were many at Adam's Peak that night. The nationality doesn't matter, nor religion, nor sex. It's the driving force of their lives, whether they're intellectuals or fanatics, civil servants or laundrymen."

"Strange that you chose that example," I said. "My laundryman is a seeker. He is in the dhoby caste, and his ancestors for generations have been laundrymen at a specified rock in the river. But he has learned English, and the other day he gave me a pamphlet about the salvation of mankind. Buddhist socialism will do it, the pamphlet said."

We came to an enormous building with a high wall around it. "What's this?" Moss asked.

"The women's dormitory," I told him. "They call it 'Walled-off Astoria.' Not the kind of joke you'd expect to find twelve thousand miles from New York, but that's what the Ceylonese students call it."

On the tennis-court next to the dormitory, four girls were playing tennis. Three of them wore saris, and they looked slightly incongruous as they ran gracefully back and forth after the ball, their long saris streaming behind them and barely clearing the ground. The fourth girl wore shorts and a jersey, and her body gleamed like dark bronze.

A short, chubby, middle-aged woman stepped out of the dormitory, saw us, and walked over. Her little brown eyes twinkled and she was smiling warmly.

"Mrs. Vitana," I said, "Mr. Moss is an American visitor." She shook hands enthusiastically with Moss. "Mrs. Vitana is one of my favorite people. She lectures in Oriental history."

Mrs. Vitana asked Moss about his trip and his impressions of Ceylon. The questions were the conventional ones, but she was so obviously sincere and so genuinely interested that Moss was soon chattering away as if he had known her for years. As students walked by they stopped to greet her or ask questions. Suddenly she looked at her watch.

"Oh, goodness," she cried. "I'm late for a meeting. You'll like Ceylon, Mr. Moss. We have Sinhalese and Tamils and Moors and Burghers, and we've all lived here happily for centuries. It's a wonderful country."

She walked off towards the administration building, delayed repeatedly by students. "She's the most popular teacher here," I said. "Her husband died when she was twenty-four, but she managed to support herself and earn a doctorate in London. I've never seen her dejected or short tempered. And she isn't an irritating Pollyanna, either. She has a tremendous zest for life, a self-reliant confidence that's very rare and very refreshing."

We walked on, past the men's tennis courts where two students were playing. They were small and agile, like most Ceylonese, and they kept the ball in play a long time, but neither one could hit the ball very hard. Several players were sitting on benches along the courts.

"They're probably waiting for their opponents to show up," I told Moss. "Ceylonese don't worry much about promptness. It irritated me at first when I entered the local tournament and had to wait a half hour for my first opponent, an hour for the next one. But eventually I realized that no malice was intended. Time just doesn't mean much here. I've gotten to like it."

We reached a place clogged with laborers building a new road. Behind a large truck loaded with gravel stood a line of men passing baskets full of gravel away from the truck. The last man handed the baskets to women, who carried them in a long file to the proper spot on the road, dumped the gravel on the ground, then brought back the baskets for the men to refill and pass to the women again.

Moss shook his head. "What an inefficient way to work. A couple of men with modern equipment could do more than these fifty people."

"It may be inefficient by American standards," I said, "but it provides work for fifty people instead of two."

"You're not seriously defending this primitive method, are you?"

"I'm not defending anything," I said. "But how would the other forty-eight people earn a living? Ceylon has thousands of unemployed."

An old Buddhist monk walked by, saffron robed, head shaved, tranquil. His black umbrella was hung casually over his right shoulder, as on a clothes rack, and he swung both arms gracefully as he walked. A woman walked up to him, held her palms together in front of her chin, and said something. The monk waggled his head from left to right, in the Ceylonese gesture for 'yes,' said something kindly, and walked on.

Moss looked at the woman. "Another one. These God seekers have certain characteristics. When they first meet you they're likely to become very friendly. They give you gifts, and entertain you, and listen very intently when you talk. But when they find out that you don't have 'the secret'—that you, too, are uncertain—then they turn against you, as if you were guilty of betraying them. They're looking for the absolute, and people who don't have it disappoint them. The God seekers I've met don't like each other very much."

I nodded. "I've met some out here. What you say about them is true, but in a way they're pathetic."

"WE are pathetic," he said.

I smiled. "I suppose you've heard the story about the professor at an American university," I said. "He was sitting alone in the office the philosophy department shared with the psychologists when a wild-eyed young man ran in, looked around excitedly, and shouted, 'Where's a psychologist? I've got to see a psychologist right now.'

"The professor said, 'Can I help you? I am a philosopher.'

"'No, no! I need a psychologist.'

"'Well,' the professor said calmly, 'let me try. What is your problem?'

"The young man looked at him suspiciously, then blurted out, 'Who am I? I know what my name is and all that, but I don't know the real me. Who am I? I've got to know.'

"The professor looked at him sympathetically, then said gently, 'Who is asking you?'"

Moss laughed. "Yes, I've heard that anecdote. And of course I've thought about it in reference to myself. But without getting excited or desperate about it, I have to find a meaning for my life. I don't know why this is so. I suppose psychoanalysis could find some original cause, in my infancy or adolescence. But regardless of the cause, I'm looking for a deeper meaning in life than being a businessman in the United States, or an expatriate in Europe. I've come closer to finding serenity, in a setting of loveliness and beauty, here in Ceylon, than anywhere else in the world. I feel that these people are genuinely happier than anyone I know. I'm going to take time to live here, to learn more about Buddhism and local customs and their way of life."

We reached the edge of the campus now and admired the patterned beauty—the blending greens of lawn, trees, and tea plantations; the gentle rise of the hills; the delicate turquoise sky; the men in sarongs and women in saris; the monks in robes slowly moving across the undulating valley.

We started to walk back, and Moss said softly, "Just look at this charm, this tranquility. And then think of the contrast in the United States."

"You keep complaining about America," I said. "But what is it really you object to?"

He was silent for a while, and his voice was biting when he finally spoke. "The whole way of life is what I object to—the values, the vulgarity, the pace, the hypocrisy."

"Be specific," I said.

"Well, the United States is the first country to openly admit that money-making is the major purpose of life. Now don't misunderstand me. I know that most countries—especially Western Europe—are as materialistic and money-grubbing and intensely competitive as we are. And more stingy and selfish than we are. But they have at least pretended—and sometimes actually believed—that there are higher values in life. Our frank, outright, pragmatic worship of money eliminates morality, beauty, and spirituality from life."

"At least," I said, "you're giving us credit for being honest."

"No," Moss said bitterly, "Americans aren't honest about most things. They pretend about almost everything except the fact that money is God. They pretend in society and in politics and in religion and in art. Business groups pretend they believe in free enterprise, but they demand government protection and subsidy for their particular business. Farmers claim they want complete freedom, but they have accepted government support for years. Labor unions talk about individual freedom—and deny it to their members. Our economic prosperity is based on the continued manufacture of military equipment, which we insist we will never use. Everyone goes on record for racial equality—in some other community than their own."

"But that kind of hypocrisy isn't limited to the United States," I said. "Your criticism would apply to any country."

"Perhaps, but it's the United States I'm most familiar with. I know that other countries are hypocrites too. China, our ally in World War Two, is now our enemy, and Japan, our enemy in that war, is ostensibly our ally. Russia, our former ally, is now the foe, and Germany, ex-foe, pretends to be a friend. We recognize the fascists in Spain who won a revolution, but we reject the communists in Red China who won a revolution. Russia pretends to be dedicated to democracy but crushes by military force every democratic opposition to her power in the nations she controls. Statesmen are politicians who do their lying abroad instead of at home."

"Aren't you exaggerating a little?" I said.

"In what way? We've created an elaborate system of noble values, few of which are true and none of which we practice. The number of church members keeps rising but clergymen complain that genuine belief is declining. Many of our professional charities have been exposed as rackets. Medical organizations fight, as they have fought for years, attempts to provide government help for the ill. Magazines like *Time* create an image of the country that exists only in the delusions of their editors—and an image of foreign countries that matches the fantasies of their publishers. There is a social timidity which leads to ridiculous conformity and to ridiculous reactions against conformity, like the silly, purposeless beatniks. There is a sameness in our clock-watching civilization, eyes glued to television sets with such devotion that during the commercials millions of toilets flush simultaneously all over the country, and the water level in thousands of cities suddenly drops. And on these television sets a new art form makes brutality acceptable, vulgarity respectable, and sentimentality patriotic. Advertisers have replaced the creative spirit, 'the gimmick' has superseded imagination, the stereotype has eliminated character. The people have been fed pabulum so long that they don't want anything original, different, realistic, honest—almost all of the attempts at serious drama and at information beyond the level of the moron have failed to attract viewers and have been dropped. It's not just a witticism that the bland are leading the bland."

"Come, come," I said, "you sound as if you were personally involved."

"I am," he said, "as a citizen. We live in a world where nuclear energy may at any moment destroy us, where communism is spreading, where cynical opportunism has outstripped creeping socialism. And what our popular media—books, movies, magazines, newspapers—offer as a solution is sentimentality, chauvinism, and advertising. If it weren't tragic it would be very funny. Our lives depend on the proper toothpaste, deodorant, breakfast cereal, liver pill, tranquillizer, pep pill, vitamin pill, pain reliever, cold eliminator, or stomach soother. Our status is clearly revealed by our choice of automobile, cigarette, suit style, tie, shoe, and hair oil. You may say that no one believes these ads and commercials—in that case you have the most cynical civilization in history, recognizing that it's surrounded by a constant barrage of lies. Our universities are famed not for scholarly achievements but for football teams. And football coaches are often paid—with perquisites—more than the presidents of their universities."

I smiled. "You said something about pace."

"Thoreau said it long before I did. He said we are all hurrying, but no one knows where. Thoreau would go mad today, with radio news every hour on the hour, electronic calculators giving immediate answers to foolish questions, everything being 'rated' and 'measured' and 'labeled' by computers and calculators so that we can do almost everything—but we don't know what is worth doing or why. We know how many people watch a cowboy show, or read a book about small-town sex. But the childishness of that program or the cheapness of that book is not measured by the mechanical raters. We get excited over the census because it counts the bathrooms in America and gives us more figures useful for businessmen and tax collectors. But the nature of the soul the census does not reveal."

We were approaching my house now and Moss stopped talking. "You don't agree, do you? You think I'm exaggerating and repeating the intellectual's standard complaints."

I shrugged. "I don't think Americans are more materialistic than other people. It just happens to be easier to make money in the United States. It's been my observation that every country that has a chance at materialistic comforts grabs them immediately—in spite of the idealism or spirituality that country may otherwise profess."

We were standing in front of my house now, and Moss looked at the landscape. "Perhaps," he said, "what you say is true for other countries I've visited. But from what I've seen so far, Ceylon is different."

I opened the door. Piodasa was waiting for us in the living room. "Lemon cream pie ready now. Come in kitchen see."

We followed him into the kitchen and he showed us the filling he had made.

"Very good," Moss said, "but where is the crust?"

Piodasa slapped his forehead violently. "I so forgetful," he said unhappily. "I forget make crust."

After dinner, when I walked with Moss to his car I said, "Something more than the condition of American culture is bothering you. You're much too emotional about it to pretend that a detached criticism of a vulgar society is really your motivation."

    Moss shrugged but didn't answer. The Sikh opened the door to the Mercedes-Benz and they drove off smoothly into the night.

Three

Moss became interested in fire walking after Mrs. Vitana took us to a Hindu festival. She was a Buddhist herself, but she had friends in all communities and she thought that Moss and I would enjoy watching it. Her driver parked her old Hillman at our door and we climbed into the back seat with her. As usual, her eyes were twinkling and she entertained us with cheerful folk tales while the car climbed steep crags and edged around precipices. It was a short journey but a slow one to a large Hindu temple in the hills behind Kandy.

When we arrived we were told that the fire walking was delayed for an hour, until six p.m. A Muslim couple greeted Mrs. Vitana warmly and insisted that we all go to their home while we waited for the ceremony. The house was less than a mile away, but when they saw an old bus rumbling along the dusty road our hosts hailed it and led us onto it. The bus was full, but several men in sarongs immediately stood up and urged us to take their seats. I tried to pay the fare and everyone laughed good naturedly. Mrs. Vitana explained that our hosts were the wealthiest family in the community and owned, among other things, the bus we were riding on.

After a number of stops at which frolicking and genially perspiring people got on and off, we reached our hosts' house. No one on the bus had spoken English and the dozens of children around the ramshackle plaster house stared at us, astonished. One came up timidly, gingerly touched Moss's bare arm, rubbed hard with his finger, then ran away giggling. "He was trying to see if the color would rub off," Mrs. Vitana explained. "Some of these children have never seen a white person."

There was a great deal of bustling and scurrying around when we entered. Obviously Western visitors were not an everyday occurrence. The house was large—at least ten rooms—but there was no inside plumbing and we had to go to a pump outside to wash our hands. The toilet was a slit in the earth in a nearby cubicle. When we got back to the large room, plates of candies, pastries, and fruit had been put out and we were urged to try everything. Then a young man and seven girls came in and were introduced to us.

"My friends will have to give seven dowries," Mrs. Vitana told us. "It's fortunate they're wealthy."

The young man had smiled politely but had not spoken, and we assumed that he knew no English. But suddenly he said, "Would you like to come to my room?"

Moss and I went with him to a small room. There was a thick, rich Persian rug on the floor, and a desk and chair in the corner. On improvised shelves over the desk were a couple of dozen books in English.

"I was at the university for two years," he told us.

We talked a little about the school, then Moss asked why he had left. The boy frowned.

"My father took me out of school. He heard that I was friendly with a Buddhist girl."

Moss made a sympathetic remark but the young man kept frowning. Then he said, half apologetically. "But times are changing. In the society of tomorrow there will be no religious prejudice." He put his hand in the desk, took out a little button, and showed it to me.

"You know who that is?" he asked belligerently.

I nodded. "Lenin," I said. "An important man."

"A great man," he said. "socialism is the only hope for Ceylon."

I didn't say anything. Moss asked whether he had become a marxist at the university.

"Yes," he said. "Most of the students are marxists. It's the wave of the future."

"But yours is the wealthiest family here," Moss said.

The boy agreed. "We own all this land, most of the houses in town, the three stores, and the bus company."

"Under socialism, you'd lose it."

The boy shrugged. "Under socialism, a man can marry whom he wants. Besides, after seven dowries there won't be too much left here."

I noticed small heads peeking in through the window, trying to get a look at white men. When I smiled, the heads abruptly disappeared and excited jabbering broke out beneath the window.

"It's time to start walking to the temple," the boy said. "There's no bus due now."

He accompanied Mrs. Vitana and us back to the temple, then shook hands, looked at us wistfully, and disappeared in the crowd. The custodian of the temple, a bald brown man with a long white beard, who resembled my mental image of Noah, escorted us to the front row and provided some mats to sit on. The atmosphere at the festival, Moss observed, was similar to that at a state fair in the United States. It was a pleasant summer afternoon. Children played around us; family groups gossiped pleasantly; vendors sold candies and drinks; and an elephant roamed amiably through the crowd. The fire pit was about fifteen feet along and three feet wide. After the logs had burned for a while, an attendant smoothed the embers with a long branch. The leaves burned the first time he did this, and the second and third tie. It was not until after the fourth leveling that the fire walking began. Three of the walkers, led by a thin old man with a scraggly goatee, ran quickly through the fire. But the fourth one, a thin, dark young man in a short white dhoti, stopped at the edge of the pit, clasped his palms together, looked up at the sky, and prayed aloud. He prayed, intensely and jerkily, for ten solid minutes, while the crowd laughed and jeered at him. His knees were shaking, his hands trembled, and his body swayed. When he was through praying he walked unflinchingly and painlessly through the fire. As soon as he stepped out of the pit he jumped over the shallow pool of water into which the other walkers had stepped, pressed his palms together again, raised his head to the sky, and prayed aloud for a long time, still impervious to the now good-natured raillery of the crowd.

Later we talked to the goateed leader and asked how he happened to become a firewalker. He told us that he had a dream one night in which a voice ordered him to become a firewalker. He reported to the local group's leader on the following day. Years later *that* leader had a dream in which he was ordered to appoint a successor, and the man who was telling us this story had a simultaneous dream in which he was appointed successor. After the transfer of authority took place, the former leader retired and, a few days later, died. "I will be told in the same way," he said, "when the time comes." He was a cheerful little man, but he seemed quite tired. When one of the young men who had walked the fire said something to him, he looked at me, hesitated, then asked whether I would be good enough to sign a petition for the young man. He gave me the petition, which was addressed "To Whom It May Concern," and requested that personage to extend all courtesies, aid, and assistance to the young man whose remarkable performance I had personally witnessed. I objected that my name couldn't possibly obtain anyone's courtesies, aid, or assistance, but the notion that any American's signature could fail to bring forth floods of money was obviously inconceivable to them. We had reached an impasse, when Moss volunteered to sign with a name more appropriate for the occasion than either his or mine, and the young firewalker was very happy to add Billy Sunday to his list of sponsors.

Moss was so impressed by the fire-walking exhibition that I suggested he go to the mass fire walk at Kataragama in August. I couldn't go myself, but when I learned that the Gunesenas and Chiltons were planning the trip I arranged to have Moss accompany them. Two days after the trip I received a long letter from him.

Four

Moss wrote:

The visit to Kataragama turned out to be the most extraordinary experience in my life. To start with, the travel plans were changed at the last moment. Siri Banda and Ranjini were supposed to come too, but he couldn't make it and Chilton asked me to take Ranjini in my car. So we made a caravan, the Gunesenas leading in their Renault, the Chiltons next in a Vauxhall, with me bringing up the rear in the Benz. The Chiltons, as usual, were dressed as if they were on the way to a directors' meeting. His double-breasted suit was sharply creased and his mustache neatly waxed. Chitra was wearing a new sari, but Lakshman had dressed casually.

The drive south from Colombo was lovely. We took the shore road and saw palms leaning out to the sea, great big outrigger canoes up on the beach, catamarans sailing on the greenish-blue ocean. Really charming. There were thatch-roofed huts along the road, shaded by palms and jak and breadfruit trees and beautifully colored trees whose names I don't know.

Ranjini told me that Siri Banda is Mavis Chilton's lover, and for appearances' sake Ranjini sometimes makes a fourth on their trips, as she did at Adam's Peak. She doesn't like Siri—he is too cynical, she says—so she was pleased that I came along.

We all had lunch in the picturesque port of Galle. It's dominated by an enormous thick-walled fort built by the Dutch two centuries ago. The walls enclose quaint little Dutch houses along the harbor. While we ate rice and curry at the rambling, old-fashioned hotel, the manager talked to us. He had heard that we were on the way to Kataragama, and he warned us to obey the local customs if we wanted to avoid bad luck. He was about thirty years old, he spoke English well and wore Western clothes, and he obviously believed every word he said.

The Hindu god Kataragama, he told us, is a handsome, seven-foot tall, six-headed, twelve-armed god, with two women and a blue peacock for companionship and transportation. Although he is technically a Hindu god, many Buddhists also worship him, or at least ask his help when they're in trouble. Originally he was the god of war and revenge, and I gather that he is more fervently worshipped and more genuinely feared than any other god in Ceylon. He has an A-1 reputation for protecting his congregation, and he exercises an absolute and somewhat whimsical control of the area within a fourteen-mile radius of his temple.

The hotel manager warned us there are two special taboos that every visitor to the Kataragama territory is supposed to observe. We were not to announce an expected arrival time; that was an infallible way to be delayed. And we were not to say anything in the slightest way critical of Kataragama. Lakshman immediately remarked that, the weather being ideal, we ought to arrive in Kataragama by six o'clock. And Mavis said that all this fear of Kararagama was nonsense; she had been there once before, had ridiculed the whole procedure, and nothing had happened. She seemed to be in a foul mood.

When we finished eating, Ranjini and I got into my Benz and followed the other two cars. Suddenly it began to rain. It rained only for five minutes and, we learned later, only within a few hundred yards. As I carefully rounded a curve on the slick road I saw that the other two cars were now facing us. The Renault's hood was stuck halfway into a rock fence, and the Vauxhall was resting its side on the same fence. It turned out that Lakshman skidded and started turning in the road, and to avoid hitting him Chilton put on his brakes. By the time the cars stopped skidding they had both smashed into the fence. The radiator of Lakshman's Renault was broken, but no one was injured except Mavis. She had a painful but not serious bruise on the spot where an irritated parent might have been expected to spank his child. It took a long time to disengage the cars and tow them to a garage. The narrow road inland ran jaggedly through the jungle, and we didn't get to the temple until just before midnight. I suppose all of these coincidences and superstitions can be logically accounted for, but I noticed that neither Lakshman nor Mavis made any more jeering remarks about Kataragama.

There was an aura at the temple totally different from anything I have ever experienced. It was the night of the full moon, and fire walking was the climax to a full week's ceremonies in honor of Kataragama. From all over the island, worshippers and spectators, Buddhists and Hindus, had converged on this little settlement in the jungle. During the early part of the week, we were told, devotees had paid tribute to Kataragama by hanging colored papers on trees near the temple, or by breaking sacrificial coconuts on a large rock provided for that purpose. But towards the week's end the nature of the sacrifices intensified. We saw some zealous worshippers who had perforated their cheeks with pins, some who walked on nails, and one man who had imbedded into his naked shoulders meat hooks with which he pulled a heavy cart along the pitted dirt road.

By midnight the crowd was feverishly tense. It was rumored that the fire walking in the twenty-five-foot by six-foot pit would take place about 4 a.m. But the tradition against making any sort of prediction about the immediate future is so strong that when the priest was asked by a German tourist when the fire walking would begin, he replied that there probably wouldn't be any walking at all. The crowd surged away from the pit slowly and steadily—slowly because every inch of the temple grounds had been packed for hours, and steadily because the heat from the pit was becoming unbearable. The men and women nearest the pit had held their places for days, eating and sleeping on one spot.

I know that the Ceylonese are ordinarily very clean and bathe frequently, but the activity at Kataragama is clearly more important to them than sanitation, and as the hours passed everything intensified—the heat, the excitement, the odors of sweat and urine and incense. A wave of expectation permeated the air, a powerful undercurrent that made an intruder like myself feel dilettantish, uncomfortable, and slightly ashamed. Fire walking is much more than just a spectacle to most of these people. It's a physical manifestation of deep wish fulfillment, a visible symbol of intimate contact with a supernatural power. From time to time men shouted "Hora Hora," the Oriental form of "Amen" in honor of a god whose power transcends the science of the West. Ranjini cried "Hora Hora" too.

It was about 2 a.m. when people near us suddenly scurried to make room for a young woman carrying a clay pot. The packed mob gave way so quickly because the pot she was carrying was full of burning coconut husks, and remaining in the immediate vicinity of the red-hot pot was distinctly uncomfortable. The young woman was carrying the pot in her bare hands, and she didn't seem to be feeling any pain. She did seem to be abnormally excited as she staggered to the outer sanctum of the temple. There she threw the pot down, exultantly showed the crowd her hands—gray, but not burned—and began knocking on the temple door. I think she wanted to show the priest, or the god, what she had accomplished, but no casual visitors were being admitted that night, and she was still pounding frantically at the massive door when the attention of the crowd shifted to another woman. This one too had a red-hot pot full of burning husks, but she carried it in the conventional Ceylonese fashion—on top of her head. And when she removed the pot, neither her hair nor her hands showed any sign of scorching.

Shortly before four a.m. an ominous grumbling swept through the crowd. Then angry shouts, threatening arms, protests. Lakshman climbed a stone wall and reported to us what the trouble was. A row of chairs had been reserved for several wealthy Ceylonese from Colombo and their European guests. But when they arrived they found that a group of Buddhist monks had occupied the seats and refused to move. Chilton told me that as a calculated technique of growing nationalism, monks have been usurping reserved seats at public gatherings. A police official tried to persuade the monks to give up the seats, but he found it a frustrating task. The yellow-robed figures leaned placidly on their black umbrellas and pretended that he didn't exist. There was no doubt that the mob supported the monks, and when the protests of the crowd became loud the police officer shrugged his shoulders and motioned to the legal holders of the seats. They dispersed to the edges of the standing mob, far away from the pit.

At four in the morning wailing flutes and pounding drums announced the arrival of the walkers. White-robed priests, their faces streaked with red, yellow, and white ash, led the long procession. By this time the flames had stopped spurting and the pit consisted of a red-hot mass of burning wood, which attendants were leveling with long branches. The heat of the fire was still intense—within ten feet of the pit it was difficult to breathe. Then the priests muttered incantations, the drums built up to a crescendo, and the fire walking began.

Among the eighty persons who walked the fire were ten women. But in the mad excitement of the crowd's cheers, the drumbeats, the odors, the tension, it was hard to identify individuals. Some men skipped lightly through the fire, as if doing a restrained version of the hop, skip, and jump in three or four steps. Some raced through, determined, somber. Some ran through exultantly, waving spears. One man danced gaily into the center of the pit, turned, did a kind of wild jig for a few moments, then turned again and danced on through. Another man stumbled suddenly and the crowd gasped—he fell forward, hung for an awful moment on the coals, then straightened and stumbled on. The crowd sighed. Two women ran through, close together, holding hands, taking five or six steps. In the phantasmagoric blur of roars, screams, and incantations, the firewalkers looked less like human beings than grotesque puppets in a macabre shadow play. For a long moment one person stood out in the hectic cavalcade of charging, gyrating figures: a short, slim man in a white sarong walked slowly and serenely through the fire, strolling along casually and unconcernedly, and stepping on the solid earth at the end of the pit as gently as he had stepped on the embers.

After going through the fire, the walkers, some shuffling, some running, a few helped or led by attendants, went to a spot beside the temple where the head priest placed a smear of saffron ash on the forehead of each participant. The ash had been taken from the pit and blessed, and the firewalkers strode off proudly.

On the long drive back, Ranjini told me some things about herself. She was working as a typist in the office of a wealthy businessman when he noticed her and she became his mistress. She didn't like him especially but she was glad to be kept by him because then she could let her fingernails grow long. It's very important for her, she explained, to have those long, exquisitely *manicured fingernails. That's why she hated typing, because she had to keep her fingernails short. What subtle symbolism do you see here?*

After a while the man who was then prime minister took a liking to her and she joined his ménage. Since then she's been married and divorced, and at the moment isn't attached to anybody. She's so casual about sex that I would call her amoral rather than immoral. What attracts me most about her is not her beauty—though she is stunning—but her tremendous zest for life. She gets such a kick out of everything it's delightful to be with her. I'll be seeing a lot of her from now on, I think.

We stopped for a late lunch in Galle, and the hotel manager came over again and asked about our experience. When we told him about the car accident he shook his head gravely and said we were lucky Kararagama had not punished us more severely. Then he asked how Westerners explained the secret of fire walking.

Chilton did most of the talking. It turned out that he had read everything he could find on the subject in preparation for the trip. "Twenty years ago," he said, "The London Council for Psychical Investigation arranged a series of fire walks at Surrey. The Council members took charge of digging the pit and burning the logs. They provided several English physicians, chemists, physicists, and professors to examine every stage of the proceedings. Then they watched two Indians walk through the fire-pit several times.

"Afterwards, the Council published their official report. They decided that fire walking is a gymnastic feat, based on the principle that taking three quick steps on a poor conductor of heat does not burn the flesh." But last night we saw some of the walkers take six or seven steps without getting burned. Most people assume that the tough calluses of Orientals' feet protect them. But the Indian walkers at Surrey had soles as soft as those of Englishmen. Another theory is that some mysterious substance is applied to the soles to harden and protect them. But the English experimenters carefully wiped the walkers' feet before they started. Some chemists say that a film of water on the walkers' soles provides, at certain high ranges of temperature, complete insulation against heat. And it's true that at the fire walk you saw last month the walkers stepped into water before walking the pit. But the people last night had dry feet. As for the theory that the pit is dug shallow in the middle, *deep at the sides, so that the fire has burned out in the place where the walking is done, that too was disproved in the Surrey tests."*

Chilton paused, but everyone was listening intently and no one said anything. He seemed a little embarrassed at being the center of attention, but he fingered his sandy mustache and went on.

"*Those are physical explanations. The psychological theories are harder to test. One suggestion, of course, is that the firewalker is hypnotized so that he feels no pain. It's true that hypnosis can control subjective feeling, but above certain temperatures protoplasm burns—hypnosis or no hypnosis. The theory that mass-hypnosis occurs—that the audience just thinks it has seen fire walking—is nonsense. Cameras have taken many photographs of firewalkers in action. And the mystic explanation that the firewalker, like the yogi and fakir, has dissociated his soul from his body doesn't help either. Even a dead body will burn. So there you are.*"

Chilton stuffed his pipe and lit it. Mavis took a deep breath and everyone turned, but she didn't say anything. Unconsciously she rubbed the bruised spot on her body. Then the hotel manager spoke up.

"*To us who believe, the secret is simple,*" he said. "*The secret is faith in Kataragama. Sometimes a man is desperate. His wife is ill, or he is near bankruptcy, or a hated rival is defeating him. The man vows to walk the fire in exchange for Kataragama's help. The people who walked the fire last night were either asking Kataragama's help or thanking him for having given it. Some of them began their preparations three months ago when they arrived at Kataragama and put themselves under the instruction of the chief priest. All that time they lived very strictly. No relationships with the opposite sex. Eating only vegetables. Drinking only water. Bathing in the holy river near the temple. Following the religious rituals that the priest conducts. Those who did all this, and who had absolute, unquestioning faith in Kataragama, walked the fire unharmed.*"

As he escorted us to our cars, the manager kept talking. "*You haven't heard about it yet, but twelve of the people who walked last night were burned enough to go to the hospital. One of them died.*"

"How do you account for that?" I asked.

The manager shrugged. "They lacked either faith or preparation." He paused, then added slyly, "There was one other man who lacked at least one of those qualifications."

We waited, then I asked, "Who was that?"

"A young English clergyman who visited Ceylon two years ago. He reasoned that the faith of a Christian was as strong as a Hindu's, and he volunteered to walk the fire with the others. He did. The doctors barely managed to save his life, and it was three months before he got out of hospital."

The manager clearly enjoyed telling us about this incident, and he was still waving happily when we drove away. Mavis sat gingerly in the Vauxhall as it followed the Renault with the smashed radiator. I wish I knew what the secret of fire walking really is.

Five

The following Saturday night we watched the Perahara, the climactic night of the ten-day long Perahera festival from a balcony of the octagonal tower in the Temple of the Tooth. Moss had brought Ranjini, and my companion was Sheila Dawson, whose brother owned a tea plantation near Kandy. A century earlier only the King of Kandy would have been permitted to sit where we were, but the last Kandy King had long been dead and we were enjoying Ramanathan's hospitality. He was a good friend of the head priest and had arranged for us to have the coveted spot.

We had not seen Ramanathan since the climb to Adam's Peak, and he admitted that he now left his home in northern Ceylon only on special occasions. He knew most of the local dignitaries and patiently explained the activities to us. The Kandy Perahara, he told us, was the most colorful festival in Asia. "Perahara" means procession, and this particular procession dated back more than eighteen hundred years, originally celebrating a famous victory of the Ceylonese King Gaja Bahu. In the eighteenth century, the festival began honoring the tooth relic of the Buddha, and it became the most famous Buddhist celebration in the world, climaxing with 100 caparisoned elephants and 1000 dancers.

In the past months I had seen the temple so often that I had begun to take for granted the three-storied yellow building with its red-tiled roof, and the large temple joined to it by a handsome entrance. On the steps below the carved arches, flower vendors urged newly arrived pilgrims to purchase a gift for the Buddha. On previous visits I had seen, inside the temple, brilliantly colored frescoes depicting incidents in the Buddha's life. In the inner courtyard was a pool in which giant turtles, said to be a thousand years old, swam.

While we sat waiting for the parade to start, Moss told Ramanathan about an amusing experience we had had earlier in the day. On the mall near the temple a large tent had been put up in which relics of Buddha were being exhibited. There was a long line of people waiting to get in, but everyone generously insisted that we enter immediately. We objected politely, but the spirit of hospitality was overwhelming and we took off our shoes and stepped in. Rows of tables had been pushed together and on each was displayed a different object associated with Buddha during his lifetime. When we came to what seemed to be a handful of small dried bones, Moss asked the monk standing behind the table what the exhibit represented.

The man in the saffron robe spoke very slowly. "*This* is a relic of the Buddha," he said.

"Yes," Moss said, "but what *is* it?"

The monk enunciated deliberately. "This *is* a relic of the Buddha."

"I understand that, but what kind of relic is it?"

"This is a *relic* of the Buddha."

Moss tried once more, but I think he knew what to expect. It came. "This is a relic of the *Buddha*," the monk said, repeating with obvious satisfaction the only English sentence he knew. We thanked him and moved on. In the octagonal tower, Moss asked Ramanathan what the relic was.

Ramanathan shrugged. "There's no way of telling. Buddhists have more relics of the Buddha floating around than Christians have of Jesus."

From the balcony we could see crowds solidly lining the parade route, two hundred thousand people in the streets of Kandy, Ramanathan estimated. They were peering out of the windows of stores and houses, hanging in trees, clinging to protuberances of large buildings. For hours previously, the traffic from side-streets had been blocked off by trim, efficient Ceylonese constables, the left brims of their large hats turned neatly upward like the brims of Australian soldiers.

The most sacred object of Buddhism, Ramanathan told us, was the Buddha's tooth. Its presence in the Temple at Kandy drew Buddhist pilgrims from all over the world. Once a year, on this night, the tooth was taken out of the temple and paraded through the streets of Kandy. For hundreds of years the possession of the tooth was a necessary requirement for the ruling dynasty of Ceylon. In 1560 the conquering Portuguese announced that they had destroyed the tooth. But the next Kandy King imperturbably produced it, accounting for its enormous size on the grounds that everything in the world has been steadily shrinking since Buddha's time. He explained that the tooth, after being ground up by the Portuguese and thrown into the sea, had reassembled itself and flown straight to Kandy. We cold not see the tooth itself, for it was enclosed in seven containers and only the outer casket, covered with cobachon rubies, sapphires, and emeralds, was exposed to view.

"Have you ever seen the tooth?" Moss asked.

"Yes," Ramanathan said.

"Well?"

Ramanathan smiled amiably. "It was bigger than any other human tooth I've ever seen," he said. "Let's leave it at that."

Ramanathan said he doubted that the tooth itself would be paraded. "The priests won't chance losing it. As for accepting its religious significance, if you Christians can believe in the mysteries of the Communion service, I don't see why Buddhists can't have a symbolic tooth."

From our balcony over the courtyard inside the temple walls we watched the loading of the elephant, which was to carry the casket. He was a large gray tusker who walked very slowly and carefully up the steps of the inner temple and stood patiently below the platform on which priests and assistants placed the casket into an elaborately decorated howdah. The howdah was lowered slowly, by pulleys, with fits and starts and shouts, until it hung over the elephant. Then the mahout and the attendants attached the howdah to the elephant, and adjusted evenly the brilliantly emblazoned canopy above the howdah. The elephant then slowly walked down the steps, one ponderous foot at a time, and waited inside the large gate.

"Elephants are quite intelligent," Ramanathan said. "I've seen them play practical jokes on motorists, clogging jungle roads with tree branches, then standing back and trumpeting with glee when drivers had to get out and clear away the obstruction. And I know of an elephant that suddenly turned on his mahout and trampled him to death. Then he carried the dead man to a side, gently covered him with logs, and guarded him until another mahout led him away."

We looked admiringly at the giant tusker below us. His whole body was covered with gold, silver and jeweled embroidery, and his tusks were encased in silver sheaths. The festival had actually begun ten nights earlier, Ramanathan told us, with a small parade of six elephants, a few dancers, and a dozen attendants. Each night the size of the procession increased, until tonight we would see over a hundred elephants and thousands of human participants. "Now it starts," Ramanathan said, pointing.

First came six muscular, bare-chested whip crackers, snapping and cracking long whips that sounded like repeated rifle shots. They were driving away whatever demons might be lurking along the road. Behind them came men holding aloft the insignia of each temple, and then the torchbearers, bare-chested old men mostly, carrying large poles with a kind of cage at the top in which coconut husks were burning. Next walked the priest of one of the temples, splendidly bedecked in a purple turban, a crimson velvet tunic, and dark green satin trousers. He was barefoot, and behind him walked, barefoot and slightly less flamboyantly attired, three assistant priests. Then came a bevy of entertainers—drummers, flute blowers, little boy dancers, and men alternately juggling and swallowing flames. They were followed by the first group of Kandy dancers, practitioners of the unique, world-famous dance, performed while walking in procession. It is an intensely masculine, athletic, exuberant dance consisting of a series of gyrations, leaps, and stomps that build up to an incredible speed, with jumping and shaking and arm-waving of unbearable intensity—then suddenly they stop and continue walking on quietly, leaving the spectator limp with orgiastic excitement.

Ranjini was vibrant with delight. She was clearly an aficionado and she bubbled with information. "The Kandy dance originated in South India, before the Christian era. But it's been completely changed in Ceylon. The Kandy Kings used to sponsor it as court entertainment, but now the temples have taken charge. They give money and food to the dancers, and they supply the teachers and the training and the places to practice. All that the dancers have to do in return is perform at festivals. But it takes many years to become a good Kandy dancer. Those boys you saw dancing near the head of the parade will practice another ten years before they're good enough to join the dancers."

Sheila asked about the dancers' costumes. "Almost all of it is beaten silver," Ranjini said. "The cheapest of these costumes is worth more than five hundred dollars. Look at that headdress, the silver cone above the wide brim. And the silver spangles dangling from the brim, just above the eyebrows. See them shaking as the dancer jumps. And look at those silver cups hanging down beside each ear. They're loaded with gems, blue sapphires usually. And the bracelets on both wrists—those are silver, too, and studded with sapphires. That enormous belt looks fantastic, doesn't it? It helps hold up the long white skirt they're wearing. They're barefoot, you see, and attached to each foot is a little silver container full of silver grains. You can't hear it in this noise, but it sounds like bells tinkling. And look at the long tasseled string, hanging down behind the headdress, almost reaching the ground."

Ranjini pointed out that the dancers' knees were always spread, and that the arms were held out at shoulder level while the torso wove back and forth and hands and fingers made traditional gestures. We watched the dancers—all men, Ranjini said proudly, no women Kandy dancers permitted—go through their violent steps. They spun around, throwing themselves in the air in a complete circle. In the next group, the dancers kept turning their bodies around and around until the tasseled strings spun around them like shimmering webs. Then they suddenly went into an entirely different step, keeping their bodies rigid while their shoulders shuddered convulsively up and down, up and down. They passed us, and the dancers of the next temple did still another routine, rolling their eyes upward and shaking their heads from side to side so violently that it looked as if each man had a number of faces flashing simultaneously.

While the dancers gyrated, the drummers stood near them, wearing only white half-turbans and long narrow white skirts. One end of the drum, Ranjini said, was made of deerskin, the other from a monkey's hide. The drums hung down from the drummers' necks and the players beat them with their hands, sometimes separately and sometimes together.

After the processions of two temples had passed, the gate of the great temple was opened, and the old man who was chief priest of the Temple of the Tooth stepped in golden slippers out into the street. The longest procession of all followed him into line, with more flame jugglers, more drummers, more boy dancers, more Kandy dancers, more flutists, and more torch bearers. Finally and majestically, the elephant bearing the tooth of Buddha marched out into the street, escorted by a smaller elephant on each side. The crowd roared, the drummers drummed, and the dancers danced.

A hundred and twenty elephants paraded that night, magnificently caparisoned in gorgeous tapestries, florid textiles, gaudy cloths. Here and there, elephants strewn with electric lights, the battery concealed under the howdah, looked like grotesque walking neon signs as the red and blue and white electric bulbs formed patterns and chains and crisscrosses, and the crowd shouted admiringly. Drums beat, flutes sounded, pipes whistled. Carts with coconut husks, to refill the burned-out stock in the torches, were spaced at short intervals. At longer intervals, other carts followed to pick up the dung that the elephants were dropping.

In the general excitement, Ramanathan quietly pointed out that little red ants were crawling on our balcony, having made the long climb all the way up the octagonal tower, unaware perhaps that where Kandy kings had once reigned and we now sat there wasn't much demand for red ants. Far below, the procession elephants moved steadily, persistently, interminably, and the image of the great beast dominated every aspect of the Perahara.

"Where do they go now?" Moss asked when the last dung cart disappeared down the street.

"They go to a designated spot just outside Kandy," Ramanathan said. "From there the priests proceed to the bank of the Mahaweliganga for the water-cutting ceremony."

"What does that consist of?"

"A priest from each of the temples that took part in tonight's procession brings a metal pot full of water. The water was put into the pot at the same spot on the river one year ago. The priest throws the old water into the river, cuts the river with a sword, then fills the pot with fresh water and returns, escorted by attendants, to his temple."

"Why do they do that?"

"It commemorates King Gaja Bahu's invasion of India. According to legend, the king crossed the strait between Ceylon and India in a miraculous way. He stepped on the shore, struck the water with his scepter, and the waters parted in two so that he and his soldiers could walk across."

"But that's just like the story of Moses crossing the Red Sea," Sheila exclaimed.

Ramanathan smiled indulgently. "If Jews are permitted to believe it, I don't see why Buddhists should be deprived of a charming legend."

We climbed down and walked along beautiful Kandy Lake towards Queens Hotel. Two Ceylonese women, their breasts partially exposed, passed us, turned, giggled, and walked on. Ranjini was furious. "Those damn Rodiyas," she sputtered. "They shouldn't be permitted in town."

"Who are Rodiyas?" Moss asked.

"The lowest caste in Ceylon. The men are worthless and the women whores. In the old days they were restricted to their own villages, and I think they should be again. They're not fit to associate with decent people."

Ramanathan left us at the entrance, but Moss and Ranjini invited us to have a drink in their room. When the waiter brought the drinks up, Ranjini served us with excessive politeness, apparently enjoying the role of hostess. Earlier in the evening the attendant had turned on the large wooden fan in the ceiling and had lowered the mosquito netting over the double bed.

Sheila and I stood by the window, watching the dispersing crowd and marveling at the beauty of Kandy by moonlight. At varying heights in the blackness of the hills, lights shone from houses and were reflected in the waters of the lake. The hills were etched sharply against the star-sprinkled sky, and tiny fireflies glowed everywhere.

When I turned around I saw Ranjini hanging her dressing gown up in the closet. She looked at it dreamily and slowly rubbed her palm across the nipple of her left breast. I had to drive Sheila back to the tea plantation, so we left soon afterward.

Six

A few days later Moss's Mercedes-Benz was again in my driveway when I came home. Lakshman had invited us to a pirith ceremony in his parents' house and had arranged to call for us at five. The big Sikh driver was sitting on a chair in the garage. When I came in he stood up lazily.

"Have a good trip from Colombo?" I asked.

"Yes, Master."

"And how is Mr. Moss?"

The Sikh smiled and showed a broad expanse of white teeth against brown skin. "Master fine," he said. "Master very nice. He give me raise."

"Oh. Fine."

He touched his turban proudly. "Master now pay me two hundred rupees a month."

"Very good," I said. "That must make you the highest paid driver in Ceylon. Are you saving your money?"

His beard popped up aggressively. "No save. I hire houseboy for my own house now."

I chuckled and went in to greet Moss. An hour later, at five-thirty, Lakshman came in a new Renault. He had traded in the one damaged on the trip to Kataragama, he told us as we got into the car.

"Just what is a pirith ceremony?" Moss asked as we rode off.

"It's a Buddhist thanksgiving ceremony, to celebrate a happy event or ask the gods' protection on a forthcoming venture."

"This isn't a birthday party, is it?" Moss asked, frowning.

"No. Actually it's to celebrate my younger brother's safe return from England. Why?"

"I don't like birthday parties," Moss said curtly.

I was sitting next to Lakshman and as he drove I looked thoughtfully at his delicately featured, gentle, intelligent face. Like his wealthy father and grandfather he had graduated from Cambridge and now, in his English suit, suave and articulate, he seemed to belong more to England than to the Orient—except for his dark skin. But I knew how deeply Ceylonese he was. He was managing director of the large department store his family owned in Kandy, and at work he was always meticulously attired in Western clothes. Every time I dropped in unexpectedly at his home, however, I found him lounging around barefoot in a short sarong. His table manners at formal affairs were impeccable, but at home he ate with his fingers, admitting that he found that method much more comfortable. And although he had lived in England four years, he had not broken away from local customs. When I first met him, Chitra had just borne their first child and was staying with her parents in Colombo. Two months later she was still there, seventy miles from their home in Kandy. When I asked about her return, he said apologetically, "Her family is waiting for an auspicious day before they let her go. The astrologer says next Monday will be a lucky day for the trip, and she'll come back then."

Lakshman was a devout Buddhist. He was a vegetarian; he touched no liquor; and even the eggs he ate had to be unfertilized ones. Chitra liked meat and a drink once in a while, and he never objected, saying that each person had to make his own choice. But he did object when Chitra slapped a servant, and that was the only time I saw him angry. He made it clear that no one was to be beaten in his house, and there was a hard integrity about him that made people obey. But because he assumed that most people were as honest and decent as he was, he was in some ways surprisingly naïve.

Now, instead of going out on the main road to Kandy, Lakshman swung the Renault towards the hills. "This is the back way to town," he said. "It's not really planned for motor traffic, and it will take us longer. But I want you to get a glimpse of a Sinhalese village that is off the beaten path, the real thing."

After a few minutes' driving he stopped the car. We got out and followed him quietly down a footpath that skirted a long grove of trees. Lakshman paused at the edge of the grove, and I saw a tiny cluster of thatch-roofed huts. There were twelve mud-walled huts scattered on both sides of a narrow dirt road. The roofs were cadjun, dried palm leaves. The trees around the little settlement isolated it completely from the outside world, and I felt an awareness of eternity as I looked at the ancient village in a beautiful country on a late summer afternoon. A man in a short gray dhoti walked slowly towards the tall palms behind the village; three women in light blue saris and pink cholis strolled casually along the road, water-jugs balanced effortlessly on their heads. Two men sat in the doorway of one hut and two women in the doorway of another. A naked little boy played on the ground. The humid heat was almost stifling, but the boy, the men, and the women accepted it resignedly. It occurred to me that the village must have looked exactly the same a thousand years ago, and the villagers knew little more now than they knew then. I wondered whether it mattered. The peace, the beauty, the quiet, the strong sense of continuity overwhelmed us, and we stood there a long time without realizing or caring that time was passing.

Then Lakshman turned, reluctantly, and led us back to the car. We walked slowly and Moss said, "They don't need what we have. They're happier without it."

Lakshman smiled. "Sometimes I think you're right," he said, his thin, sensitive face crinkling. "I used to visit this village with my father when I was a boy. It looks just the same now—beautiful, peaceful, self-sufficient, ignoring as it always has the frenzied, changing modern world outside. But I know what their infant mortality rate is, and how short their life span, and I wonder."

There was no other traffic, and the car stayed in the middle of the narrow road, but as soon as we reached the main highway we got into the left lane again and were caught in a stream of bullock carts, bicycles, pedestrians, cars, motorcycles, children, buses, and elephants on their way to the river to bathe after the day's work. "In England people complain about what the lorries do to the highways," Lakshman said, "but in Ceylon it's the bullock carts that slow up traffic, cut ruts in the roads, and crack the asphalt. Just look at them."

We looked at a stolid bullock pulling a bright red gasoline barrel. Another bullock was pulling a dull brown barrel. "What is that?" Moss asked.

"Toddy," Lakshman said. "Local beer. Down south, where they manufacture it, they usually deliver it to nearby taverns by rolling the kegs on the ground. It's rather pleasant to watch, a man directing the rolling barrel with a long heavy stick. But it ties up traffic even worse than this."

We stopped at a petrol station and while the attendant serviced the car, a bright-eyed young man in a shabby sarong came over and spoke to Lakshman in Sinhalese. Lakshman listened, then gave the man a coin and sent him away.

"You can't resist beggars either, can you?" Moss said.

Lakshman seemed puzzled, then he laughed. "That wasn't a beggar. He used to be a houseboy of ours. A very lazy scamp, but he has a wonderful sense of humor." He chuckled and we waited politely.

"His name is Mahadeva, which means 'great god.' My father didn't like having a servant with a name like that—he felt it was blasphemous, I suppose—so he offered the boy twenty rupees to get his name changed officially. The boy agreed, took the money, and had it taken care of."

Lakshman paused, savoring the memory. "Well," Moss asked, "what did he change it to?"

"To Mahamahadeva. That means 'great great god.' That's when my father sacked him."

A few blocks up the road we passed the river where elephants were bathing. The huge animals, mottled with pink about the ears and trunk, were playing like ponderous children, spraying water at their mahouts, sprawling on their sides, rolling, trumpeting happily. Near them, three men had driven a tractor into the river and were washing it.

"An odd car wash," Moss said.

Lakshman shrugged. "They reason that if a river bath is good enough for an elephant it's good enough for a tractor. Can't say that I'd let them wash my car, though."

We passed a group of Tamil women, barefoot, in cheap cotton saris, wearing gold necklaces, earrings, and rings. "They don't believe in banks," Lakshman said. "They put all their savings in gold and let the women wear it. You'd think there'd be more robbery than there is, with all these women walking around like that, but they seem to take care of their own. A kind of unwritten law. The gold necklace is the wedding gift from the husband. That's all he is required to give."

When we came to a stop light Lakshman pointed down the side street. "A few blocks from here is an orphan home for boys, the first one in Ceylon."

"The state operates it?" Moss asked.

"No. It's supported by private contributions. Chitra and I founded it."

Now we were nearing the center of Kandy and passing rows of neat bungalows, the brown and pinkish plaster walls and red-tiled roofs providing a fairytale picturesqueness. Lakshman's store, a block-wide, three-story building, bulged imposingly. I remembered the first time I had gone in there, to shop in the food department. One clerk took my order, a second gathered the items I was buying, a third wrapped the purchases in a newspaper and carried them to the cashier, and a fourth eventually carried them to my car. There was a fifth character standing around, observing the procedure and intervening at times to slow it up. Later, when I remarked lightly to Lakshman that it was inefficient to have four men do a job that one could easily handle, he strenuously defended the practice. "No, no," he said, "all these men need jobs. What would they do if I fired them? Would it be efficient to triple the number of unemployed? That's what would happen if we fired all our unnecessary help. No, human beings are more important than statistical charts." I had used the same reasoning when Moss commented on Ceylonese inefficiency.

The constable directing traffic under the clock tower held us up and Lakshman pointed. "That's where the beggars line up every morning and assign the territory for the day."

"I know they prey on tourists," Moss said, "but do Ceylonese themselves give to beggars?"

Lakshman shrugged. "We are not supposed to, but we often do. We know most of these beggars are faking but Buddha taught that charity is a virtue, so we give anyway. I try to give only to cripples, but it's hard to tell. One man in town pretends to be blind one day, have only one leg the next, and be decrepit the third."

A Ceylonese in Western clothes clapped his hands impatiently until a taxi-driver heard him and drove over. Lakshman smiled. "We don't whistle or shout for cabs, as people do in some countries." We followed the cab, then turned off after we passed the temple. A man wearing his hair in the old-fashioned bun at the back of his head stood outside the temple, his palms pressed together before his face, his head bowed. Two boys in short sarongs walked by without stopping. An old bus crammed full of people lumbered by, and then a group of men carrying enormous bales on their heads crossed the street, swinging their arms jauntily and chattering unconcernedly as traffic swirled around them. Moss shook his head. "Transport and transportation here are more colorful than comfortable," he said.

I agreed.

"Look," Moss cried. "There is a swastika painted on the temple."

"Yes," Lakshman said calmly. "There is."

"You mean there are Nazis here?"

"If they are, they've been here a long time," Lakshman said dryly. "The swastika is an Oriental religious symbol that goes back about three thousand years."

As we approached the house of Lakshman's parents, his little boy Ananda came out to greet us. I had once asked whether there was any special ritual in choosing children's names, and Lakshman nodded earnestly. "The astrologer said 'A' would be a lucky letter to begin our boy's name with. I'm not sure how important it is, but the women take it very seriously so it's easier to go long. And it might be very bad luck if we didn't follow the astrologer's advice."

It was just before the sunset that always seemed to come startlingly early in the tropics. The house to which Lakshman took us was at the very top of a large hill in the center of Kandy. From it one could see much of the beautiful city—the tall octagonal Temple of the Tooth, the massive Queens Hotel with its red-tiled roof, the lake with the little artificial island where queens of Kandy were sometimes sent when the King was displeased, the Hindu temple surrounded by shops and vegetable stalls, the open market a few blocks away, the squat, square new government secretariat, the hospital and the coffin shop next to it—and, dotting the hills beyond, tea plantations, coconut palms, breadfruit trees, richly hued frangipani, and wide-spread banyan trees. The house of Mr. Gunesenas was very large and very modern. All of the windows on the higher floor were floor to ceiling; on the staggered lower levels of the house, the windows jutted out of the hillside into which the house was built.

When I had visited the senior Gunasenas before, they had worn Western clothing and the meals had been served in elegant English style. There had been four servants at the table, and nine separate courses, and finger bowls with flowers floating in them. But tonight we saw rows of shoes in the entrance hall, so we took ours off. The living room was filled with people, all in white Sinhalese clothes. The women were wearing saris—some rich silks threaded with silver, others exquisitely thin materials. Chitra, sitting on the floor in a beautiful silver sari, winked at us. Near her, in a Benares sari weighted down with gold thread, lounged a long-lashed Sinhalese dowager named Dissanayaka who regarded herself as Ceylon's fashion leader.

A pale, dignified, middle-aged Englishwoman, sitting on the floor in a simple white sari, saw me and pressed her palms together. It was the widow of Lakshman's uncle, and although Moss assumed the gesture was mere courtesy, I knew that she was completely sincere. She was a devout convert to Buddhism, and when her eldest son became a bhikku she donated a large building to the temple he had joined. The men, many of whom I recognized, were wearing long-sleeved tunics and ankle-long sarongs called longues. All of them, and the women, were barefoot. It was the first time I had seen these men—a cabinet minister, two doctors, a lawyer, a judge of the Supreme Court, several wealthy businessmen—wearing anything but smart Western clothes. The prime minister was present, but he always wore the national costume in public. They were all sitting on the floor, their attention focused on the east end of the room.

The last time I had been there, that end of the large room had been a sunroom—an area of about 150 square feet, raised four feet higher than the level of the living room and approached by steps on two sides. But now a 15 x 10-foot paper house called a "mandala" filled the room, its roof barely clearing the ceiling. The walls and canopy of this "house" were daintily cut into various shapes of filigree, some thin and delicate, others wide and sweeping, all graceful and intricate. Within its walls were green plants and a variety of Oriental fruits, symbols whose meaning I didn't know and could not ask because everyone in the living room was silent. Moss and I sat down on the floor against the back wall.

In the mandala sat sixteen monks, two of them at the table. At the moment we came in, all of them had been chanting in unison the sutras of Buddha, but by now they had completed the introductory section, and fifteen of the yellow-robed monks sat back while the head priest chanted alone in Pali. He was an old man, but his voice was strong and loud, and the long-dead language seemed vibrant and flexible as he expressed sympathy, warning, sarcasm, kindliness, and consolation. I looked around and agreed with Moss that the wealthy society women listening raptly understood no more of Pali than we did. The men too were rigid with attention, and a young businessman whom a couple of evenings before I had seen drunk at the country club was now lying on his stomach, his palms pressed together above his head, his face reverent and intent.

After the head priest stopped, an old monk continued the chant. But now the mood relaxed. All of the monks except the one chanting, and one other, stood up and walked down the steps, single file, the electric lights gleaming on their shaved heads. When they had disappeared the men began to move around, and the women to whisper quietly. Lakshman came in from a bedroom. He had changed from the Western-style suit he had been wearing to a white longue. Chitra joined us.

"Is this all?" Moss asked.

"Oh, no," Lakshman said. "The pirith will go on for about forty hours. The priests take turns from now on, two of them reading the sutras continuously while the others rest. When all the sutras have been read, we will give gifts to charity and the pirith will end."

"Is sixteen priests the required number?" Moss asked.

Chitra shrugged. "Some people use only two priests. But a wealthy family like ours is expected to use the maximum number. Let's go downstairs now, and have a bite."

The large table in the dining room was covered with food, most of it candies and pastries. The priest, an old man with a pleasant round face and lively brown eyes, put a few nuts and a mango on his plate.

"Please have some more," Lakshman said.

The priest smiled politely, then recognizing us as foreigners said, also in English, "I do not need much."

Lakshman introduced us to the priest, and we held our palms together for a moment. The priest seemed pleased. Lakshman explained that Moss was interested in Buddhism and the priest said he would be glad to talk to us. He told us that he had learned English from an Oxford graduate, and he had a strong Oxonian accent in his speech, but his speech pattern was sing-song, like that of most Ceylonese, and like them he pronounced "th" as "t", and "w" as "v". We sat down in a corner of the large room.

The priest spoke slowly, liltingly, and although we sometimes failed to understand his pronunciation of a word here and there, we had no trouble following what he was saying. "Buddhism is a very reasonable philosophy, very logical, psychologically modern and totally devoid of superstitions. It is a happy medium between sensual indulgence on the one hand and excessive asceticism on the other. It is the middle way, the path of reasonable restraints for the layman.

"Lord Buddha—'Buddha' means 'the enlightened one'—taught that there are four great truths. The first truth is: life is full of suffering. Birth pain, illness, melancholy, death, work that one hates doing, separation from loved ones, such things. The second truth is: suffering is caused by desire—that is, self-centered desire. The third truth is: suffering can be cured by overcoming desire. And the fourth truth is: the method of overcoming desire is the eightfold path."

The priest paused to eat a couple of nuts and Moss said, "I have read about the eightfold path."

"Yes, it is easier to read than to practice. The path consists of right knowledge, right aspiration, right speech, right occupation, right effort, right-mindedness, right absorption, and right behavior. You Westerners are most likely to be familiar with some rules of 'right behavior.' It prohibits killing—man or animal or insect. It includes vegetarianism. It forbids lying, stealing, drinking intoxicants, or being unchaste. For priests it includes many more prohibitions, of course. Under 'right occupation,' certain jobs are objectionable. In reference to 'right effort,' willpower is tremendously important. Schopenhauer was very much interested in Buddhism for that reason. As to 'right-mindedness,' all that we are is the result of what we have thought. And 'right absorption' involves certain practices of yoga, certain techniques for achieving concentration and reflection that we have known for thousands of years, which permit yogis to perform feats that the West finds incredible."

A young man who had been standing near us took advantage of the priest's pause and came forward. The young man, whom I recognized as the owner of a large bookstore, approached the priest with his head bowed, and offered on extended palms a package of leaves. The priest smiled, pressed his hands together, then accepted the gift and began to unfold the leaves.

"It's a traditional gift to elders and eminent persons," Lakshman whispered to us. "Betel leaves, usually wrapped around areca nuts. Makes very pleasant chewing."

The priest unwrapped the last betel leaf and found a package of Chesterfield cigarettes. His face beamed with pleasure. There were no pockets in his robe and after shuffling the package from one hand to the other he put it on the table beside him and turned back to us.

"Do Buddhists believe in God?" Moss asked.

The priest shrugged good naturedly. "Not in the sense that Western religions do. It is rather difficult to explain to you, with your conception of a kindly grandfather sitting up in heaven. We believe in Nirvana, which is the highest state man can attain—an identity with Godhood. It is the achievement of life's essence, a very affirmative act, not at all the negative annihilation that you Westerners seem to visualize."

Moss hesitated. "Well," he said, "does man have a soul?"

The priest smiled. "This is another difficult problem. Even Buddhists themselves disagree. In theory, as Lord Buddha taught, there are no individual souls. That is, the soul is not a separate spiritual substance, having an individual identity. Rather, it is like a flame that is passed from candle to candle.

"That, as I say, is the theory. But in actual fact I must confess that most Ceylonese Buddhists do believe in the existence of individual souls. And they believe in reincarnation. The kind of life one leads determines whether in the next existence one's soul will inhabit a higher level of man, or an animal, or an insect. According to this belief, a soul goes through a thousand rebirths. In this long journey, some souls keep walking in the same place, so to speak, neither improving nor degenerating. A few keep purifying themselves, reaching a higher stage each time until eventually they attain Nirvana and break the cycle of desire forever. But many keep moving downward, through the animals and insects, until they end up as stones."

Moss spoke eagerly. "You do believe then in reincarnation?"

"Many do," the priest said. "But very few are able to remember their previous existences. Very few."

A mosquito had been buzzing around the priest's face, without having disturbed him. Now the mosquito settled on his cheek. The priest lifted the insect gently, delicately, off his face and let it fly away.

"And karma?" Moss asked. "What is karma?"

"Again, it is not what most Western writers think it is. It is not fate in the abstract. Nor is it destiny in the sense that the Greeks described it, as an inevitable plan. No, man creates his own karma or destiny by accumulating all of his actions and desires. Everything he has done, down to the most minute action, and everything he has wished, down to the most deeply repressed desire, combine to shape his destiny. But man's will remains free. If it is strong enough, he can shape his destiny. In that sense, the Buddha was an optimist. He is a very modern thinker. He anticipated the materialist philosophers like Hume; he agreed with William James; he transcended Freud. The Buddha knew of the subconscious, repressions, psychosomatic illnesses. A man's impressions, feelings, thoughts—these are the things that create his destiny, and these are the *only* things that create his destiny. He is not fated to fail if he really wants to free himself. There is no outsider, no god planning his future. Only man himself is responsible for himself."

"That's a terrifying idea," Moss said.

The priest bobbed his head in a side to side motion vigorously, indicating agreement. "Terrifying—or sublime. Every man has the chance to attain Nirvana. Every man can break away from the limitations of the physical."

He paused to cut a piece off the mango and put it in his mouth. "I'm afraid the priest is getting tired," Lakshman said.

"Just two more questions," Moss said. "May I?"

The priest waggled his head, so Moss asked, "What is the difference between Hinayana Buddhism and Mahayana Buddhism? I know that Hinayana means 'Little Raft' and Mahayana means 'Big Raft.' And that they refer to the vehicle used for the journey across the sea of life to the shore of enlightenment."

The priest laughed out loud and wiped his mouth with his robe. "You keep asking for simple answers to complex questions. For more than two thousand years Buddhists have been debating these problems. I suppose the basic difference is that we of the Hinayana faith believe that the highest virtue is wisdom, and that man's highest duty is to concentrate on his personal chance to attain Nirvana. The Mahayana Buddhists say that compassion is the highest virtue, and that man's highest duty is to help others." The priest smiled impishly. "I cannot say," he lowered his voice, "that the Mahayana Buddhists of China, Tibet, and Korea have a convincing record of helping others."

The mosquito had come back and was buzzing around again. The priest waved it off, absent mindedly.

"Well, then," Moss said, "isn't Western civilization on the right track? It is based on the compassion of Christianity, implemented by modern technology."

The priest smiled sadly. "Young man, let me tell you what your civilization is accomplishing. And I will use the words of your own Western philosophers to do it. Thoreau said, 'The mass of men lead lives of quiet desperation.' I would change that to noisy desperation. Hobbes said that man's life is 'nasty, brutish, and short.' I would say that the twentieth century has made it nasty, brutish, and long. Was there anything else you wanted to ask?"

Moss started to shake his head, then said, "Yes. I still don't see what satisfaction the life of a monk offers. Why do you do it?"

This time the priest did not smile. He looked at Moss earnestly and spoke slowly and carefully. "I wish I could explain that to you. All I own—and am permitted to own—is a robe, a begging bowl, and the Buddha's book. But if, as Thoreau said, a man is rich in proportion to the number of things he can do without, I am as wealthy as anyone in the world, because there is nothing else I want. Millionaires want more millions, rulers want more power, but Buddhism emphasizes detachment, aloofness, non-involvement in worldly affairs. I have retired from what you call the real world to lead a full-time life of disciplined search for enlightenment and release. Study, meditation, self-control—these are my activities. I follow the path of the Buddha. Other paths hold no attraction for me. Have you been to Polonnaruwa?"

"Yes," Moss said, surprised. "I've seen the ruins of the great city."

"Ah. The city had beautiful palaces, splendid assembly halls, magnificent swimming pools. But you don't know that there was one group of monks at Polonnaruwa for whom the king built living quarters exactly as they requested. It turned out to be a simple, primitive building with one unique feature. Only one section of this building was elaborately carved, exquisitely fashioned, and aesthetically beautiful. It was the urinal."

We didn't say anything. The priest put his hands on Moss's shoulders. "You mean well, young man," he said softly, "but you are only playing at the surface of life. There are depths in the human soul of which you haven't the slightest understanding. And it is only in those depths that the answers lie."

The priest stepped back, pressed his palms together, then turned, picked up the package of Chesterfields from the table, and went into one of the bedrooms.

"He will rest," Lakshman said, "until it is his turn to chant again, early in the morning."

We went to the food table and there found Lakshman's father talking with the prime minister. The tall, thin man with gray hair stood at the table, but his shrewd black eyes roamed constantly. When he saw us he motioned us to approach. Mr. Gunesena introduced us, and we all went out on the veranda, which ran the length of the house, at the top of the mountain, and we looked down at the lights of the city. An old servant came out, carrying a tray with homemade candies. He pointed to an especially tasty one for me, and I took it. After he had gone, I told Mr. Gunesena about the servant's friendly gesture. He smiled. "Simon is a good boy," he said. "He's been with us thirty-two years. Only the cook's been here longer."

"How many servants do you have?" Moss asked.

"Eight or nine full-time ones, I suppose," Mr. Gunesena said. "My wife would know. Six of them have been with us more than ten years. And, of course, there was an ayah for each of the children from infancy until they went away to college."

"That style of life is gone in the United States," Moss said.

"We enjoy it," Mr. Gunesena said. "And we confess that Simon did not wait on the queen. He seems to be the only servant in Ceylon who didn't."

Moss looked puzzled, so I explained that the biggest social event in Ceylon's history was Queen Elizabeth's visit in 1954. After she departed every servant who had waited on her anywhere on the island immediately demanded higher wages and was thereafter proudly introduced by his employer to guests with a good deal of reverence. Within a year the number of servants who claimed to have waited on the queen jumped to ludicrous proportions.

We looked out, under the clear sky, at the lights of the city below us. In the room behind us, dozens of people milled around the table and talked quietly, while servants unobtrusively offered trays of pastries and sweets.

"This is a beautiful country, Your Excellency," Moss said.

The prime minister nodded. He was the only Ceylonese I saw do that, but he had lived in England a long time and had acquired many Western mannerisms. "I'm glad to have Americans here to see what we're doing," he said, looking at me solemnly. "Some of your statesmen can't seem to understand why we don't take sides in the Cold War. We want the best of both your societies, the personal freedom of the West and the social consciousness of Russia and China. Our island is ideally suited for the transition to the utopia of the future. Our people are good natured, easy going, and intelligent. They have a long tradition of tolerance—Buddhism fosters that, you know. We've had Sinhalese and Tamils and Moors and Burghers living peacefully side-by-side for centuries. And Ceylonese Buddhists and Hindus and Christians and Muslims respect each other's religion. These are wonderful people, Mr. Moss—witty and lovable and charming. And because there has always been enough to eat here, they are gentle and kind."

Mr. Gunesena smiled complacently. "The people feel about the prime minister as he does about them. He's a wealthy man who was elected by the poor—and who devotes all his efforts to improve the conditions of the poor. The people call him the millionaire socialist."

The prime minister nodded. "That's true. I believe in socialism—up to a point. But I also believe in private enterprise, up to a point. My problem now is to decide exactly how much of each is best. But when we work that out, Ceylon will truly be the pearl of the Pacific. My enemies say that I have a catchall platform, promising something to everybody. They don't understand that politics requires compromise, that everyone has to give up some things for the greater good. Campaign promises are not intended to be carried out literally. But if any country can serve as a model Ceylon can. The Ceylonese are generous, honest, devout people. And they are dramatists, all of them. They love to act."

Moss nodded politely and the prime minister said, "The people have been good enough to produce a few small things I've written for the stage."

"What sort of things?"

He made a self-deprecating motion with his hands. "Oh, nothing important. For years I've amused myself by writing horror stories. Recently some of them have been staged in public, quite successfully I must say. I am working now on an adaptation of *Dracula*, which will be presented, at a big pageant next month. I hope you'll see it."

There was a slight commotion in the other room, then Lakshman's sister came in and apologized for being late. She and her husband had started to leave the bungalow on the tea plantation when their little boy pointed to the sofa and cried, "Naga." He was right. A cobra was lying between the cushions. Her husband got his stick and killed the snake. After things were cleaned up they were preparing to leave again when the boy pointed to the bookcase. The cobra's mate was coiled on a shelf. She was trickier than the male, and they finally had to shoot her. That delayed them somewhat, and she was sorry they were late.

Mr. Gunasena went out with her and we were left with the prime minister. "Forgive me, Your Excellency," Moss said hesitantly. "I've heard and read a lot about caste distinctions and race discrimination in Ceylon."

"In what way?"

"Oh, I've heard people say that the Sinhalese feel superior to the Tamils. And that within each community certain castes are superior to others and won't intermarry, and that sort of thing."

The prime minister bent his head to a side. "I'll say this, Mr. Moss. We have no more caste discrimination than you have."

"We don't have any," Moss said.

"Oh," the prime minister pursed his lips. "You mean that when a stranger is introduced at a party in your country, the group reacts exactly the same whether his name is Crawford or Karpinsky?"

Moss hesitated. "It makes a little difference."

"Or Olson or Cohen?"

"It makes some difference."

The prime minister laughed amiably. "That's what I meant. Everybody has some caste discrimination. I don't think we're very guilty." He started to walk out.

"I am puzzled by one thing," Moss said. "Buddhists don't believe in God, but you are now having a forty-hour ceremony giving thanks to God."

The prime minister smiled blandly. "You cannot expect to learn all about Buddhism in an evening, Mr. Moss. It's a very complex philosophy, and some things which at first seem contradictory, eventually become clear."

The prime minister said goodnight and left. Moss walked to the end of the veranda and looked up at the sky. From the expression on his face, I judged that it would be some time before Buddhism became clear to him.

A little later Lakshman drove us home. We talked about the prime minister, and Lakshman told us that all the workers and servants on his vast ancestral estate loved the premier.

"I noticed," Moss said, "that the prime minister isn't living at the official residence. Why is that?"

"It's been bewitched," Lakshman said gravely. "A few years ago a rival of the man who was then prime minister hired a charmer to put a black spell on the residence. The prime minister became ill, and the rival was appointed to replace him."

"Does the spell carry over to this administration?" I asked.

"You can't be sure," Lakshman said as he drove to my doorstep. "But the prime minister's astrologer told him to take no chances, so he is living at home. Goodnight."

We stood on the front steps a few minutes after he left. "It's hard to believe that people this intelligent can so superstitious."

I looked up at the clear sky and remarked that an astrologer who calculated the influence of all the stars would have a busy night ahead of him. Moss agreed and shook his head perplexedly as he went to his bedroom.

Seven

A few weeks later the Burtons invited Moss and me for an excursion into the country and a visit to a devil-dancing ceremony. Marian stopped for us at Moss's apartment in Colombo. She asked casually why Ranjini wasn't coming, and Moss replied that he hadn't seen much of her lately. I thought he sounded relieved.

We picked up George at his office and he took the wheel of the big Plymouth. Moss and I sat in back. George had with him what he called his "spy" camera. It had two lenses at right angles to each other, permitting George to take pictures of unwilling subjects by pretending that he was photographing something else. George was very proud of the camera and remarked once that he enjoyed outwitting fools.

The road south out of Colombo wound along the shore, with the ocean never more than a few yards away. Everywhere along the beach tall graceful palms leaned out to sea, almost embarrassingly lush and picturesque, like an elaborately arranged Hollywood set for a tropical movie. The sky was a pale blue, the ocean deep green, and high on the beach stood large outrigger canoes. Women in long colorful cloths and white blouses, children in tiny loincloths or naked romped around near the thatch-roofed huts scattered along the shore. Now and then the huts grouped together into tiny villages bordered by small Buddhist temples with white round roofs or, at rare intervals, by Muslim mosques. Here and there were small Catholic churches, vestiges of the sixteenth-century conquest of coastal Ceylon by Portugal.

To the west were palms leaning out to the water, large outriggers, the ocean. To the east was a thick, solid growth of jungle, sometimes broken by even rows of rubber trees. The massive breadfruit trees were green; the frangipani were luminous with bright red and orange and purple blossoms. Monkeys swung in and out of trees, and twice we had to stop to let thalagoyas—iguana-like lizards, about four feet long—cross the road. We drove slowly, weaving in and out of bullock carts, buses, trucks, cars, bicycles, and more bullock carts.

On the southern coast of the island, off the town of Weligama, we saw the famous stilt fishers. The men had planted poles deep in the sand while the tide was out. Then they attached foot bars just high enough to remain above the water when the tide came back, and on these bars they perched precariously through the evening, casting with baited hooks for little fish in the surf. That was how their ancestors had fished, one of them haltingly told us, long before white men first came to Ceylon.

About three hundred yards off shore a stately modern house almost covered the tiny island that it occupied. The waves of the ocean lapped just outside the palms that surrounded the house and gave it complete privacy.

"Shangri-La," Moss said thoughtfully.

"That's what the French count who built it thought," George said. "It's supposed to be fabulously luxurious inside. But the count doesn't live here any more. The house is up for sale."

After we had eaten dinner at the resthouse on the shore, Marian said, "I have a pleasant surprise for you. George learned just this morning that there's going to be a folk play performed near here tonight. We're going to see it."

So at eleven o'clock that night we were sitting in the open-walled schoolhouse of a little village deep in the jungle. To reach it we had driven along a narrow, rutted dirt road, then parked the car and walked a mile on a footpath overhung by thick branches and enormous leaves. George shone his flashlight, and we followed, single file, peering suspiciously into the darkness around us and flinching when we heard a sudden noise. When Moss suddenly found a leech sucking blood from his leg, Marian lit a match and held it by the little black worm until it let go and dropped off.

Only one person, an old man in a dirty sarong, was on the grounds when we reached the school, but he assured George in halting English that the performance would begin immediately. Actually it was after midnight before the fifty or sixty villagers who composed the audience arrived. They had gone to bed at sundown, as they usually did, and had awakened and dressed for the performance.

"This kind of theatre is called *sokari*," Marian told us while we waited. "It's the last trace of native Ceylonese drama. We're lucky to see a performance. They're very rare now."

There were five actors in the play, all men, although two of them played women's parts, and they had learned their parts by heart from their fathers, each of whom had in turn learned his part from his father. The plot was a long, involved series of episodes about an old doctor with a young wife. He was traveling from India to Ceylon in order to implore a local god for help in making his wife pregnant. The wife eventually became pregnant, obviously with more help from the youthful manservant than from the god, and in the entre-acts the characters improvised with satiric comment on the hypocrisy of contemporary politicians and the sexual habits of prominent local citizens. They were still going strong at six in the morning when we had to leave.

"I can see why the performances are rare," Moss said as we walked back through the jungle in the dawn light. "They're much too long."

"No," George said, "they've always been all-night affairs, intended originally to keep people awake during the harvest season so they could drive off pilfering animals. They've been popular for centuries. But now the radio and movies have spoiled the natives' taste. Now there are radios in every village, and these people get to see Indian and American movies. They don't care any more about their own traditional drama."

We drove as rapidly as the dirt road permitted back to the rest-house and slept till noon. Then we ate a lunch of freshly caught seir fish and got into the car again.

But our progress was slow. Just outside of town George took a side-road and five minutes later we stopped by a small stucco house. A middle-aged man in a red sarong greeted us politely, spoke to George a few minutes, then led us to an open shed behind the house. There, under a circular roof supported by a half a dozen posts, a fire was burning in an open pit, and around it five men in short dhotis sat on mats, working. The host offered Marian a chair, an intricately carved Victorian piece with faded red velvet, incongruous in a Ceylonese hut. This was a tortoise-shell factory, the man explained, showing us how the men made bracelets, napkin rings, pill boxes, combs, and letter openers. Each man made a different object, holding it by iron tongs in the fire until the shell was soft enough to bend, then sticking the cool end between the toes of the right foot and holding it in that convenient vise while he filed and manipulated the shell into the desired object. The men were arranged around the fire in the order of seniority, and the leader with his long white hair tied in a bun at the back of his head quickly carved an elaborately decorative bracelet. When the shell had to be bent again, he held it patiently in the fire with the iron tong. We watched for a while, then the owner escorted us back to the car. He had to send to the Maldive Islands for the shells, he told us proudly. There weren't enough in Ceylon.

A mile further on we stopped to visit another small factory, where wooden elephants were carved. At the entrance to the barn-like, open-walled building were stacked logs of ebony, teak, satinwood, coconutwood, and several Ceylonese trees for which there are no English names. Here too there were five men. The first, with a rough saw, cut the logs into blocks. The second man put each block into a vise and with a chisel and mallet hewed out a roughly shaped elephant. The third man, with a thinner chisel and smaller mallet, put in the details—trunk, ears, tail, and toes—and passed them on to the fourth man, who sandpapered the wooden animal. The fifth man applied a dark stain and piled up the elephants behind him, ready for the salesmen.

"That isn't real ivory they use for the tusks, you notice," George pointed out. "Real ivory is too expensive, especially the Ceylon variety."

"What's special about it?" Moss asked.

"The Ceylon elephant, unlike the African, never digs the earth for roots or for water. As a result, his tusks are less brittle and of a smoother texture. They're more valuable on the world market."

It was almost two o'clock when we took the road again, and George said regretfully, "I'm afraid we won't have time to visit the lens grinder near here. There's a family a few miles away that makes glasses for spectacles. Their ancestors have been doing it for a couple of hundred years, and the workmanship is so good that one of the cabinet ministers has them make his glasses. They know nothing about optometrists' prescriptions or modern methods, but the lenses they grind are as good as anything you can buy in New York."

We rode for two hours inland and up the central mountains toward Ratnapura, "the city of gems." The road hung along the side of the mountain, the curves were sharp, the drop-off was hundreds of feet, and the views were magnificent. George slowed up as we passed on dry earth under a four-thousand-foot waterfall, the narrow stream of water dropping past us like the jet of a giant faucet.

In Ratnapura we ate lunch at the home of George's friend, a businessman named Jinadasa. He was a short, fat man with glazed black eyes and an earnest desire to be cordial. He insisted that we see gem mining, and after a short rest we took a dead-end road a few miles out of the city. Then we walked a half a mile across cleared jungle to a shallow river. The river had been dammed off, and a dozen men stood next to each other, waist deep in the river, scraping the river-bottom with twelve-foot-long shovels. They dumped the dirt they brought up into broad, shallow baskets held by two men standing in the water behind them, and those men shook the baskets and panned for gems.

After watching them for a while, we walked a few feet away from the shore to look at open-pit mining. Ten men had sunk a twenty-five-foot shaft into the earth and were now sending up baskets of what looked like colored rock.

"What kind of gems do they find here?" Marian asked.

Jinadasa waved his fat arms expansively. "All kinds. Blue sapphires, star sapphires. Rubies—red and yellow. And less valuable stones—topaz, tourmaline, spinel, garnet, amethyst, aquamarine, cat's eye. Lots of moonstones—the image of the moon is supposed to be reflected in the stone. But moonstones are so common here they're very cheap."

"I'd like to get a few," Marian said, looking at George.

He nodded. "I've already spoken to Jinadasa about it. When we get back to town he'll take us to a gem merchant."

The foreman had been watching us and now came over and said something to Jinadasa. "He wants to know if you're thirsty." When we said we were, the foreman yelled something to one of the boys helping the workers. The boy disappeared for a few moments, then returned with a basket of king coconuts. The foreman drilled each one open and handed them to us, and we drank the cool, thin, watery liquid direct from the coconut. It tasted wonderful at first, then suddenly became flat.

On the drive back to Ratnapura, Jinadasa told us that gem mining was a weekend hobby for him and several of his land-owning friends. Sometimes they found valuable stones, but usually the gems barely paid for the labor. It was the thrill of the gamble that lured them, Jinadasa said. Then he turned to Marian.

"Mrs. Burton, I must warn you about the gem merchant we're going to see. He has the biggest stock in town but he is as crooked as a man can be and still stay out of jail. You'll have to bargain very hard with him, and if you do decide to buy any valuable stones from him I'll have my own appraiser examine them before the deal is closed."

Mahomet Rahim's store was in the center of the busy Ratnapura shopping district. Large gems were casually exposed on newspapers in the window seat, and toward the back a dark old Muslim was polishing stones on an emery wheel. A brown, middle-aged man in a shabby sarong came toward us, smiling ingratiatingly. Jinadasa shook hands with him and introduced us to Mr. Rahim.

"Americans," Rahim said genially. "Always a pleasure to do business with Americans. You are very fortunate. Just this morning a shipment arrived from the mines, and I am badly overstocked. I am ready to give stones away today. Now this star sapphire, lady, is one of the most beautiful stones I ever had. Look at that star shine. Isn't it beautiful?"

Marian looked and frowned. "But it's a gray stone. The best stones are blue. Everybody knows that."

Rahim shook his head sadly. "Ah, lady, lady. The foolish notions people spread who don't understand gems. Many connoisseurs prefer the gray sapphire because the star shows up more clear. But what can a man do? I'll tell you. Since you're a friend of Mr. Jinadasa, I give it to you for three hundred rupees."

Marian looked at the stone. "Thirty rupees."

Rahim beamed. "Lady, lady. Even Mr. Jinadasa I would have to ask two hundred rupees."

"Forty," Marian said.

While the bargaining was going on, I looked at the wall of the shop. It was covered with what seemed to be testimonials, and I looked at one closely. It said:

To Whom It May Concern:
Mahomed Rahim is a gem merchant and property owner in Ratnapura. He has a wife and four children. Signed,
       James P. Andrews
       Government Agent, Ratnapura

This seemed such a restrained endorsement that I read the next testimonial.

To Whom It May Concern:
Mahomed Rahim is a property owner in Ratnapura. He has paid his property tax. Signed,
    K. Jayatillika, Mayor

The other testimonials were similar in tone, limiting their endorsement of Rahim to what was clearly an absolute minimum. But on the center wall, under glass and beautifully framed, was a long document which, I thought, would surely pay some tribute to Rahim. I read it carefully.

The framed statement was a letter from the office of the Lord Chancellor of England, signed by his private secretary. The letter was addressed to Mahomed Rahim and said, in effect, that Mr. Rahim's letter had been received; that every statement in it was false; that Mr. Rahim was either a fool or a knave; and that the Lord Chancellor wanted to hear no more, on this subject or any other, from Mr. Rahim. If Mr. Rahim should choose to annoy the Lord Chancellor again, appropriate legal action would immediately be taken. The letter was dated fifteen years earlier, so apparently the affair had stopped there. The frame and the glass over the letter were quite expensive, and there was an electric light immediately above it, presumably so that evening visitors would also have the opportunity to see the Lord Chancellor's opinion of Rahim.

I turned away from the testimonial and heard Rahim say, "Lady, you win. I give you the star sapphire for sixty rupees."

While he was wrapping it, Marian said apologetically, "I realize you have to make a profit, Mr. Rahim."

Rahim took her money and put it in a steel box. "Don't worry, lady, I make a profit. One American like you every day, and I stay in business a long time."

Before we left Ratnapura, George insisted on stopping at a store and buying a bottle of Haig and Haig. He had a quick drink before we said goodbye to Jinadasa, and a long one as the car rolled along the mountain road toward the village where the devil dancing was going to be held. The rest of us dozed quietly, resting up for the long night ahead.

"We'll be there soon," George said, loudly enough to wake us. I looked at his bottle and saw that it was one-third empty. But he seemed quite alert and only a slight slurring in his speech revealed how much he had drunk.

Moss awoke, too. "What's the occasion for the devil dancing?" he asked.

"There's a sick woman in the village," George said. "She's been ailing for a few months. The family is pretty well off, and one of the sons works in our office in Colombo. That's how I heard of it, and that's why we're welcome tonight. At first they tried the native medicine—an Ayurvedic doctor. When that didn't help she went to a doctor trained in England. But he couldn't cure her either, so now they're going back to the traditional method. They've hired devil dancers to drive out the evil spirit who inflicted the illness on her. It's going to be a long and colorful ceremony. The dancers will wear fantastic, terrifying masks; they'll chant long incantations; they'll go through rigidly prescribed rituals; and they'll dance with increasing wildness through the night. The fire will cast eerie shadows and the dancers will toss gunpowder in scarlet flashes. The children will be petrified with terror."

"But—what religion does this family believe in?"

"Buddhism."

Moss frowned. "I don't understand. How can a Buddhist, who isn't supposed to believe even in God, believe in devils?"

"It's not a matter of understanding," George said brusquely. "It's simply a matter of fact. These people are Buddhists, but they do believe in devil dancing. Hell, the world is full of contradictory religions. Why should the Ceylonese be any different? But if you want a historical explanation, there is one. By the third century B.C., when King Asoka's son brought Buddhism to Ceylon, the Sinhalese already had a firmly established religion. They believed that evil spirits caused the illnesses and misfortunes of human beings—call them devils if you like. Each of these devils has charge of a separate disease—malaria, dysentery, toothache, miscarriage, anything. And other devils have charge of various forms of bad luck—ruined crops, loss of love, failure in business, whatever trouble a person can have. There are special rituals for placating these spirits, for ingratiating or frightening. Now this concept is totally different from the calm logic of Buddhism. But logic has nothing to do with it. They accepted Buddhism in principle, and they continue to apply this indigenous exorcism in practice, and there you are. It isn't really very different from the way South American natives adapted Roman Catholicism. Or American Indians adapted Christianity."

"And all Ceylonese Buddhists believe in it?"

"Oh, no," George said. "Educated Ceylonese ridicule it, and even out here in the villages devil dancing is dying out. Not, I think, because of growing rationalism but simply because the ceremony is cumbersome, expensive, and inconvenient. My guess is that the Ceylonese are just as superstitious as they ever were. They do their placating of devils and gods in socially more restrained ways, such as the pirith ceremony for instance. Very few Ceylonese leaders make an important move without going through a prescribed ritual—from the prime minister down."

We were all quiet for a while, then George blurted out vehemently, "I wish to God *we* had a way of placating devils." He said it so bitterly that Marian turned to him immediately and pressed his arm. I said quickly, "If you want someone who's full of superstitions, Piodasa will do nicely."

Marian looked at me gratefully. "Tell us about him."

"Well, I hired him because he showed up at the door just when I needed a cook. I asked him later what made him come then. He looked at me haughtily. 'Stars know everything,' he said. 'Astrologer say that my lucky hour. I come near bungalow, wait all day till lucky hour come, go to door, ask for job. Not smart make fun astrologer.'"

"I suppose your first cook had passed the word that he expected to be fired at any moment," George said.

"I suppose. Piodasa complained immediately that there were *yakas* in the bungalow."

"What's a *yaka?*" Moss asked.

"An evil demon. Piodasa came to me and said in a low voice, 'Yaka come at night, knock on door, make noise, eat people.'

"I asked him whether he had heard them in our bungalow. He waggled his head solemnly. 'Every night.'

"'Well, what do you do when you hear them?' I asked him.

"He seemed surprised. 'I close my window and lock my door. What you think I do?'

"I told him to call me the next time he heard *yakas* and I would see what was going on. 'Sure, Master,' he said. 'I call you. But I no tink they come tonight.'

"I understood by that remark that he was frightened and had no intention of calling anybody; but, like most Ceylonese servants, he had gotten into the habit of never saying 'no' to a Western employer, so he pretended to agree. A week later I heard someone knocking on the front door at two in the morning. I went to the door and called out, but no one answered, and when I turned on the entrance light and opened the door there was no one there. The next day Piodasa admitted that he had heard the knocking. "many *yakas* here, Master. This bad bungalow for *yakas*."

"Why?"

"Bungalow hopeless,' he said. 'Hopeless' is his favorite adjective, and he uses it indiscriminately to criticize tradesmen, movies, politicians, and the houseboy. 'Bungalow face wrong direction, bad-luck direction. That's why *yakas* come.'

"He was delighted when, a few weeks later, I told him that we were moving to another bungalow, much nearer the campus. But he absolutely refused to move that Saturday. 'Now, Master. Very unlucky day. Must not do big thing like move this Saturday. Best not do anything this Saturday.'

"'That's ridiculous, Piodasa,' I said. 'You don't really believe that.'

"'Master,' he said earnestly, 'I not even go to toilet this Saturday.'

"It turned out that the moving van couldn't, or wouldn't, come that Saturday, so we moved on Monday. Whether Piodasa would have accompanied me otherwise, I'll never know."

The car was going slowly now, down a narrow dirt road surrounded on both sides by thick jungle. The sun was shining, but the jungle was dark and impenetrable and faintly menacing. "You know," Moss said, "it's much easier to make fun of superstitions in the safety of modern civilization than when you're exposed to wild nature. A man living in semi-primitive conditions is constantly in danger from snakes, wild animals, diseases that we've eliminated. It's natural for him to turn to charmers and astrologers to help him fight the evil forces that surround him."

"Natives aren't the only ones who are superstitious," Marian said. "Millions of Americans read the forecasts of astrologers and thousands of them have horoscopes cast. Gambling is a form of superstition, and we have hundreds of taboos, like walking under a ladder or three on a match or knocking on wood. Many Westerners who live in an environment like this become much more susceptible to local beliefs."

"Are you thinking of Major Perrin?" I asked.

"Yes," Marian said. "As a matter of fact I was. He left before you came, Anthony. Major Perrin was the British military attaché here for a couple of years. On the table of his living room he kept a damaged wooden figure of an African god. It's called a juju. He didn't mind telling people why it was there. It seems that during the war the major was in charge of an African territory. The natives had been stealing and he punished them. In revenge, they pooled together twenty-five dollars and paid a native sorcerer to kill Major Perrin by magic. The sorcerer went through his whole ritual, with magic formulae and incantations and hexes. The next day, he said, the major would die.

"The following morning the major lost control of his car on a hillside curve and rolled down the hill. The car was a total wreck but he came out unscratched. In the car, considerably damaged, was this "juju" that a more powerful African sorcerer had once given him and that he always carried with him. Now he keeps it in full view in his living room."

A few minutes later we arrived at the village. A thin young man in a white sarong came to the car and greeted us in English. He was Kapilla, the son who worked in George's office, and after exchanging palm-pressed salutes we followed him to a mud-and-wattle hut near the center of the village. Water was brought for our washing, then we were served fruits and nuts. There were no chairs in the small, dark room, so we sat on the mats that covered parts of the dirt floor and ate. We had barely finished when the sun went down, and Kapilla lit a torch and led us outside.

The devil dancing, he told us, would take place in the garden behind his parents' house, a few huts away. He led us into the garden, enclosed by coconut trees. Large flaming torches encircled the area and provided the illumination. At the end of the garden was a temporary dais on which we could dimly see a person lying. "My mother," Kapilla whispered huskily. We could not distinguish the women's features or see the expression on her face. There was an area in front of the dais reserved for shrines and for the devil dancing itself. We sat down on mats at the edge of the prescribed area.

Villagers were arriving and sitting down behind us, men wandered around making last-minute preparations, and Kapilla sat near us explaining what was going on. The devil dancers themselves belong to a special caste—a low caste, he indicated contemptuously. (Later George told us that in Colombo Kapilla proudly insisted that Ceylon was a true democracy.) The main shrine, at the end of the dance area, was woven of braided palm stalks and stems. Into the walls of the three smaller shrines near it patterns and flower designs were woven out of yellow palm leaves. From the ceiling of matted palm fronds narrow strings of leaves hung over the dance area, undulating slowly in the slight evening breeze. White flowers were scattered profusely along the walls. On one side was a long arrow whose mission in the ceremony, Kapilla explained, would be to compel recalcitrant devils to identify themselves. Each of the shrines was dedicated to a different demon, one of whom was suspected of inflicting the illness on Kapilla's mother. By appealing directly to the devils, the dancers would entice them to approach the vicinity and inveigle the responsible devil to enter the sick woman's body. Then the dancers would, through the prescribed ritual, threaten and beg, terrify and bribe the evil spirit until he promised to release his suffering victim.

A boy came out of the house and spoke to Kapilla. He explained that there would be a delay and suggested that we go into the house for a while. Marian and Moss went in, but George curtly refused. Seeing that he had almost finished the bottle he had been carrying, I decided to stay with him and keep an eye on him. He was muttering angrily to himself.

"Think I'm drunk?" he asked belligerently.

"You know what you're doing," I said.

He glared at me, then looked away. "Yeah, I know damned well what I'm doing. Jesus, how I wish you really could drive out demons by hiring dancers. I'd hire every goddamned dancer on the island, so help me. I'd have the biggest exorcism they ever saw."

His head drooped for a while, then he looked at me again, his face gaunt in the moonlight. "But we know better, don't we? For some crimes there is no exorcism and no atonement. Even if you've been sorry every moment since you did it. And wished you had just one more chance to undo it."

A spasm passed over his face. "I'm talking like a child. Just one more chance. But nobody gets a second chance."

I picked up his bottle and put it down near me where I hoped he wouldn't notice it. He was looking at the dais where the woman lay quietly. The moon drenched the garden in pale silvery light and the coconut trees formed a stockade around us. Indistinct Sinhalese voices murmured behind us, but George was not aware of them.

"I lost my nerve," he said tensely. "It was my fault, but I couldn't help it. I just couldn't help it."

He stopped and I waited. I knew that he wanted me to ask, that it would make it easier for him if he were urged to talk. But I did not want to initiate my own involvement. If I became involved I would accept the responsibility, but I didn't want to force myself into his destiny. It was a foolish hesitation, and meaningless, since these things work themselves out and neither hesitation nor encouragement on my part could have changed his fate in the slightest degree.

George sighed softly. "He was my best friend at college and I betrayed him. I didn't want to, but I've always been afraid of physical pain, and I thought they were going to hurt me. They came to initiate us and I thought if I told them about Peter they'd let me alone. I told them he once belonged to the communist party. He was only a kid then and he quit the party when he was nineteen and I was the only one who knew about it. After I told, they took away his scholarship. He had wanted to be a doctor and now he couldn't, and he dropped out of school. He called me a Judas." He paused and looked down at the ground. "I'll never forget the way he looked at me. He couldn't understand that I didn't want to hurt him. I just couldn't help it."

George looked around for the bottle, reached over near me, and took a long drink. "Wouldn't it be fine if I could arrange a devil dance to drive it out of my mind? Our Western technology just hasn't gotten around to inventing that kind of device. It would be a hell of a lot more useful than color television and juke boxes to me."

Kapilla came back with an elderly Ceylonese in a long white sarong. "My father," he said. We pressed palms. Kapilla explained that his father didn't speak English but wanted us to know that we were very welcome. The skin on the old man's face was smooth, and he looked at us calmly and benignly.

"Ask him if the devil dance is sure to be successful," George said.

Kapilla translated. The old man smiled placidly, and spoke, quietly and confidently. "Absolutely," Kapilla said. "He has no doubt at all."

"Why is he so sure?" George asked.

The father and son talked for a moment. "Because evil spirits cause diseases. They can be persuaded to remove the diseases, and devil dancing is the only way to do it. My father never wanted to try the Western doctor in the first place. He knows the devil dancers can cure Mother. He says everybody knows that."

George nodded somberly. "Everybody knows that," he said. Kapilla's father said goodbye and the two of them went back to the house. George took another drink. "How about that?" he said bitterly. "That ignorant old fool is better off than I am. He believes. What he believes is nonsense, but it satisfies him and gives him peace of mind. And I know all about psychology and philosophy and superstition, and I can't find a moment's peace."

Marian and Moss returned, saying that the dancing was about to start. They had barely sat down before four bare-chested drummers appeared at the end of the arena. Their hair was tied behind their heads in a careless bun, and later, when they excitedly increased the rhythm to a feverish pitch, the buns bounced up and down absurdly. Near them stood six singers. Now a dozen dancers suddenly began cavorting around the dance area. They were all men dressed to look like women. Their heads were covered with a red cloth from which hung strips of palm leaves resembling a woman's hair. On their chests were brief cloths intended to represent a breast covering, and they wore long skirts down to the ground. Sometimes when they kicked their legs we could see the large bells tied above their ankles, clanging discordantly throughout the dance. The dance steps themselves were primitive. The men walked or trotted, arms outstretched and waving, the feet in rhythm with the beat of the drummers and the chanting of the singers. After a series of simple steps, the dancers began spinning and whirling, building up to a twirling leap during which the body remained parallel to the ground but spinning rapidly for fantastically long periods of time. Another dancer suddenly stood still and began swaying his body more and more rapidly until the coconut hair twirled around him like a huge dark halo.

The dancers rested, then started again. On and off for hours the ritual went on, while the chief exorcist murmured and shouted the magic formulae which established contact with the demons. Then a new element was suddenly introduced into the dance. The chief dancer, carrying a tray of charcoal in his left hand, threw a handful of gunpowder over the tray. It ignited immediately, setting afire a long white cloth above the shrine and exploding into a flash of reddish white flame, which raced across the garden. The other dancers, holding burning torches, spun and whirled and jumped around the area, forming a ring of blazing, racing fire. They were so close to us that sparks constantly landed on and near us, and a young attendant ran around stamping out the incipient flames. The dancers themselves were not disturbed by the flames at all, pausing at intervals to dip their faces and bodies in the fire spurting from the torches. In the exuberant finale of the fire dance, the dancers held the torches under their chest-coverings, ignoring the flames licking their bodies and shining through the cloth. Not one dancer showed any sign of burning.

After a long interval—it was almost dawn now—the dancers came out for the last phase of the ritual. They had discarded all the feminine paraphernalia—the long hair, the breast coverings, and the skirt—and now wore masks representing the demons, which had been summoned. Some of the masks symbolized specific diseases, one a vicious-looking demon holding a tiny human corpse in her teeth, another a bird swallowing a snake, a third a face composed of writhing cobras. Each of the demons ran around the area, calling out his identity. They had been forced to do so by the chief exorcist, Kapilla excitedly whispered to us. His eyes were gleaming, and there was no doubt that he accepted the authenticity of the ceremony.

The chief exorcist shouted to the disease-causing demon, and the demon shouted back. They harangued each other for a while, then the devil dancer turned and left, followed by all the others. "He promised to leave Mother," Kapilla said happily. "The Kapuraia forced him. But he said he will come back some day. Mother is cured now."

We stepped forward toward the dais. The old woman was lying asleep, breathing quietly and regularly. George stood staring at her while the rest of us walked back to the house. Marian took me aside.

"Did George say anything to you?" she asked.

"He told me about Peter. He feels very guilty about him."

She breathed what I thought was a sign of relief. "Yes, Peter. What did he say?"

I repeated what George had told me. She hesitated. "That's all?"

"Yes," I said.

She turned away and started to walk toward the table covered with fruits and sweet pastries.

"Was there more to the story than that?" I called after her.

She turned slowly. "A year later Peter killed himself," she said. Then she went back to the food table. I went outside. George was still standing by the dais, looking at the peacefully sleeping woman.

Marian took the wheel on the drive back. We were delayed once by a python stretched out across the rarely traveled road. The huge snake wasn't looking for trouble. He apparently found the road a pleasant place to rest, but he responded to Marian's repeated honking by eventually slithering his fifteen-foot body off the road and into the jungle. Marian drove fast until we reached the main highway.

Eight

When Moss finally realized that he was getting only a superficial view of Ceylon and said he wished he could talk to an expert, I arranged a meeting with a Ceylonese journalist. I thought that Chris Van Langenburg, sub-editor of the leading newspaper, certainly qualified. That Saturday we left my bungalow about ten in the morning and I drove the Volkswagen slowly along the Kandy road. The traffic was heavy, but we were in no hurry, and I patiently followed the stream of bullock carts, bicycles, automobiles, buses, and trucks. The vividly colored Peradeniya Botanical Gardens filled the landscape on our left, and crows kept croaking in the trees and flying across the highway. Moss said that he found them vaguely disturbing.

On the porch of a small house two women were sitting, one carefully picking lice out of the other woman's hair. A little farther on two monkeys sat at the foot of a tree, one carefully picking lice out of the other monkey's hair. Moss looked at me and smiled.

A large lizard waddled out on the highway, and the Austin in front of us stopped and waited until the lizard got off the road. "That lizard is protected by law," I explained. "It's harmless, and it eats snakes."

"An awful lot of snakes around here," Moss murmured.

"The newspapers publish daily lists of snake-bite deaths," I told him, "the way American papers list traffic deaths. But the people don't seem to mind them. I once mentioned that we had rats and the veterinary-medicine professor offered to give me a ratsnake to keep in the house. It's five or six feet long, and as thick around as your bicep. You saw one that day we took a walk. I told him I preferred the rats. And last week I was watching a cricket match at the university when the players started scurrying around and yelling. It turned out there was a cobra on the field, and there was a wild commotion before one of the boys killed it with a cricket bat."

"The students aren't superstitious, then?"

I hesitated. "They select their superstitions, just as American students do." I pulled the car around an elephant standing in the road, and Moss said, looking back, "No one seems to be concerned about elephants here."

"There are all tame, and each one is handled by his mahout. It's the rogue elephant you have to keep away from."

"What's a rogue elephant?"

"An elephant that's been kicked out of his herd for antisocial activity. Elephants living in the wild have a very strict organization, and the elephant that violates their rules is thrown out. A rogue elephant is a bad elephant, and is likely to attack anybody. He tramples rice fields, crushes huts, kills people. The villagers usually ask for a hunter to come out and kill him. They can't handle him themselves."

A man was squatting nonchalantly by the roadside, his sarong spread out carefully around him.

"Resting?" Moss asked.

"Going to the bathroom," I said. "They usually use the fields, but the roadside is a popular place. That's one of the reasons eating fresh vegetables is risky. Too much 'night soil' around."

As we neared Kandy we saw more men walking towards town. In spite of the blistering sun, none of them was wearing a hat. Some of the women and many of the monks carried umbrellas. The monks' saffron robes dotted the landscape and sometimes, when the sun hit them, their shaved heads gleamed. A cow appeared suddenly in the middle of the road, and I headed for its tail. The cow kept moving and I passed it safely. Someone had told me that cows rarely change direction on Ceylon roads, and so far the advice had proved sound.

The highway was a wide ribbon of asphalt, laid out by the British before the war. At frequent intervals the sign "slippery when wet" warned the driver. Along the roadside were stalls selling mangoes and jakfruit, and near the edge of the city a small factory manufactured spurious Dutch antiques. When we reached the market I stopped to get some papayas, but before we could get out of the car, beggars surrounded us. A simpering young woman carrying an infant, a sad-faced boy, and an old man in a dirty sarong crowded around us, all holding out their hands. I brushed by them and went to the fruit stall.

"They seem so pathetic," Moss said. "Especially the woman with the baby."

"She seemed less pathetic last week," I told him, "when she was fighting with another beggar-woman over a week-old baby. The baby didn't belong to either one of them, any more than this baby does. They both wanted to use the baby in that day's begging, and they had almost torn it apart before a constable chased them away. I don't know where the real mother was."

"I knew that many beggars are fakers, but I didn't know it was this bad," Moss said.

"It's a lot worse. India has passed a law making life in prison the punishment for master beggars who maim children and put them out to beg in streets. There are organized gangs like that in parts of India."

I bought the papayas and we were returning to the car when another beggar woman stepped in front of me and put out her palm. She was an attractive middle-aged woman with a wistful expression, and she was wearing a cheap, torn, dirty sari, a heavy gold necklace, a gold nose-stud, gold rings on all ten fingers, rings on the two large toes, and two pairs of gold earrings, one in the ear-lobes and the other in the ear-tops. Moss shook his head in amazement. We walked around the woman, got back into the car, and drove past fly-covered slabs of meat hanging in the open stalls.

I parked near the Queens Hotel and Dasa came over, bowing and smiling. Dasa was an old Sinhalese who pretended that he protected the cars parked on that street. What he protected them from, I told Moss, I never learned, but he was enthusiastic about his self-appointed job and he was happy with the rupee a month I gave him. It seemed simpler to go along with the gag.

A woman with a heavy jug on her head strolled by us, window-shopping as she walked, swinging her arms gracefully. Just outside the hotel a snake charmer was folding up his cobra and putting it away in a flat round box, like a tailor stuffing a tape-measure back into its container. The doorman came towards us, bowing and smiling. He had a grenadier type of mustache, a big red sash across his chest, and a crimson cylinder-hat on his head. "Mr. Van Langenburg inside," he told me. I gave him a rupee every month too, although I wasn't sure why.

Queens Hotel, four-storied, its walls brown-and-cream colored, the roof red-tiled, towered massively over the center of Kandy. Across the street was the artificial lake of the Kandy kings, and a block away the Temple of the Tooth from which we had watched the Perahara.

Van Langenburg came over to greet us, and I introduced Moss to him. Van was a short, squat Eurasian with olive skin, thick features, and very dark eyes. He took us to the lobby, where he had been drinking beer, and we all sat down. Then he turned to Moss and smiled. "Westerling tells me you're interested in the inside story on Ceylon," he said crisply. "I suppose that means you're familiar with the pap about Ceylon being the Pearl of the East and the Eden of the Orient, that Solomon mentioned it in the Bible and Marco Polo called it the most beautiful island in the world. And you must have seen Bishop Heber's remark, 'in Ceylon every prospect pleases.' The guidebooks are less likely to quote the remainder of his statement: '—and only man is vile.'

The Bishop made that statement more than a century ago, but it's still accurate.

"If you want the truth about Ceylon, I can give it to you. The first Van Langenburg came here from Holland in 1684. I was born here. I took my degree at the University of London, and I've been a journalist here for twenty-three years. With the exception of Western experts who make three-day visits to Ceylon, I suppose I know as much about the country as anyone does. But I should admit at the start that I'm prejudiced. Ever since Ceylon got its independence, we Burghers have been discriminated against by the Sinhalese majority. I can understand why they do it—for four centuries the whites have discriminated against them—but that doesn't make it any easier for me."

He signaled to the waiter, and the old man in a white coat and white sarong padded over in his bare feet. "Yes, Master," he said, bowing a little. His gray hair was combed into a bun at the back of his head, and a large tortoise-shell comb stood up above the bun. Van Langenburg ordered beer and the waiter went away.

"You were looking at the comb on his head. It used to be a mark of differentiation between servants, signifying that he was high enough up in the servant hierarchy to never have to carry packages on his head. Very few people still follow the custom. All it means now is that he's too old-fashioned to keep up with the times. He's an anachronism. But Ceylon is full of anachronisms. And paradoxes.

"For instance, Ceylonese Buddhism is famous as the religion of reason and restraint, but Ceylon has the highest murder rate in the world. Instead of nodding, we Ceylonese waggle our heads from side to side as a sign of agreement. We wash ourselves carefully—before eating food so unhygienically prepared that ninety percent of the people have dysentery. We once had a tropical paradise where everyone had enough to eat and malaria was the only serious problem. Now Western medicine has almost eliminated malaria and the population has quadrupled and we have to import half our food. Outside of Japan, we have the highest standard of living in the Orient. We are also the most dissatisfied nation in the Orient. We wear white clothes to funerals but carry black umbrellas to protect ourselves from the sun. The Westerner gets out into the sun so that his skin will darken, but the upper-class Ceylonese avoids exposure in the hope that his skin will become lighter. A friend of mine, a wealthy Ceylonese merchant who makes frequent trips to Europe, is convinced that after a few months in England he becomes considerably lighter-skinned than he is here.

"Our political leaders have degrees from leading European universities, but almost all of them regularly consult astrologers before making decisions. Many educated Ceylonese—and all of the uneducated—wait for an astrologically auspicious moment before taking a trip, or giving an infant his first solid food, or choosing a wedding date."

The waiter with the comb in his hair brought the beer and Van poured it. "You're right about auspicious days," I said. I mentioned Lakshman waiting three months for his wife to return home with the baby, and Piodasa refusing to move from the bungalow.

Moss laughed, but Van Langenburg didn't. "Of course," he said. "We're all superstitious. Thousands of people in Ceylon got married one day last month because the astrologers said it was an auspicious day. Next April, for instance, on the day of our New Year, the proper moment for kindling the first fire will be 11:21 a.m. The time to eat the first meal will be 1:54 p.m., facing west. Since emerald green is the auspicious color for this particular year, everyone connected with official festivities will be dressed in that color. The time for anointing the head with oil will be 9:07 p.m. And the following morning, at exactly 4:17 a.m., millions of people all over the island will face north and leave their homes, for that is the auspicious hour for returning to work. What they'll do when they get to work at that hour, I don't know.

"Last week I had to take the bus to Polonnaruwn. Before we started, the driver broke a coconut at a shrine to ensure a safe journey. I know a man who writes scurrilous verse in the vernacular—or refrains from writing it, for a fee. His father is a devil dancer, his uncle is a professional charmer, and he himself is regularly consulted by leading Colombo families to help them choose auspicious days. On top of that, man for man the Ceylonese bet more money on horses than any other country in the world."

A boy wandered into the hotel, looked around, and came to our table. He took a batch of tickets out of his pocket. "Lottery tickets, masters?" he said. "Lucky numbers." Moss took out a rupee and bought a ticket just before the servant with the comb spotted the boy and shooed him out of the hotel.

"Did you win anything with the tickets you bought on Adam's Peak?" I asked.

Moss shook his head.

"Did anyone in that group win?"

"No," he said, "But you never can tell. I don't need the money. It's just fun to gamble."

Van Langenburg smiled wryly. "The average Ceylonese is kind to guests and cruel to servants—a large number of whom are children under twelve, in spite of laws forbidding both the employment of children and cruelty to servants. He imitates the English by driving on the left side of the street, by pretending that he believes in parliamentary democracy, and by wearing English coats—sometimes with a sarong instead of trousers. But he publicly blames England for most of Ceylon's economic, political, and social problems."

A man in a dirty gray shirt and bright red sarong sidled up to our table. "Best star sapphires, master," he whispered as he put a piece of folded newspaper on the table and opened it up. There were gray and light-blue stones in it. When Moss held one up to the light, we could see a hazy white star in the middle. Moss put it back on his newspaper.

"Very good price, master," the man said.

"I don't need any," Moss told him.

"Best price, master. Very good price."

"How much?" Moss asked.

The man looked quickly at Van Langenburg. "Three hundred rupees," he whispered.

"No," Moss said. "I don't want any."

Van Langenburg said something angrily, in Sinhalese, and the man smiled at Moss obsequiously. "You friend Master Langenburg. I give you better price."

"What price?" Moss asked.

"Thirty rupees," he said eagerly.

Moss finally convinced him that he didn't want to buy and the man went away. "He knew you were an American," Van Langenburg said. "The local gem merchants assume that Americans are keen on star sapphires, Englishmen on diamonds, and Dutch on emeralds. But you didn't come here to talk about gems. You want to know the truth about the Ceylonese people."

He played thoughtfully with his beer glass. "The average Ceylonese disapproves of racial discrimination everywhere in the world, and is especially indignant about American race prejudice. But, if he is a Sinhalese, he tries to keep his child from marrying a Ceylonese Tamil. He uses the word 'fair' as synonymous with attractive, and 'dark' in a critical sense. I've heard students at the University of Ceylon sing 'Poor Old Joe' instead of "Old Black Joe.' And the educated Ceylonese was conspicuously silent when Sinhalese mobs murdered Tamils during the recent racial riots. The Sinhalese has created a stereotype of the Tamil—cunning, over-diligent, thrifty, business minded, clannish. If that portrait reminds you of the Jew in Europe, don't blame me. And don't think me a cynic when I tell you that what happened to the Jews in Germany may one day happen to the Tamils here."

A male servant with a long black braid of hair approached the table and said something to Van Langenburg. "Excuse me," he said. "I'm wanted on the telephone."

We sat for a few minutes, watching tiny brown lizards crawling on the hotel walls. Then we walked across the lobby and stood on the open balcony, looking at the heart of Kandy. The artificial lake was across the street, and we could see the little island where, according to local tradition, Kandy kings sent recalcitrant wives to spend the night. Behind the lake the hills towered, steeply and gracefully, showing off the handsome buildings perched along their sides. At the very top was the streamlined glass mansion of Mr. Gunesena where we had attended the pirith ceremony.

The road was crowded. There were no sidewalks at that point, for the lake and the hotel encroached on the main street, and trucks, buses, automobiles, bullock carts, and bicycles streamed past, at varying rates of speed and with varying amounts of noise. A colorful conglomeration of people hugged the walls of the hotel as they sauntered by—women in red, pink, purple, and blue saris, a few Englishwomen in Western frocks, men in white, gray and striped sarongs, other men in Western coats and long sarongs, a few in Western suits, carrying umbrellas. An English planter, in a short-sleeved white shirt, blue shorts, knee high stockings, and a scarf around his neck strode by briskly. Few of the men, even those in suits, wore ties, and none of the shoe wearers, except for the Englishmen, had socks on. A policeman rode by on a bicycle, his brown shirt and shorts neatly pressed, the left brim of his broad hat tucked rakishly up.

Buddhist monks strolled by, heads clean shaven, saffron robes thrown casually around them, the right shoulder uncovered. Some of them had black umbrellas, others carried large palm leaves, which they held over their heads to protect them from the sun. None of these monks carried a begging bowl, and none of them stopped to beg. Three young monks did stop to stare at the merchandise displayed in the ground-floor windows of the hotel, and the youngest of them, a thin-faced teenager, had the wistful look of an American boy at Christmastime. Another group of monks came by, chattering merrily. One of them, a jolly, extroverted, cheerful young man, was apparently telling a joke. Then they all burst out into loud laughter. A couple of young Ceylonese boys in shorts walked by, swinging tennis rackets, on their way to the tennis club at the other end of the lake.

A beggar woman strolled by, looking for prospects. The baby she was carrying was about a month old, not the same baby I had seen her carrying at the market. The street was covered with red stains, the residue of thousands of betel chewers. Suddenly an elephant appeared, led by a walking mahout. On top of the elephant, languidly holding up a black umbrella to protect himself from the sun, sat a middle-aged Ceylonese gentleman in a Western coat and a white longue.

"Colorful, isn't it?" a voice behind us said. Van Langenburg was looking at the elephant. He led us back to the table.

The servant with the comb appeared and Van ordered more beer for all of us. "Kandy was the capital of the Sinhalese kings, you know, when the last of them surrendered to the British in 1815. The Kandy kings were colorful—you've seen the Perahara—but they were very cruel, and the street you were just looking at was regularly the scene of a rather unpleasant ceremony. The usual way of punishing a convicted criminal was to have an elephant trample him to death in this public square."

Moss grimaced, and Van said apologetically, "Oh, well, the Ceylonese had a shortage of public entertainments. They took what they could get. And the modern Kandyan isn't really bubbling over with the milk of human kindness. He won't hurt an insect but he kills people. He doesn't kill animals—but he doesn't feed them, either, and just last night a pack of hungry dogs tore a cat apart in my neighborhood. There's one caste in Ceylon, which corresponds to India's untouchables—the Rodiyas. Legally, of course, there are no castes in modern Ceylon. But the Rodiya men are pretty much limited to begging and garbage carrying, and the women are supposed to be available for prostitution—incongruous, of course, for an untouchable. Until recently Rodiya women were supposed to go naked above the waist, but now they're permitted to wear two thin strips of cotton. Last week a Rodiya woman dared to come into Kandy wearing a blouse. A mob, mostly women, tore all her clothes off and chased her out of town. And a Rodiya man who tried to move into another village recently was permitted to build his new home. The day he finished it all his new neighbors came over and burned it. They let him go back to the Rodiya village. But we Ceylonese are very bitter about racial discrimination in the United States."

Moss asked how the Rodiyas had been allocated the lowest rung on the social ladder. Van grinned sardonically. "We have a very convenient legend for that, to justify our superiority and cruelty. It seems that many years ago there was a Kandyan princess who developed a taste for cooked children. She persuaded a young hunter to bring her, daily, a young child properly prepared for the table. When the king discovered this he put a curse on her and the hunter, and sent them out into the jungle. The Rodiyas are their descendants, and you can hardly expect decent people to treat them with much respect."

"I thought Buddha eliminated all castes," Moss said.

"Oh, he did. He certainly did. Buddha established a very reasonable, very tolerant philosophy. But human nature being what it is, there is considerable difference between what Buddha taught and what most Buddhists actually practice. Actually, the caste system is breaking down. In the cities more rapidly than in the villages, and among the educated more than the ignorant. But even sophisticated urbanites are very conscious of the subtle social distinctions that permeate Ceylon society. The tradition is especially strong here in Kandy, which prides itself on being the center of 'genuine' Sinhalese culture. One of my best friends in town, a capable, intelligent descendant of Kandy kings, has been frozen out of the upper echelons of Kandy society because he married a charming, university-educated Tamil woman."

A short brown-skinned woman with a large diamond imbedded in the side of her nostril walked by us. She was an elderly woman and her gold-bordered Benaras sari trailed on the floor behind her. Two servants followed her solicitously until she sat down at a table in the corner.

"Enormously wealthy woman," Van said. "Not high caste, though."

A short, husky Ceylonese, about sixty, came briskly into the lobby, accompanied by a beautiful young woman and followed by servants carrying luggage. He saw Van, smiled, said something to his entourage, then left them and came to our table. Van immediately stood up to shake hands with him and to introduce us. "Mr. Nayake is the minister of security," he told us.

Mr. Nayake chatted for a few minutes. He oozed vitality and even as he stood there talking kept shifting his feet, as if bored with physical inactivity. Finally he said goodbye, patted Van on the back, and hurried to the elevator, followed by the young woman and the luggage.

"His daughter is a stunning woman," Moss said.

"She is not his daughter," Van said. "Nayake is the undisputed Don Juan of the island. His nickname is '365.' They claim he sleeps with a woman—though not necessarily, a different woman—every night of the year. For a man of sixty-seven that's not bad."

"He doesn't look sixty-seven."

"He is. There's a charming story about him. The priest at his temple tried to persuade Nayake not to spend so much time with women. 'The important things in life,' the priest said to him, 'are detachment, restraint, self-control. Do you agree?'

"'Absolutely,' Nayake said. 'And lots of beautiful women.'"

A monk walked into the hotel and looked around angrily. He had an aquiline nose and a round face, and as he approached our table I realized that he was the man whom Ramanathan rescued on the climb to Adam's Peak. He spoke in Sinhalese, softly but very intensely, to Van Langenburg. Van listened for a long time, then replied. The monk spoke again, then shook his finger angrily in Van's face, turned, and stomped out of the hotel.

Van shrugged. "A crackpot. He took literally the prime minister's campaign promises. Now he wants Buddhism to be made the state religion. He wants me to write an editorial about it. I told him to talk to the prime minister, not to me. He says he has talked to the prime minister, and to leading politicians, and they're all betraying the nation. He may have to take things in his own hands, he threatens. How about that?"

Van laughed and drank his beer. Then he excused himself and went to the bathroom. Again we stepped to the veranda and looked out. A man with rows of pins stuck in his face and in his bare back danced slowly down the street. Nobody paid any attention to him and cars simply drove around him in the crowded traffic. A bullock stopped drawing his cart long enough to drop a large turd and the dancing pinman barely avoided stepping in it. "He's fulfilling some kind of vow," I told Moss.

Van joined us at the table a few minutes later. "I was talking about Buddha's influence," he said. "In 1956, to celebrate the 2,500th anniversary of Buddha's birth, the government of Ceylon gave amnesty to hundreds of prisoners—and the crime rate shot up to a new high. Buddha urged humane consideration for all living things, but in Ceylon there is a brutal indifference to suffering and a disregard for children outside of one's own family group that is more callous than the materialistic selfishness of the West.

"Buddha taught that there should be no images made or worshipped. But there are more images and statues of Buddha in the Orient than of any other individual. Buddha taught that there are no gods. But the majority of Ceylonese either worship demons or fear them. This is understandable. Buddhism concerns itself with ultimate spiritual questions, so the ordinary Buddhist has to look elsewhere for help for his day-to-day problems. Buddha taught that each man must work out his own destiny and that no one can intercede for him. But the temples are full of men and women sprawled in fervent supplication before statues of Buddha. Buddha taught that mechanical gadgets cannot be substituted for genuine faith, but today his monks are using loud speakers to broadcast their chants in the central squares. On the other hand, a monk who tried to take a driver's test was jeered by the mob until he failed."

Van paused to take a long draught of beer. Then he went on.

"Buddha taught that his monks should take no part in politics, but monks now campaign in elections and intrude in government at every level, pushing religious and nationalistic legislation. Ironically, the socialists also helped elect the present government, and one of the main planks in the party's platform was land reform. They promised to break up the big estates and give them to small farmers. But the largest landowners in Ceylon are the Buddhist temples, which have been deeded land by the rich and royal down through the centuries. Now the monks are fighting bitterly against land reform and hinting that it was the wrath of the gods that caused the recent floods.

"As far as nationalism is concerned, the monks want the days of rest to be moon-days, not Saturdays and Sundays. There's nothing special about Sunday, as far as Buddhist scriptures are concerned. And of course they want Buddhist holidays made national holidays. The Tamils are demanding that Hindu holidays be made national holidays. The Muslims of course insist that Islam's celebrations are sacred. And sheer inertia keeps the Western holidays, like Christmas, January First, and weekends in effect. It's getting hard to get through a week without a national holiday of some sort—and this in a country which insists that it has to work overtime to catch up to Western technology."

Van Langenburg stopped to take another drink and Moss looked at him unhappily. Van smiled. "Don't be shocked," he said. "I've been emphasizing the worst things, of course. Some of the practical compromises between religion and society are rather charming. The Buddhist monk, forbidden by his religious vows to ask for extra food, has devised an interesting solution. He points at someone else at the table and says, 'He wants more rice.' The host understands and brings a second portion to the monk.

"And most poor Buddhists in Ceylon obey the Buddhist injunction against drinking alcohol—in the form of expensive whiskey, that is. They drink alcohol in the form of cheap local arrack instead. And they're likely to obey the Buddhist rule against eating meat—since meat also is expensive. But many Buddhists who can afford to buy meat eat it."

Moss shook his head sadly. Van went on, earnestly.

"Believe me, in spite of the spiritual virtues popularly associated with Buddhist philosophy, the upper-class Ceylonese is no more calm, objective, or indifferent to physical pleasures than the American, European, Indian, or Japanese. Nor does Buddhism affect his ethical behavior any more—or any less—than Christianity, Hinduism, and other religions influence the day-to-day morality of other individuals.

"The upper-level Ceylonese are wealthy, well educated, intelligent, sophisticated, and cosmopolitan. But in the privacy of their homes they prefer wearing a sarong to trousers, eat curry with their fingers, and revel in being called 'Master' by their servants. I've noticed, incidentally, that even Americans, after they've lived in Ceylon for some time, learn to enjoy the pleasures of class superiority. Many Americans find that their attempts to treat servants democratically result not in greater respect for democracy, or for Americans, but, instead, in laziness, slovenliness, and contemptuous familiarity. In self defense, Americans learn to adapt themselves to the master-servant relationship and to develop the detached indifference to servants' personal problems that is necessary for gracious living. A contributing factor to this insensitivity is the appalling inefficiency and unreliability of most Ceylonese servants, to the extent that many American women wish they had their American gadgets instead of Ceylonese servants."

The servant with the comb brought more beer and Van Langenburg poured it. We looked at each other and each took a long drink.

"Like most Eastern countries, Ceylon has a small upper class, a relatively small middle class, and a tremendous number of poor farmers and workers. It's mainly this proletariat that is now having problems, trying to shift rapidly from peonage to independence, from ignorance to education, from total lack of political power to theoretically absolute political control. But the habits of centuries die hard, and the servants, like the ones you see at the hotel here, are still likely to put out both hands, palms up, and bow deeply when given their wages or tips.

"The servants go barefoot and chew betel, and they are just as prejudiced as the upper-class Sinhalese. They look down on lower castes than their own, and on Tamils and Muslims. No one forces them to like brutal American movies, or rock-and-roll music, or slot machines, but those are the examples of American culture that the Ceylonese masses have selected as their favorites. And they love American gadgets—refrigerators, washing machines, cars, and radios. It may be, as Buddhism teaches, that material objects are unimportant, but every Ceylonese who can afford these objects tries to get them.

"There's another class in Ceylon, the farmer or *goya*, who works hard in the paddy field or loafs blissfully in the village. Not much entertainment is available in the hinterland, although the movie has largely replaced the folk play, and the radio station broadcasts all day in Sinhala, Tamil, and English. Still, life is dull, and people throng to funerals and political meetings, where they stand around patiently, wearing their best sarongs and saris, listening to encomiums to the dead and attacks on the living. Then they go back to the village and sit around and breed more children. The birthrate in Ceylon is very high. After all, what else is there for the men to do in the villages?"

Van Langenburg paused, but we had no suggestions to offer.

"The murder rate in Ceylon—the highest in the world, as I told you—has been analyzed by a number of experts. Unfortunately, they haven't agreed on the cause. The popular culprit is the heat. Bad enough most of the year, it becomes stickily unbearable during March and April when many of the murders occur. If you're here then, you'll feel the depression, the irritation, the heat-sapped melancholy of spring in the low country. One of our prime ministers, an ardent prohibitionist, insisted that arrack, the potent local substitute for whiskey, is responsible. But many of our murders are committed by sober citizens. And a leading police official blames the illicit stills, which sell a more potent brew than the taverns closed by temperance workers. On the other hand, a prominent psychologist says the cause of the murders is Buddhism itself, because it demands an unnatural amount of self-control from ordinary human beings who find it necessary to explode, violently, at intervals. And an educator at the university suggests that the murders are a symptom of the national maladjustment, due to insufficient participation by Ceylonese in creative activity."

One of the small birds that had been flitting unobtrusively about the room now perched on our table. Van Langenburg smiled. "It's a house sparrow. Very common here."

I remarked that house sparrows attended my lectures at the university regularly. "Ah yes," Van said. "The university. And the social scientists there. The fad for explaining nations in terms of individual types has reached Ceylon, and there are now available several scholarly, profound, and contradictory analyses of the Ceylonese character. One expert tells us that the laziness of the Ceylonese goes back to generations of easy living. The rich soil gave rice to the casual laborer, and there were coconuts, papayas, pineapples, mangoes, bananas, and exotic tropical fruits for anyone willing to pick them—or, sometimes, pick them up from the ground after they fell.

"But a Ceylonese physician insists that no nation can be very energetic when most of its population suffers from amoebiosis; when eye changes occur at thirty, ten years sooner than in the West; and when fifty-five is the legal age for retirement. And a Ceylonese philosopher suggests that the Ceylonese emphasize that aspect of Buddha's teaching which urges the fatalistic acceptance of one's status during each brief stage of the soul's long journey to the final reincarnation.

"It's this fatalistic attitude which explains what may seem to you Westerners a lack of gratefulness on the part of the Ceylonese. Strictly speaking, there's no word for 'thanks' in Sinhalese. Buddha taught that virtue is its own reward. So the Ceylonese sees no reason to thank the donor of a gift for an act that, in the eternal scheme of things, the giver is performing for his own benefit and for which, in the eternal scheme of things, he will eventually be rewarded by a more permanent evaluator than the particular recipient of the gift. Nor is there, strictly speaking, a Sinhalese equivalent of the word 'please,' on the theory that in a social order where each fatalistically accepts his position, there is no more need for politeness than for gratitude. Your ambassador sent an expensive gift to a prominent Ceylonese and his wife on their wedding anniversary. Six months later, having received no acknowledgment, he asked the lady whether the gift had been delivered. 'Yes, it has,' she replied nonchalantly. 'And a lovely piece of jewelry it is.'"

Moss lit a cigarette and Van Langenburg refilled his glass.

"An English tea planter recently wrote, in a book published in England, that the typical Ceylonese is lazy and ungrateful. He may have been prejudiced by the government's threat to nationalize the tea estates. The Ceylonese political theorist who told me, after the fifth drink, that the typical Ceylonese is hypocritical, egotistical, and cruel, may have simply been expressing a momentary irritation. A German anthropologist characterized the average Ceylonese as the spoiled product of an over-coddled childhood. He may have been oversimplifying. And my editor was unusually bitter the day he insisted that the national stereotype is a lazy, malicious, cunning, superstitious, immature personality—an individual poised insecurely between an outdated native culture and an unfamiliar foreign one, and choosing with ironic consistency the worst aspects of both. Including, of course, myself."

A waiter walked by our table with a glass of milk and a glass of ginger ale on the tray he was carrying. Van Langenburg watched him serve two teenage tourists. "I hope that boy isn't drinking that milk for its calcium," he said dryly.

"Why?" I asked.

"Because Ceylon cows give milk without calcium. I'm not joking. It's something about the composition of our soil. Our milk looks better than it is. Which is true of Ceylon in general, I would say. The tendency to promise far more than one can perform seems to be an Oriental characteristic, and we certainly share it. Even Ceylonese at the top level—intellectually, politically, commercially—make grandiose promises very casually. Later, just as casually, they ignore those promises. Another of our national characteristics—as popular with men as with women—is an irresistible fascination with gossip. The Ceylonese, at every social level, is preoccupied with purveying, exaggerating, and distorting facts and rumors into gossip that is usually malicious and sometimes sadistic. It's a national disease, characterized by a complacent contempt for such irrelevant details as the actual facts of the matter. As a result, the private lives of our prominent citizens are open secrets, and the most intimate details are purveyed everywhere with avid enthusiasm. It's hard to keep assignations secret in our country—for one thing, too many servants are involved—and we all know, or think we know, that a prominent woman legislator used to live with a communist leader, but is now the mistress of a leading Buddhist priest. Her political views, of course, have conformed to the change of bed-partners. And it may interest you to know that one of the political parties in our country was formed simply because its present leader resented his former colleagues' informing him that his wife was being unfaithful. He resigned from his leftist party and organized a new marxist faction—a Freudian innovation that old Karl Marx hardly anticipated in his blueprint for revolutions. But what do you expect in a country where a jury consists of seven men—on the sensible assumption that seven is about as many competent jurors as one can normally expect to find. And though our people have not had democracy long they've quickly learned the market price of their ballots. It's an expensive business being elected to office in Ceylon."

Moss had been looking out of the window while Van talked. Now he jumped up, walked out on the veranda, looked down the street for a while, then came back. "I just saw two monks in pink robes instead of saffron."

Van Langenburg smiled. "No, you didn't. You saw two Buddhist nuns."

"Nuns? But their heads were shaved."

"Of course," Van said. "Having renounced physical pleasures and vanity, what do they need hair for?"

Moss signaled for another drink and I said that I had personally found the Ceylonese people generous, helpful, and very cordial.

"Oh yes," Van Langenburg said. "If anything, we exaggerate this cordiality to a ludicrous degree. After three centuries of white man's rule, many Ceylonese have become so accustomed to agreeing orally with a Westerner that they still tend to tell him whatever they think he'd like to hear. As a result, workers glibly agree to do things they know they're incapable of doing; businessmen promise to deliver merchandise they haven't the slightest chance of obtaining; and friends promise entertainment they have no facilities for providing. One young tourist guide here in Kandy carries this congeniality to its logical extreme. When asked his name, he saves tourists the difficult task of trying to pronounce 'Wickremasinghe,' and instead offers a name that he thinks will please his employer of the moment. He tells Americans that his name is Elvis, or Clark, or some other popular entertainer. He tells Englishmen that his name is Winston.

"But although the Ceylonese are polite to tourists, generous to guests, charming at parties, witty in conversation, and brilliant in print, their behavior in ordinary everyday life is as imperfect as that of other human beings. It isn't easy to ignore the cruelty and physical brutality of Ceylonese to servants, animals, and each other. In a government hospital the attendants refused to serve food to those patients who didn't tip them. One bed-ridden patient's plate was left just out of his reach. Other attendants, during the flu epidemic, kicked patients who had been put on floors, saying, 'Why do you crowd this place?' Complaints of pain on the part of some patients were ignored until the patients died. The national callousness was dramatically emphasized during the recent floods, when many people refused to try to save others, who perished. When dockworkers went on strike for higher wages and refused to discharge food from ships while thousands starved. When many claimed compensation for losses they had not suffered. And when, during reconstruction, a group of men near Anaradpura who had been making good money carrying cars across a washed-out rivulet, kept breaking the bridge each night, after workers repaired it during the day, in order to keep their car-carrying business going."

Again Moss shook his head, and Van smiled wryly.

"Installing classless socialism in any society is difficult enough. In a caste-conscious community the problem is intensified. Recently all telephone service on the island stopped for two days while the white-collar workers—the term in Ceylon is 'trousered' workers, as distinguished from the sarong-clad laborers—went on strike. Their complaint: They refused to have the lower class laborers share their lunchroom and recreation room.

"A ludicrous by-product of the new independence has appeared. Inspired by Gandhi's example, hunger strikers all over Ceylon have been dramatizing their discontent. When the newly elected government ignored his recommendations, a professor of economics began a hunger fast on the steps of the legislature. The prime minister brought him a glass of orange juice, and the professor departed. A few weeks later a farm laborer who decided he was working too hard, dug a grave and announced that he would fast beside it until he died—unless the prime minister arrived to dissuade him. After four hours of fasting, the laborer accepted a pineapple from the village constable and went back to work. But the idea has caught on. We've had 'hunger' strikes by clerks passed over for promotion, unsatisfied lovers, overworked schoolboys, and weary housewives. The government art college, the university, and the technical college submitted to weeklong strikes, the latter by students demanding a larger number of excused absences. No one has starved to death."

A waiter with a walrus mustache, who had been hovering near our table, now shuffled over. "Excuse, Master," he said to Van Langenburg, "you eat lunch here today?"

"What's on the Western menu?"

"Vienna steak, Master."

"That's hamburger," Van told us. "Want to eat here?"

Moss nodded and we rose and followed the waiter into the large dining room. It had a high ceiling, tall narrow windows, and was furnished exactly the way a good hotel dining room in Victorian England had been furnished. We sat down at a small table with a white tablecloth and Van Langenburg ordered Vienna steak. Moss and I ordered the beef dinner. The few other people in the dining room were English tea planters and European tourists. Through the windows we could see saffron-robed monks, sari-clad women, and men in sarongs walking by. Behind them moved a stream of bullock carts, bicycles, and automobiles. Occasionally, an elephant passed quietly. A monk stopped, looked in through the window curiously, then walked on.

The waiter, not the one who had led us to the dining room but a younger one without mustache or comb, brought the first course. It was fish. "You should eat fish in the coast towns," Van Langenburg said. "In Negombo you can order what you want at breakfast, and they'll catch it and serve it to you for lunch and dinner. Wonderful prawns and crabs at Negombo—and in Colombo too."

When we finished the fish, a fourth waiter appeared and removed the plates. He moved slowly. Everyone moved slowly. Moss mentioned the fact.

"That's right," Van Langenburg said. "When you've lived here long enough you stop worrying about the slow pace. Everything is done in slow motion—and you aren't going to convince these people that that isn't the way it should be. The mail takes a couple of days for delivery, and a telegram may take longer. Long-distance phone calls may take four or five hours to arrange. For dinners, or parties, or appointments, no one hurries. What if he is an hour or two late? It doesn't really matter. Haven't you found that?"

I agreed. Moss remarked that surprisingly many servants spoke English. "No," Van said. "They just seem to speak English. Actually, they only know the few words dealing with their daily work. The minute you try to talk about a different subject you'll find they won't understand you."

"You know," Moss said, "I've gotten to like the slow pace here."

"Certainly," Van Langenburg said. "Ceylon's had a continuous history for more than 2500 years. It was beautiful then, and it was hot, and people moved slowly, and eventually time passed. Ceylon is beautiful now, and hot, and it's more comfortable to move slowly, and eventually the time will pass. There is time for resting, and time for playing, and a little time for working—and there's a great deal of time for just sitting around and talking. So much, in fact, that when I asked a police detective what he found most helpful in solving village crimes he said, without hesitation, 'Rumor.'"

We worked our way through the meat course, then vegetables and potatoes, then a tart, and finally coffee. Each item had been served on a separate plate, and a total of six people, including the peon in short pants and dirty coat who cleared off, took part in the serving. We called for the bill, added a tip to be distributed among all of them, and Moss observed that the meal still cost about a third as much as it would have at an American hotel.

Then we went out into the lobby again and sat down. "I heard a funny one the other day," Van Langenburg said. "I've heard a lot of reasons why political promises should be kept, but none as naïvely honest as this one. A three-man city council in South Ceylon has one Muslim member. When the council was elected, for a three-year term, the members agreed to rotate the chairmanship each year. One of the Buddhist members served as chairman the first year and, at the request of the second member, another year. But when he suggested the possibility of continuing as chairman, the Muslim member protested violently. His reason for protesting? He had accepted a large number of invitations to be the honored guest at important Muslim functions during the coming year—but all of the invitations were contingent upon his being chairman of the council at the time he attended."

We laughed, and the waiter with the comb came over with coffee. He also placed a newspaper on the table, and Van Langenburg picked it up and looked through it. "You Americans may have large insurance companies," he said, "but I'll bet none of them offers a policy like this one."

He spread out the paper and we looked at the advertisement.

ARE YOU MAKING PROVISIONS FOR YOUR DAUGHTERS' DOWRY?

You will wish to give your daughter a fair start in life when her time comes to leave you. YET the high cost of living and heavy taxation has made it more difficult than ever before what you conceive to be the right thing by your darling Daughter who has come into your life. She has brought you untold joy and blessings—and she looks up to you with innocent confidence for all her happiness: and you as an Intelligent Father can you afford to be carefree?

Take a **FREE LANKA CHILDREN'S DOWRY ENDOWMENT POLICY** for a guaranteed sum payable at the end of a selected term.

"I'd rather read an ad like that," Moss said, "than have an American insurance salesman call me by my first name when he's introduced to me. But I hadn't realized that dowries were so common."

"The dowry system," Van Langenburg said, "is far more prevalent in Ceylon than we admit. Even at the university, the majority of whose students call themselves communists or trotskyites, almost everybody expects to get or give a dowry at marriage. I asked a communist leader on campus how he reconciled his demand for a dowry with his marxist principles. 'Do you think I'm crazy?' he replied. 'All the other chaps are going to get dowries.'

"It's an ironic carry-over from the colonial system that the civil servant is still regarded as the top professional man in Ceylon and claims the highest dowry when he marries. But businessmen, engineers, lawyers, and doctors are also considered very desirable bridegrooms. The doctor less than in other countries, perhaps, because Ceylon medicine is largely socialized. There is some incentive for sending one's daughter to the university, for she can deduct the cost of her higher education from the amount of her dowry. And the amount of that will depend on a number of factors besides the profession of the bridegroom. His caste, his social class, his wealth, the location of his home. Recently, when a brilliant young Ceylonese physicist was offered a three-year appointment in the United States, he told his family to find him a bride within four days. The family was rushed but successful, the wedding was held, and the newlyweds set sail with thirty new saris and a three-week trip to get acquainted in.

"It's true that the dowry requirement is ignored more frequently in Christian homes than among Buddhists and Tamils. But the reason is less religious than economic. Many of the Christians are ordinary workingmen and can't afford a dowry. They make a virtue of necessity and marry other poor Christians. But the wealthy Christians in Ceylon, like the wealthy Buddhists and Hindus, accept the dowry principle.

"Hindus follow the dowry system rigidly, and marriages are arranged without consulting the principals, even when they're professional men and educated women. And the process is not as simple as you might think, for even when the financial arrangements are satisfactory it's still necessary to consult the astrologer. If he finds that the horoscopes of the prospective bride and groom do not indicate a happy marriage, the wedding preparations are immediately canceled."

Moss lit a cigarette. "But you told me that most people are poor. What do they do about dowries?"

"Some go in debt heavily to get their daughters married. But many poor Ceylonese solve the dowry problem very simply. They neglect to go through an official marriage ceremony and simply set up housekeeping. We have a great many common-law marriages. Separations under such conditions are obviously frequent and hard to prevent."

Van had been leafing through the paper. Now he stopped and chucked. "You Americans are always being criticized for vulgarity. But it's amusing that when we borrow things from your culture, it's almost always the cheapest and most objectionable element. Your high-pressure advertising is irritating, we say. But listen to this ad, by a native physician. He says one bottle of his remedy 'cures catarrh, neuralgia, short-sight, premature gray hair, dandruff, dental and ear diseases, bleeding of nose, falling hair. Its application immediately relieves headache, sunstroke, and fatigue.' All that for three rupees—that's sixty cents in your money."

"Hard to beat," Moss agreed. "But, Mr. Van Langenburg, if you'll forgive my saying so, you seem to get pleasure out of pointing out Ceylonese faults. Almost a perverse pleasure."

Van looked up angrily and started to say something. But he stopped, snorted, and drummed his fingers rapidly on the table. Finally he relaxed. "I hope it isn't perverse pleasure. You've put your finger on a sore spot—not just for me but also for most of our intellectuals. It's true that the Westernized Ceylonese is always criticizing—even more than the European, who at least has a positive tradition behind him to give him more security and more tolerance. Our intellectuals can only attack. And I'll admit many of them become neurotic about it."

Van pulled an expensive English pipe out of his pocket, filled it with tobacco, and lit it. "Many of our writers are incapable of praising anything, of being 'for' something. There is an almost pathological need to criticize, to ridicule, to expose. We share the Western European intellectual's contempt for American culture—but, unlike the European, we don't have a superior culture of our own to point to. We've adopted the European values, but we have a sneaking suspicion that the Europeans don't really feel we're entitled to them. And since we've rejected the Sinhalese culture as primitive, we're left stranded—and bitter.

"A friend of mine is a novelist in Colombo. He turns to European friends for literary advice and criticism, because Ceylonese writers and critics are too jealous of his success to offer anything except vituperation. Our intellectuals are not so much angry as peevish and churlish and quarrelsome. They spread so much malicious gossip that there simply isn't any way of distinguishing truth from falsehood. They lie and distort and complain with a compulsive nastiness that reveals how insecure they really are. A Colombo psychoanalyst claims that the Ceylonese custom of saying 'Hard luck' when an athlete makes a mistake reflects the national inability to confess inadequacy or failure. But I think the psychoanalyst—as usual—overstates his case and makes it ridiculous."

A woman on the street put her face in through the window and looked around. Moss started to get up. "She needs help," he said. "Her mouth is bleeding."

I pulled him down and Van laughed. "She's not bleeding," he said. "She's just been chewing too much betel." The woman's teeth and lips were covered with a red stain. After a long moment she pulled her head back and walked on.

Van Langenburg took some letters out of his pocket and pasted stamps on them. "This is a Buddhist country," he said, "and Buddha taught absolute honesty. But this is also a poor country, so there's a good chance that the stamps will be stolen off these envelopes before they're delivered. That's why most refrigerators in Ceylon come equipped with a key in the door. And that's why telephones in the Colombo YWCA are under lock and key."

He signaled for the waiter with the tortoise-shell comb and paid the bill for the beer. He also left a small tip for each of the servants who had been involved in the morning's activity. The headwaiter from the dining room came over to bow us out, and all the waiters who had been tipped in the lobby. We stopped at the desk, and Van put his letters in the mailbox.

Moss shook his hand. "Thanks, Mr. Van Langenburg. I hadn't realized how hypocritical the Ceylonese really are."

Van Langenburg seemed genuinely startled. "We Ceylonese are no more hypocritical than anybody else," he said earnestly. "In some ways we're better than Westerners, and in some ways we're worse. We are normal human beings—that's all."

The doorman with the grenadier mustache, the red sash, and the crimson cylinder-hat bowed repeatedly as we went out the door. By the time I reached the car, Dasa was opening the door, smiling ingratiatingly, and saying, "Yes, Master."

I drove back down the main street, past bullock carts, bicycles, automobiles, and elephants. On the sidewalk the beggar woman with the rented infant was smiling forlornly at a tourist. A tall, muscular Afghan moneylender pushed her aside as he walked past. Nearby a peon sat against a wall, eating rice with his fingers from an outspread newspaper. A woman with a basket on her head, a package in one arm, and a baby cradled in the other was walking quickly across the street, and I slowed down to let her pass. A bearded man on a motorcycle passed my car.

I turned off the main road so that Moss could see another part of Kandy. In back of an elaborate mansion, two blocks from the center of town, cows and chickens roamed behind a short fence.

"Many Ceylonese keep domestic animals on their grounds," I said. "There are no zoning laws. But this particular family has a rooster they're very proud of. He crows only in the evening."

I drove past the municipal hospital and the coffin store next to it. Moss looked at the coffins but didn't say anything. Than I turned back to the highway. Again I stopped once to let a three-foot lizard cross the road, and slowed up a little later while a snake slid across the highway. Just before I made the turn for home I had to wait for a bullock cart to crawl past me. It was holding up traffic at the crossroads, and a truck on the other side honked impatiently. The bullock plodded on slowly, pulling the heavy cart, utterly oblivious to the commotion he was causing, a look of sad, stupid, unquestioning resignation in his big glazed eyes. Big crows kept flying noisily across the highway.

Nine

In Colombo a few weeks later I finished my business two hours before the train for Kandy was scheduled to depart. Since Moss's apartment was only a few blocks from the station, I decided to visit him. I telephoned, but the line was busy, and rather than waste more time I called a quickshaw, Ceylon's smaller version of the rickshaw, and rode to his house. I didn't bother ringing the bell but walked up to the second floor and knocked on the door of his apartment.

The door opened almost immediately, but it was not Moss who opened it. Marian Burton was standing there in sheer green pajama bottoms.

"Oh, it's you," she said. "I thought it was Anthony." She looked down at her small rigid breasts, hesitated a moment, then said, "You may as well come in."

She turned and went into the bedroom. I closed the apartment door, took a cigarette from the package on the coffee table, and lit it. The phonograph in the corner was playing "Le Coq D'Or." I had barely sat down when Marian returned. She had put on Moss's bathrobe but was still barefoot. I gave her a cigarette and lit it, and we looked at each other for a long moment. Suddenly she smiled impishly.

"Caught in the act, aren't I?"

I nodded. She extended her lower lip playfully like a child who had committed a slight misdemeanor but knew that it didn't really matter and that the friendly adult who had discovered it also knew that it didn't really matter.

"You're a good friend of all of us," she said finally. "I don't want you to misunderstand."

"It would be hard to misunderstand," I said gently.

"For some people, perhaps. But you know us too well."

"I didn't know you this well," I said.

She walked over to the window and looked out. "I thought you were Anthony, but he must have gone down to the Fort." She came back to her chair. "All right. I am sleeping with Anthony. But I love George, and Anthony knows it."

I didn't say anything. "Do you remember the night of devil dancing, when George told you about betraying his best friend?"

"I remember," I said.

"It's been preying on his mind, bothering him more and more. For the last two years George's been impotent."

"Because of his guilt?"

"I think so, and he thinks so, but we haven't been able to help him. I love him and I understand him but I need sex—and Anthony is a safe way of getting it."

"Safe in what way?"

"Because he doesn't love me. He's fine in bed, and he satisfies my physical needs. But there isn't the slightest chance of his becoming involved emotionally with me."

"Why?"

"Because he can't really love anybody. He's kind and generous but it's too late, I think, for him ever to fall in love."

I put out my cigarette and automatically lit another one for myself and one for her. She inhaled deeply and blew the smoke out through her nostrils. "Ironic, isn't it?" she said, lightly but with quivering lips. "George loves me but can't make love to me. Anthony makes love to me but can't love me."

I looked at Marian pensively. She was short and heavy, and I was surprised that her breasts had seemed so small a moment ago. Her hair was dark, her eyes greenish, and the snub nose perched inconspicuously above her thick wide lips. I had always thought of her as a genuinely friendly person, but never as a passionate one. She had never shown any concern for clothes, status, or the petty gossip that so many of the Western women in Ceylon thrived on. I found it difficult to fit her into the relationship I had just discovered.

"Why do you say that Moss can't love anybody?" I asked. "He's searching for something, and it may simply turn out to be a woman who can give it to him."

Marian shook her head decisively. "No. What do you think is bothering Anthony?"

"I know what he told me. Materialism, hypocrisy, the purposeless rushing around of modern society—all this alienates him."

Marian burst out laughing. "Nonsense," she cried. "Horse manure. He's no more frustrated by modern society than you are, or I am, or any other sensitive human being. Oh sure, he's disturbed by the vulgarity and brutality, but millions of people feel like that. No, that isn't his problem."

"What is his problem?"

She looked at me steadily. "You really don't know, do you? I thought you might. But I suppose I really am closer to him than any one else.

Love or no love, our kind of intimacy breeds confiding. And over the weeks, Anthony's confided."

"Well, what is it?" I asked impatiently.

"It's very simple, really. He is afraid of being rejected again."

"Again?"

"Yes. As a boy he was denied love so many times that he trained himself—subconsciously—to do without it. Whether he knows it or not his basic impulse in life is never again to put himself in a position where his love can be rejected. That, and only that, is his motivation. The rigmarole about looking for a happy land is just delusion, a romantic rationalization to justify his behavior."

"And that's why you're sure he doesn't love you?"

She nodded soberly. "He doesn't, and he won't. That's why our relationship is perfect. We get, and give, exactly what we both need. And nothing more."

I stepped to the window. In the scramble of Colombo traffic a quickshaw pulled around a bullock cart, a bus bulging with people lumbered down the street, bicycles wove in and out, and a woman with a large basket on her head waited to cross the street. Marian came over and stood next to me.

"Does George know?" I asked.

"No," she said. "I hope not. I don't want him to be hurt, he's suffering enough. Not that there's any reason—really—for him to be hurt."

I looked at her quietly. She pouted, then smiled. "I hope he never finds out," she said. "Will you have some wine?"

I sat down while she poured a dry white wine into two glasses. The music of "Le Coq D'Or" stopped and the phonograph turned itself off.

"Is there any hope for George?" I said.

"Yes," she said vehemently. "I'm sure of it. If he gets another chance, I know he'll do the right thing. And after that I'm sure he'll get his virility back and his peace." She slapped her knee. "It's this damned guilt that makes him so cynical about everything, so sarcastic. George isn't really like that—or wasn't, once. But now he has a compulsion to find out people's weaknesses and secrets and shames. By dragging them down to his own level he has company in his misery, but the pleasure never lasts, and so he has to start all over, aggressive and suspicious and biting, spreading malicious gossip, believing the worst of everybody."

We drank the cool pleasant wine. I tried to remember, from my conversations with Moss, whether he had revealed his real feelings. But I couldn't think of anything, so I asked Marian what frustrating experiences he had had.

"Anthony's mother died when he was born, you know," she said. "He was brought up by governesses. They were competent and correct but of course it was just a job with them and he got no love from them. It's interesting that of all the governesses he had—and they seemed to come and go every year—he remembers the name of only one, a redheaded woman whom he liked because she tickled him when he misbehaved. When his father saw where she tickled him, he fired her immediately."

"Hasn't he ever been in love?" I asked.

"When he was a sophomore in college he became infatuated with a town girl. Her mother ran a boardinghouse for students, and the girl had quit school at sixteen. She was attractive, I suppose, and knew her way around, but she was about as suitable for Anthony as a brooding sow would be. But he didn't see it and wanted to marry this idealized virgin. And he might have too, if she hadn't become obviously pregnant. He just couldn't believe it, until his roommate told him, 'Look, Anthony, everybody in town's laid her except you. Why should you be the one to marry her?'"

Marian stepped to the window again and looked out. "There's no sign of him," she said. "I have to go now. George will be home by five."

She went into the bedroom and came out a few minutes later, dressed for the street. "You still have an hour before your train," she said. "You may as well stay here. There's wine in the kitchen, and some records by the phonograph."

After she had gone I looked out the window for a while. The street was heavily crowded now with home-going traffic, and a mass of cars, bicycles, buses, bullock carts, and people in sarongs and saris moved with gelatinous slowness in both directions. Then I turned to the pile of records and put the top one on the phonograph. It turned out to be Tchaikovsky's "Sixth."

A few minutes later Moss came in. I told him that Marian had had to leave and he nodded. "I got tied up at the Fort," he said. "Transferring money from one country to another is a complicated business—at least, that's what my banker's been telling me for the past hour."

He poured himself a drink and filled my glass. Then he stood by the window and looked out at the mass of traffic. "Look at them," he said, pointing with his wine glass. "All of them going places. When I was a boy in Manhattan I used to watch the cars at night. It fascinated me to see all those lighted automobiles moving quickly and purposefully toward their destination. I had a comfortable image of a beautifully coordinated world, with everyone having an important job to do and doing it, the whole complex organization directed by some mysterious central authority, wise and calm and omniscient. Now I know better. I know that all of these people are just moving around haphazardly, caught in the rut of circumstance or following unpremeditated impulses. They're not part of any sensible pattern at all, unless you feel that chance itself is sensible. There is no omniscient master directing it—neither government officials, nor judges, nor scientists, nor generals, nor priests really control more than a tiny portion of men's lives or destinies. We're all running around in circles, and the universe doesn't care and governments don't care and nobody really cares. We all wish desperately there was someone who cared. That's why paternalistic governments have their appeal, and that's why communism is popular. But the ones who live under these governments soon learn that you can't substitute an official love for a personal one—and Karl Marx was a much better hater than he was a lover. No, most people are wise to choose God instead—because from Him you can at least demand a personal concern. And since you never see Him, you can never really be sure that He ignored you. He might have some satisfactory excuse to offer for his negligence, if only you could get directly in touch with Him. Nobody really cares if I live or die."

He stared broodingly out the window. The cars, bicycles, buses, bullock carts, and people kept milling around, intently pushing somewhere. Suddenly a siren sounded, and an ambulance squeezed ponderously in and out of the slowing traffic and disappeared noisily in the distance. I was barely aware of saccharine melancholy as the Tchaikovsky Sixth played on in the corner.

"Doctors," Moss snorted. "Another symbol of modern science. Supposed to know everything. They're stumbling around too. I was in the hospital every day while my father was dying. He was fifty-four years old, and he had two million dollars, and he was dying because modern science didn't know how to cure lung cancer. One of the doctors said it was because he smoked too much. But another doctor said he didn't think smoking had much to do with it. Down the hall were two accident victims—a gangster who was trying to escape from police and the ten-year-old boy he ran down in the street when he lost control of the car. My father died and the boy died. The gangster recovered—he's still in prison."

"Anthony," I said, "you're picking a few melodramatic examples, and unfair ones. There are millions of enthusiastic productive men and women. Don't be morbid. Many people enjoy life."

"Do they?" Moss said, looking down at the endless traffic.

"You've been alone too long," I said. "Many people care. They really do."

"Like that?" Moss asked, pointing to a spot on the sidewalk below us where pedestrians were walking past an old woman who had collapsed and was lying sprawled helplessly. She made a pocket in the swirl of humanity as dark figures in sarongs and saris converged, looked, then quickly edged around her and moved on. For a long time no one stopped. Then a man in a long white cloth stopped, bent and spoke to the woman, and signaled a taxi. He put her in the cab and gave the driver money, but the car did not move and the man talked a long time.

Then he shrugged and climbed into the cab with the woman. The cab quickly drove away.

Moss turned and stopped the phonograph.

"My train will be leaving soon," I said. "I'd better start for the station."

"I'll walk with you," he said. We walked slowly past the spot where the woman had fallen. It was packed with a milling crowd now, intent on getting wherever they were going, and there was no longer an island in the traffic. A little girl pushed her way toward us and put out her palm, begging plaintively. Moss put a coin in her hand and walked on.

We stepped into the drab, dark station and walked over to the ramp where the Kandy train was waiting. People were scurrying around, porters were carrying luggage and bags, and children clustered around parents and chattered.

"What happened to Ranjini?" I asked.

Moss smiled cheerfully. "Oh, she's living with an important Buddhist priest. He's very active in the nationalist movement, a powerful politician, and Ranjini is a fanatical patriot now. She's sincere about it, too. She has a tremendous zest for life."

"When did you two split up?"

Moss laughed. "A month ago. I woke one morning to find her gone and all her clothes missing. But she had left the American dictionary I had given her—so I knew that she had left for good."

The train whistled and the crowd began to surge forward. "You don't seem disturbed," I said.

He looked at me with unaffected surprise. "She did exactly the right thing. Look for a new experience. That's the only way to live. Keep looking for new experiences. Try never to repeat one—it's never the same."

"Even happy experiences?" I asked as I boarded the train.

"Happiness doesn't last," Moss said, "I know now there isn't any happy land, and I'm not looking for one any more. But there is always a new experience, and I'm willing to settle for that."

The train pulled away slowly and I waved to the receding figure in the station.

Ten

The monkeys chattered noisily in the distance as George Burton's black Plymouth wound slowly around mountain corners. The car was really too wide for Ceylon, taking up more than half of the narrow road, but George had not been able to resist his company's offer to pay for shipping it from the United States. He was taking Moss and me to what he had described as a fabulous estate in southern Ceylon, where an unusual kind of meeting was to take place that evening. George had mentioned an unconventional group to which he belonged, but this was the first time he had invited us to visit the Gurdjieff gathering.

"This really isn't a regular meeting," he explained, making a hairpin curve on the steep road ten miles south of Kandy. "The group is fairly well advanced, and we now do exercises that novices couldn't handle. But the new international leader of our organization has just arrived in Ceylon for a visit. He's a famous guru, and he has agreed to give an introductory lecture tonight, for the benefit of people like yourselves who don't know anything about the Gurdjieff method."

"What kind of guru?" Moss asked.

"In this case, a master teacher. This guru knew Gurdjieff many years ago, and later he was a student of Ouspensky, whose books explain the Gurdjieff method."

"Who belongs to this group?" I asked.

George paused a moment and we all looked admiringly at the loveliness of the green landscape, mountainous but not overwhelming, symmetrical but not artificial, restful and yet stimulating. Three farmers were working in the paddy fields, swinging their hoes in graceful choreography.

"I have to give you a little background about the group," George finally said. "Many intellectuals in the Orient are finding the traditional religions inadequate. You know that in the West many educated Christians have rejected traditional Christianity. In Israel, most of the intellectuals have substituted nationalism for religion because old-fashioned Judaism seems to them archaic. Well, many educated Hindus and Buddhists also consider their religions outdated, and they are trying to find a faith that can satisfy them at an elevated intellectual level. The Gurdjieff system is a mixture of science and mysticism. It takes into account their scientific knowledge, and it satisfies the emotional needs that they, like everyone else, have. They're what Moss calls 'God seekers of the twentieth century.'"

"And yet we in the West have always been told about the superior spiritual qualities of the East," Moss said.

George shook his head vigorously. "After living here three years, I'm just not very impressed by the spiritual qualities of the Orientals. They may be no worse than we are, but they're certainly no better. And in many ways they really are more cruel than we are."

Moss interrupted. "More cruel than the Nazis in Germany, the fascists in Italy and Spain, the communists under Stalin?"

George hesitated. "I suppose not. It depends on the circumstances. In general, they're like ourselves."

We drove through a series of tight, sharp turns as the mountains of central Ceylon sloped quickly toward the Western plain. The altitude was too low for tea bushes, and few rubber trees grew in this area. Instead, the land was covered with small wet rice fields, neat, trim, and green, separated by raised earthen embankments called bunds.

"I was born a Lutheran," George went on, "but I gave it up in college. The pastor kept telling me that food, sex, and comfort aren't important, but I kept feeling that for me they were. There may be people who don't need physical pleasures, but I'm not one of them. And there may be people for whom the Bible is an adequate explanation of the universe. I'm not one of them.

"Unlike evangelists and mystical historians, I just didn't see how a new spiritual revival would save the world. We've had 'salvation' available for a couple of thousand years without getting a very satisfactory society. Religious leaders tell us that lack of religion is wrecking the earth. But the centuries when the Church dominated Europe are now called the Dark Ages. And with good reason. No, the churches have nothing new to offer, except violence in support of old ideas.

"I'm not talking about the well-known contradictions, of Christians having for centuries fought Christians, Moslems slaughtered Moslems, and Buddhists warred against Buddhists. I can understand the logic of religions that teach that everyone outside their faith is doomed to eternal damnation. I can sympathize with the Massachusetts Puritans who left England to get religious freedom and then forbade it to everyone else. I know about the denial of high public office to non-Catholics in Spain and to non-Lutherans in Sweden. All that doesn't bother me. What I am concerned with is a very practical problem: I want a religion that works. As I see it, all traditional religions have failed to work, in the sense that they teach values that people praise but can't practice, that people mouth but don't believe. If they were honest, all these worshipers would admit that men really want God to be responsible to them, instead of their being responsible to God. If they were honest, they would admit that they really want God around only when they need help, not all the time."

We were approaching Colombo now and the traffic thickened. George stopped talking and concentrated on driving around bullock carts, bicycles, and occasional groups of sarong-clad gossipers in the middle of the road.

The city itself was teeming with cheerful crowds. In the Fort small cars kept cruising around, looking for non-existent parking spaces, moved along by efficient constables in short-sleeved brown shirts, broad-brimmed hats, and brown shorts. The native shopping area was so full of people that pedestrians moved faster than we did, and George remarked that all half-million inhabitants seemed to be shopping at that hour. Sarong-clad natives with ingratiating smiles offered cheap gems to naïve Western tourists while other shifty characters tried to buy dollars at black-market rates. In the stalls of the bazaar riotous colors displayed melons, pineapples, mangoes, coconuts, and dozens of tropical vegetables. The carcasses of meat hanging in the butchers' stalls were covered with flies. A few rickshaws appeared here and there, but they were clearly being pushed out by the more maneuverable quickshaws. The lion flag of Ceylon waved over the shabby government buildings as we finally pulled out into the faster traffic flowing beside the long, grass-covered sea walk extending from the Galle Face Hotel. That massive red sandstone edifice faced the sea, ignoring with staid Victorian dignity the tumult of the city behind it.

In front of George's house an enormous fan-palm tree dominated the grounds. It was about a hundred and twenty feet tall and the lowest branches were at least thirty feet above the ground. From a distance the tree looked like an enormous fan, the twenty-six branches evenly spaced and elegantly spread. One of the leaves could have covered a dozen men. George noticed our admiration and said that the tree was supposed to flower only once, in its fiftieth year, and then die. None of us had ever seen a fan palm in bloom.

We had lunch and a short rest in George's house, a large, modern house handsomely and comfortably furnished. Marian supervised the meal, but she didn't have to work very hard because the Burtons' servants were among the best—and the best paid—in Colombo. Marian was not coming with us, and when we left she shook hands with Moss and me, and kissed George warmly. We drove leisurely south on the ocean road for about forty miles, then turned inland to the road leading to Mauvais' estate.

George had told us no more about the meeting place than that it was the home of a rubber plantation owner.

"Ceylonese?" I asked.

"His mother was Ceylonese. His father was an officer in the French army. The family was wealthy and Mauvais was educated at the Sorbonne."

Moss became interested. "Christian?" he asked.

"Technically," George said. "What he actually believes, nobody knows. Existentialism, nothing, black magic—take your choice. Mauvais is over fifty and a bachelor. He has never shown any interest in women. Marian doesn't like him but I think he's interesting. He is an aesthete, and he lives for beauty."

We were driving on a primitive dirt road now, through flat country. In the wet paddy fields dark men in g-strings urged on wide-horned water buffaloes pulling wooden plows. A family of gray monkeys jabbered away in a clump of trees. It seemed to me they were noisier than I had ever heard them. Then the road turned and we drove through acre after acre of rubber trees, tall, straight, evenly spaced in neat rows. The road curved again and we went up a hill and came, suddenly and unexpectedly, to two tall concrete pillars with Notre Dame gargoyles at the top of each. Behind them an enclosed courtyard led to a very large wooden door in a high wall. George got out of the car and pulled the rope of an old green brass bell. The bell made a loud clang. George came back to the car and waited. I felt that I had unaccountably drifted into a dream world.

A few moments later a servant in a white blouse and green sarong opened the door and waved us in. He was a big man but he walked and waved delicately. We drove in on a paved road comfortably shaded by tall wax palms whose vermilion trunks shone luxuriously against the rich green jungle growth. At the end of the road was another wall, whitewashed, but the door in it was open and we drove through to a magnificent approach to an enormous red-tile-roofed yellow building. We parked the car on a long driveway behind the garage. There were three stalls in the garage but they were all occupied, and another half-dozen cars were parked in the driveway. We walked around the garage, past the servants' quarters and the kitchens, back to the front entrance and George pulled the rope at the entrance. The lanterns above the doorway looked as if they had been there for centuries.

"How old is this house?" I asked.

"Twenty-six years ago Mauvais started with an open hill top. Everything you'll see—house, gardens, pools, terraces—everything has been built since then."

The door opened and another servant in a white shirt and green sarong led us through a bare anteroom, where two large stone statues of nude male bodies balanced on rough stone bases, to a large veranda that ran along two sides of the house. A powerful man, about five feet seven inches tall and weighing over 200 pounds, detached himself from a group of Ceylonese and Europeans and came towards us. He shook George's hand warmly, then greeted Moss and me politely, but with a kind of amused tolerance that I later noticed he showed to all strangers.

Although it was the middle of a hot Ceylon day, Mauvais was wearing a beige suit, a light green tie, and heavy Western shoes. He looked as if he had just had a haircut, had just stepped out of a bath, and had just finished trimming his immaculate narrow mustache. There was a faint, pleasant odor of pine about him, and his massive head was very erect. He snapped his fingers for a servant, waited till our drinks were brought, and then offered to show us the house and gardens. Before we started, though, another servant brought a large visitors' book and asked us to sign. George examined the last few names.

"I see Doc Bergland is here again. What's that son-of-a-bitch doing, trying to dun his patients here?"

Mauvais smiled faintly. "I'm sure he won't bother my guests," he said. Then he noticed our blank faces and said, "Oh, you don't know Dr. Bergland. He is a psychoanalyst in Colombo who likes to bill his patients the same day he treats them. He cures so few of them that he has trouble collecting."

George had signed his name but was still frowning. "Jayasuria's here too. The most crooked lawyer in town."

We signed our names and followed Mauvais through his magnificent palace, a superb kaleidoscope of symmetrical layout, imaginative architecture, distinctive furnishings, rich colors, a studied elegance of grandeur and good taste that would have been overwhelming anywhere in the world. There, in the center of an equatorial plantation, surrounded by muddy rice fields and rangy rubber trees, we saw old French prints, oil paintings, statuary, antique Dutch breakfronts and highboys in gleaming teak and ebony, carved brass trays and boxes, marble parquet floors, and a twelve-foot-long upholstered white couch.

Mauvais calmly watched our growing amazement as he nonchalantly led us from room to room. In a small room with black walls, on which the maps of the world had been painted in white, Mauvais's world-girdling trips were drawn in, each in a different color. There was only one figure in that room, the Japanese deity Quan Yin, which had originally been a male god but had somehow become transformed into the goddess of mercy. Next was the library, with heavy Dutch furniture, modern white carpets, lampshades made of "coolie" hats, and an ancient bronze Buddha that looked down at us from the top of the desk. One bookcase, to which Mauvais motioned languidly, was filled with expensive editions of erotica and complete sets of Gide, Proust, and Oscar Wilde. There were two editions of Wilde's trial. But I noticed, when Mauvais turned to lead us out of the room, that on his desk, concealed by a slick French journal, were Bishop Sheen's *Peace of Soul* and a Bible.

There were many other rooms. A two-walled dining room with delicate wrought-iron furniture. A bedroom with an enormous bed on a raised dais placed at an angle in a corner where the light of the moon would reflect in a mirror. A bathroom with a nine-foot black-marble sunken bathtub, black towels as large as sheets, wide slits for windows, brightly colored carved wooden figures, and a reading shelf filled with pornographic magazines. We went out on a veranda, where people were standing by black wrought-iron tables and sitting on red-cushioned divans.

"The gardens," Mauvais murmured.

George smiled. "Yes. The gardens."

If the house had amazed me with its skillful symmetry, its balance of old and new, its subtle blending of colors, the gardens overwhelmed me with opulence. A series of terraces led down a long hill to a deep Versailles pool at the bottom, next to a red-and-black pavilion. Before we had finished the hour's walk we had seen a Spanish garden, with a bathing well built into the stonewall and authentic Spanish lanterns over the doorway; a perfect Japanese garden built around a four-foot Japanese pagoda; a cactus garden, full of grotesque shapes, all suggestive of phallic symbols but slightly distorted; and a French garden, entered by an enormous Chinese moon-gate, a circle in the brick wall large enough to let the 200-pound Mauvais pass through easily. The profusion of colors in gardens, between terraces, on walls, was overpowering. Exotic Oriental flowers. Familiar Western flowers. Trees, plants, bushes. A series of green hedges separated each grouping from the others, giving each complete privacy and individuality. And everywhere the flower which was clearly Mauvais' favorite and which seemed to hold a special significance for him, the anthurium, with its heart-shaped green leaves, gaily colored spreading flowers, and a protruding slender yellow spike.

Large stone statues, scattered here and there, were sculpted by Mauvais himself. There were water pools. One of them was a flat, lotus-shaped pool white in the afternoon sun; another, around a fountain in front of the veranda, had pieces of expensive broken china which Mauvais felt contained the proper shades of blue. Heavy ferns filled in the spaces.

When we returned to the veranda Moss shook his head in amazement. George brought over a tiny bald-headed brown man with a hooked nose and small shifty black eyes. The man was in his middle thirties but the bald head made him look older, and I thought immediately of an angry vulture.

"This is T.S. Wijesinghe, my very good friend," George said, introducing the little man to us.

I was surprised. Wigesinghe was editor of the most vituperative magazine in Ceylon. All of the articles were vitriolic, and T.S. himself specialized in witty, malicious satires about prominent Ceylonese. He used a pseudonym, but every literate person in Ceylon knew who he was.

"I've read your articles with great interest," I said.

"Yes, of course," he said indifferently.

"But I didn't think you'd be interested in a gathering of this kind."

Wigesinghe cocked his head to one side and pursed his lips. "My dear fellow, you really mustn't think that only Americans are searching for the truth. You want to find the truth about nuclear energy—we seek the truth about man's soul. I assume that your state department will not deny us that privilege."

"I shouldn't think it mattered much to you what our state department did," I said. "I notice that you keep attacking us no matter what we do."

"I attack your government because it is doing the wrong things."

"But you haven't been attacking the Russians or the Chinese."

"When they do the wrong thing, Wijesinghe will attack them." He strutted a little, and the light gleamed on his skull.

I spoke quietly. "So far, the Russians and Chinese have done nothing wrong?"

"Wrong, right, what does your materialistic capitalism know about it?" He waved a hand contemptuously, and the light caught the diamond in his ring. He was wearing a light gray suit, and a gold tiepin was carefully adjusted on his tie. "When Russia and China need criticism, Wijesinghe will give it to them. And now you will excuse me. There are people waiting to speak to me." He looked at Moss quizzically, asked George whether his wife had come, then walked off briskly.

I turned to George. "Is he here to write about the meeting?"

"Oh, no," George said. "He's one of the original founders of this group. He's a very devout follower of the Gurdjieff method." George hesitated. "You mustn't take him at face value. He is sensitive about his size and his looks and the low-class school he went to. But he's really very honest, very loyal. He is convinced that Gurdjieff's soul will be reincarnated, and he hopes to have the mystic spark fanned into flame."

At the buffet table on the veranda we nibbled on curry puffs, a small pastry full of spicy ground meat. Moss and I sat down, but George wandered off to greet his friends. A few minutes later he returned with a round little dark woman.

"I think you know Mrs. Vitana," he said.

We stood up and shook hands enthusiastically. Mrs. Vitana's eyes were sparkling, and her face was creased with a broad smile.

"Yes, indeed," Moss said, "Mrs. Vitana was one of the first people to make me feel welcome in Ceylon. We're old friends."

Mrs. Vitana waggled her head from side to side. "Is your wife here?" she asked George.

George told her that Marian had not come.

"That's a pity," she said. "Gurdjieff can add so much to our lives. Last year I spent two weeks at a swami's retreat near New Delhi. There were thirty of us there and the swami's conversation was so inspiring. So heart warming. I'm so glad you've come."

George headed for the buffet table and Moss said, "Mrs. Vitana, may I ask you a personal question?"

"Of course," she said simply.

"You're a very kind person and very generous. I suppose you're the most popular teacher at the university, always helping students and arranging projects. I thought you were completely self sufficient, and I'm surprised to see you here. Why are you here?"

"No one is self sufficient," she said. "No one."

George came back with a couple. "Mr. Dhanapala. And Miss Swanson. I want you to meet my American friends."

I shook hands with the most handsome Ceylonese I had ever seen. He was a little over six feet tall, standing very straight, and he looked at me with frank and friendly eyes. I judged him to be in his middle fifties, and with his perfectly symmetrical features, his dark brown eyes, his even white teeth, he could have been typecast as a heroic Indian emperor in a Hollywood extravaganza. His voice was low, beautifully modulated, and his enunciation was perfect.

"How do you do?" he said, shaking hands with each of us firmly and making us feel that he was genuinely interested. "I hope very much that some day I can talk to you about American writers. Henry Miller, Hemingway, Faulkner, Prokosch, Thomas Wolfe, Tennessee Williams, Eugene O'Neill. I've read everything they've written, but I've never been in America, and it's so hard to evaluate the work of a different culture. For example, I wonder whether their Freudian interpretations are not oversimplified. Human relations are considerably more complex than O'Neill seems to realize."

Moss said he would be glad to discuss American literature with him. Dhanapala nodded. "When I get back to Ceylon, two months from now, we must get together. Tomorrow Miss Swanson and I leave for a retreat in India."

Miss Swanson nodded. She was a very tall blonde, with a long face and thin features. Her English had a heavy Swedish accent. "The master and I—we go to retreat—meditate."

She looked at Dhanapala intently, hanging on to his left arm. He smiled at her fondly.

"We will meditate," he said, his voice low and deep.

She turned to us proudly. "And on the way we will visit temples in South India and pray to many gods."

Mr. Dhanapala patted her shoulder gently. Her pale face glowed. "Master taught me write prayer to Krishna every morning. At night I throw old prayer in running water. Right, master?"

Dhanapala looked at us somberly. "Miss Swanson has come to the East to find God," he said softly. "Perhaps we can help her."

"Oh, yes, Master," she whispered, looking into his eyes, "you help me." She shivered voluptuously, and pressed his arm tighter. Dhanapala shook hands with us firmly and they walked out into the garden.

"He's a retired civil servant," George said. "They say he was one of the most brilliant administrators in the country."

"What is this retreat of his?"

George shrugged. "I don't know. He used to be a Theosophist, but that was many years ago. I can't keep track of all the crackpot sects that pop up."

As we stepped inside, a woman in a garish sari—large red flowers on a purple, gold-sprinkled background—flowed out of the room and smiled at us vaguely. George smiled. "That's Mrs. Dissanayake, the fashion leader. She's one of our irregulars. She comes when our meetings don't interfere with her social activities."

I commented, "What on earth would a woman like that want from your group?"

"Gurdjieff can help everybody who really wants to be helped," George said curtly.

There were two men in the room, sitting on opposite sides. In a deep lounge chair turned to face the wall sat a white man, about forty years old. He didn't pay the slightest attention to us. On the small table next to him was a bottle of whiskey and while we stood watching he finished the drink in his hand and immediately refilled the small glass. Then he resumed his blank stare at the wall.

George lowered his voice. "Hugh's been doing that for a couple of years. Everyone's wondering how long he'll last."

"Who is he?" Moss asked.

"He was on the plane that dropped the Hiroshima bomb. A couple of years ago he showed up in Ceylon, broke and listless. Mauvais brought him here and lets him live in one of the estate bungalows. But he doesn't show any interest in anything. He just drinks."

We sat down on a red divan, across from a slight Ceylonese in a white shirt and dark trousers. He jumped up when we approached and shied away, but George put out his hand and introduced himself. The man shook hands with us gingerly. Then he sat down again hesitantly.

It was hard to get him to talk, but eventually he told us about himself. He worked for his uncle, a wealthy Colombo importer. He worked in the office—"paper work," he vaguely called it. "I'm not very good at meeting people," he said. "I freeze up."

Moss smiled. "That's not unusual. A lot of people aren't good mixers. There's nothing wrong in that."

"There is in my business," Deva said sadly. "My uncle keeps telling me I'll never get ahead unless I develop a stronger personality. But I'm not a strong personality. The truth is, I'm afraid of people."

I tried to reassure him. "If you were as afraid as you say you are, you wouldn't be here now. Why did you come, incidentally?"

Deva looked at us shamefacedly and lowered his voice. "I'm afraid of death. I thought maybe Gurdjieff can give me courage."

George patted him on the shoulder. "Everyone is afraid of death. But we all learn to live with it."

"Not me," Deva said. "It's easy for you people who've been brought up to believe that everything ends with death. But I am Buddhist, and

I've been taught that the end of this life just means the beginning of another in an endless series of reincarnations. I just can't face the prospect. One life of misery is enough for me." He buried his face in his hands.

George stood up, shrugged contemptuously, and walked out. Moss waited till Deva grew quiet, then tried to comfort him. Deva whimpered, "There are so many things I'm afraid of."

"What are you afraid of?" Moss asked kindly.

Deva looked at us uncertainly. "You won't laugh at me?"

Moss shook his head. Deva spoke softly. "I don't think God noticed when I was born. Something went wrong and they never made a record of it in heaven and I'm alive but no one knows it. Not even God."

"I'm sure God knows," Moss said gently.

"No." Deva looked at us earnestly. "Will you believe me that in the thirty years of my life I have never been happy?"

"Oh come now—" Moss said.

"You can't believe that, can you? I swear to you it's true."

"Surely you exaggerate," Moss said.

"No. The devils never leave me and I've never had a happy moment."

"The devils? Oh, Deva, do you really believe that devils exist?"

Deva looked amazed. "Of course they exist."

"They do," said a deep voice. Mauvais had come in silently and was standing behind us. "We have more impressive authorities than Deva to prove that."

Moss looked at him carefully but he appeared to be in absolute earnest. "The belief in demons is older than the belief in gods. You're a lucky man, Mr. Moss, if no demon ever possessed you."

"Are you serious?"

"Has the demon of melancholy never possessed you?"

Moss looked at me helplessly. "I've been melancholic, but that doesn't mean a devil did it."

Mauvais' expression didn't change. "Has the devil of evil never possessed you?"

Again Moss looked frustrated. "I've done evil things," he said, "and been tempted to do more. But that's a psychological condition—not a supernatural one. Freud—"

"I've read everything Herr Freud has said on the subject. I find demons a more convincing explanation. And so does the Church of England."

"The Church of England?"

"Yes. At a church convocation a few years ago, an Anglican bishop proposed that the Church state officially it does not believe in devils. His resolution was overwhelmingly defeated—and remember that only clergymen voted."

"But what possible reasons could they give?"

"They gave a number," Mauvais said calmly. "One dean said that the first tactic of the Devil is to persuade Christians that he doesn't exist. The next is to persuade them that God doesn't exist. A bishop suggested that belief in the Devil explains a great many otherwise insoluble problems. And a canon of Oxford expressed his belief that most patients in English mental hospitals are really possessed by devils, rather than suffering diseases of the mind."

George came into the room with a dark, stocky young man. It was one of the few times I had seen Mavis Chilton's friend when he was not looking sullen.

"You all know Siri Banda," George said. Mauvais greeted him, then left the room with George. Deva shrank back into the corner of the divan.

"It's good to see you again," Moss said, "but I didn't expect to find you here."

"Why not?" Siri said. "You're here. How long have you been interested in Gurdjieff?"

Moss explained that he hadn't heard much about the movement in the United States.

"But there are many Americans studying Gurdjieff," Siri said.

"I realize that now," Moss said. "Why does it appeal to a Buddhist like yourself?"

He smiled wryly. "I suppose because I know too much about Buddhism to accept it and not enough about the real nature of the universe to reject it."

"And Gurdjieff knew more?" Moss asked.

"Unquestionably," Siri said. "And Ouspensky, his disciple, added his enormous scientific knowledge—he was a great mathematician and a first-class chemist, you know—to support Gurdjieff's abstract principles. But the guru will tell you all that, when he lectures tonight."

Moss looked out into the exquisite garden. "Ceylon is perfectly beautiful," he said, "and I thought for a while that Buddhism was the perfect religion. Why do you find it unsatisfactory?"

Siri looked out into the garden, at the ferns and anthurium and hibiscus. "Of all the Oriental philosophies, Buddhism is supposed to be least interested in materialism. It's true that Buddha's life was an inspiring example of spiritual behavior. And that Buddha's teachings, originally, were pure and helpful. But today most Buddhists are selfish and materialistic instead of generous and devout. We Ceylonese are now building the tallest standing statue of Buddha in the world, to compete in size with the largest reclining Buddha. I saw that one last year in a Bangkok temple. In setting the record, the Bangkok Buddhists made a few aesthetic miscalculations. The 180-foot Buddha required a lot of gilt—which is flaking badly. A building was erected around the statue, but the building is so low and narrow that you can't see the Buddha in his impressive entirety. The best you can do is catch intermittent glimpses as you walk past the forehead, the nose, the chin, down to the toes.

"The Burmese Buddhists at the Schwe Dagon Pagoda have made a different concession to the vulgar proletariat. There you may win God's favor by washing, or paying for the washing of, a small Buddha. Some of the Buddhas at this pagoda can be washed by hand, but one small statue of Buddha remains permanently under a sprinkler, for the convenience of the paying tourist.

"And Tibetan Buddhists were as inconsistent as we are. Since a Buddhist is not supposed to kill any living thing, the devout Buddhist government of Tibet for many years obeyed that commandment by forbidding the slaughter of sheep in Tibet. Instead, it put a high export tax on the 50,000 sheep annually driven to the slaughterhouses of Nepal."

Mauvais came back and asked how we were getting along. I told him that I was tired. I had recently gotten over amoebic dysentery. "There's a couch in the alcove, just off the veranda," he said solicitously. "Why don't you lie down there for awhile? No one will see you."

Siri and Moss walked out into the garden and I turned to go. In the corner the American airman was still looking at the wall and drinking. I went into the alcove, stretched out on the couch, and fell asleep almost immediately. It was almost an hour later when I was awakened by a conversation just outside my room.

Wijesinghe's shrill voice was saying, "I admit, George, that America has given us a lot of help. And I will mention it in an article soon."

"Fine," George said. "I'm going to see whether the guru has arrived. I'll see you later."

There was silence for a moment, then Wijesinghe's voice reached me again. "Stupid Americans," he said. "Vulgar children."

Mrs. Vitana cried indignantly, "I thought you liked George."

"He's useful," Wijesinghe said. "His company's money is useful. But he's a fool like the rest of them. Americans must think we're idiots, pretending that their aid is altruistic. It's not us they're trying to help, it's Russia and China they're trying to keep out."

"That's not true," Mrs. Vitana said. "They've given us money for education, for irrigation, for roads."

"They do it for their own interests," Wijesinghe said. "Nobody gives anything away for nothing."

Their voices faded away and it was quiet for a while. Than I heard Dhanapala's mellow baritone. "Professor Rao. How nice to see you. I didn't know you were in Ceylon."

A clipped British inflection was superimposed on a singsong speech pattern when the professor spoke. "I arrived yesterday. There's a Southeast Asia conference of economists in Colombo next week. I came here early to meet the guru."

They talked about the forthcoming conference. Professor Rao explained that he was to give a paper in econometrics, analyzing the statistical effects of India's new economic policy on the productivity of individual laborers in four Indian cities. He referred casually to the work of Keynes, Tintner, and a number of other Western economists.

"You find the use of statistics helpful in economic analysis?" Dhanapala asked.

"Indispensable. Classical economics is completely outmoded. With econometrics you get objective analysis of the facts, the trends, the issues. Science, my friend, not just speculation."

Dhanapala asked whether he had seen Swami Shantinaha lately. "No, no," Rao said excitedly. "I don't bother with him any more. I've found a great soul, a really great swami near Nagpur. He has done wonderful things. He creates fire without matches. He revives the dead. He divides up a loaf of bread among thousands. I tell you, everything Christ did this man can do. You simply must go see him."

"This is wonderful," Dhanapala said. "You've seen him do these things?"

"I saw him make fire. Of course there's no telling before time when he'll decide to perform a miracle. He doesn't like to do it often, because it takes so much out of him. He is more than three hundred years old. As you know, the drain of psychic energy is so great that a swami is left exhausted."

"That's true," Dhanapala said. "There is just so much psychic energy available, and when it's used up for miracles it has to be replenished. That's why Jesus always retired to recuperate after he performed miracles."

"Will you go to see him?"

There was a pause. Dhanapala said, hesitantly, "I am going to India tomorrow, but I don't think I'll visit him this time. I am taking a disciple along."

There was a hint of laughter in Rao's voice. "Another Englishwoman?"

"No. Swedish. She is a sensitive soul."

"Who isn't?" Rao said. "Best of luck, and all that. But I wish you could get up to see the swami. I tell you, he is going to achieve Nirvana. He is absolutely wonderful. A bachelor over three hundred years."

"I'll see him next time. Did you get to Nepal for the holidays, as you were planning?"

Rao's voice was full of enthusiasm. "Yes, I did. They have some very interesting customs there. Very interesting. I noticed that we barely missed hitting people in the Katmandu traffic, and I asked my driver if the pedestrians simply weren't accustomed to automobiles. That wasn't it, he told me. The Nepalese believe that each man has an evil demon who follows him wherever he goes. They reason that if a car runs over the demon, they'll be rid of him. So they try to just escape being hit by autos and hope the demon will be killed."

"That's sensible," Dhanapala said.

"Isn't it? They have another custom that's worth imitating. Like us, they choose a child's name with the advice of an astrologer. But if the child has a severe illness, or very bad luck, they change his name."

"Very efficient. I saw a variation of that in Burma. They have a sham divorce there that a couple goes through to get rid of illness or bad luck. It's for a specified period of time, until the stars are in an auspicious position to resume the marriage."

They talked on for a while, then greeted a newcomer and Dhanapala said goodbye. The new voice was that of a brilliant young historian who helped lead the communist party in Ceylon. I had met Vandenburg at a number of parties, in Colombo and in Kandy. He was a Burgher with a Ph.D. from Oxford, the son of a wealthy, archconservative businessman. Young Vandenburg collected antiques and paintings. He and Rao discussed some of the technical aspects of the forthcoming economics conference, and Vandenburg used complex mathematical formulae to challenge Rao's conclusions.

"I don't have all the figures here, my dear chap," Rao said, "but if you'll come to the conference I'll show you where you're wrong."

"I'll be there," Vandenburg promised. "Tell me, did you see my friend Tambiah lately?"

"Yes, just before I left. He is quite disappointed that he didn't get the professorship at Delhi. Of course, he is still young, but he is one of our finest mathematicians. He read my horoscope before I left."

"What did he tell you?"

"He said I should be very careful between the eighth of the month and the twelfth."

Vandenburg's voice was intense. "Well, for heaven's sake follow his advice. Or you'll have the same trouble I had."

"What happened to you?"

Vandenburg lowered his voice a little. "A year ago a friend of mine in the sociology department read my horoscope. I didn't really believe in it, so I was just humoring him. He warned me to stay in the house until midnight of the following day. Well, it happened that I had nothing to do, so I stayed in all day. But that evening a friend phoned and invited me to a party. I waited until 11:30, then I thought I was perfectly safe and went out. The minute I stepped out of the door I was bitten by a mad dog, fell down, and broke my leg. I had rabies shots, my leg had to be re-set, I was in hospital three months. I don't take any more chances with astrology."

Rao assured him that he wouldn't take any chances. They discussed recent articles by a German industrial psychiatrist who used motivational devices to stimulate factory production, and I dozed off. When I awoke, half an hour later, Mauvais was saying sympathetically, "I'm glad you told me, George," and George said, "If I only had another chance, I know I'd make up for it." I waited till their voices faded away.

When I stepped out of the alcove, no one was standing by the buffet table. I strolled out and sat on a corner of the banister, and listened to the voices in the dark garden. They all spoke English but the inflections were Ceylonese, American, Indian, and Swedish. The Swedish voice came from the far side of the garden.

"Thomas Hardy says that God is asleep."

"Koestler's character in *Age of Longing* is sure God has gone mad."

"If God is asleep, is it best to let him sleep?"

"If God is mad, is it worth sending a psychiatrist to cure him?"

"Who would cure the psychiatrist?"

"Please don't joke about God that way. He may be listening."

"Not now, Master."

"I agree with Ralph Waldo Emerson. He said, 'Know thyself.'"

"And when he got to know himself well enough, Emerson went mad. Don't forget that."

"Bernard Shaw said the will to live was inexplicable, but he didn't want to die."

"Neither did Voltaire."

"Neither do I."

"George Eastman did."

"Who was he?"

"An American millionaire who developed the Kodak camera."

"What happened to him?"

"He killed himself."

"Did he have a big funeral?"

"Why? What does it matter?"

"Oh, the ancient Egyptians hired professional weepers for funerals. Modern Chinese hire professional entertainers. Which is right?"

"I don't know. But I know a lucky spot to die."

"Where is that?"

"A temple in Katmandu where dying people are brought every day. They say it's very lucky. There's an enormous golden bull in the temple."

"The bull is a phallic symbol."

"I agree with Dr. Reich—the length of orgasm is the true test of personality."

"Not here, Master."

"I'm afraid to die."

"The Japanese professor who was in Ceylon studying our Buddhism went away very disappointed. He says we don't practice what Buddha preached, and we've added gods to a godless religion."

"How naïve can you get? What did he expect to find? And Zen Buddhism is confused too. They say Zen is amoral, but its purpose is to make men good. If it's amoral, what does Zen care about goodness?"

"The reason you Christians can't really understand Oriental religions is that you can't purge yourself of the need for self justification. Your conscience makes you confuse pleasure with guilt, and you'll never get over it."

"Still, there's something to be said for the medieval notion of the incubus—the evil spirit who gets inside a person and makes him do evil."

"Freud says the incubus is an old-fashioned version of the id. It's the id that makes people do things they shouldn't be doing."

"Gurdjieff's explanation of the id is far more subtle than Freud's."

"Idealism and schizophrenia are synonymous."

"I was reading an American psychiatrist's formula for sane living. Karen Horney says, 'No complaint, no self-pity, no self-analysis, no searching for possible motives, no perfectionism, acceptance of one's ability, diet, and rest.'"

"Not here, Master."

"You can say what you like, but homeopathic medicine is the only sensible treatment of illnesses. I've had three years of college chemistry, but it stands to reason that if you put foreign substances into the body, the body will rebel."

"I met an Englishman who didn't know that it's bad luck to buy a carved elephant with the trunk down."

"Europeans don't know that a blue sapphire brings either very good luck or very bad luck. An Asian first puts the sapphire in a cheap setting and wears it a while. If it turns out to be lucky, then he resets it in a valuable material."

"Later, Master."

"My taxi driver in Calcutta had a clean-shaven head, except for one long hair."

"He's a Muslim. That hair is for pulling him up to heaven when he dies."

"The Muslim's heaven is different from the Christian kind."

"Hells are different too. In hot India, hell is described as a very hot place. But in cold Tibet, hell is a freezing place."

"The Catholics reserve the lowest level of hell for suicides."

"The Japanese reserve the highest level of heaven for the proper kind of suicide."

"I'm a scientist, and a scientist deals with facts. Of course, there are more things on heaven and earth …."

"Scientists say that anti-matter may be the real thing, and what we call matter is an illusion."

"But Professor Whitehead thought that the laws of nature are not necessarily permanent. They may change, as customs and human relationships change."

"It's physiologically wrong to say that woman was made from Adam's rib. Man is made from the body of woman."

"Oh, Master."

"Man can find himself only in solitude."

"Solitude, shmolitude. Hermits and swamis are simply egotists—extreme egotists. Each of them is a spoiled child who wants to be master. And the only way to be master, without having your wishes thwarted and without having to worry about the wishes of others, is to live alone. They're actually intolerant, rigid personalities who can't adjust to the normal requirements of group living. That's why they live alone."

"I'm afraid to live alone."

"Christianity and competition are incompatible—but society is based on competition."

"Yesterday, Jehovah's Witnesses were parading with sandwich boards in Colombo."

"The converted natives on the island of Tonga were told that Queen Elizabeth was scheduled to visit them on a Sunday. But they wouldn't be able to eat the 1,500-suckling-pig dinner they had prepared. So they passed a law, changing the name of that Sunday to Monday."

"I'm a scientist and I tell you there is a relationship between a man's chemical composition and his political beliefs."

"But there's a limit to what a man can do."

"The limit is far beyond what you Westerners imagine. I myself have done things you people think are impossible."

"Such as?"

"I've levitated myself a foot off the ground many times. And I once cured an infection on my wife's knee by touching it while I repeated God's name thrice. But after that I felt very weak. I had used my store of divine energy for a selfish purpose. When I concentrate, I repeat the name of God a hundred thousand times."

"Don't the Naga tribes live near you in northern India?"

"I heard a story about them from an American flier. He says that during World War Two the Nagas found an American pilot who had parachuted out of his damaged plane. They brought him back to the American air base, but then they refused to leave until they were shown 'the nest from which the big birds flew.'"

"That story is true."

"I'm going to travel around the world westward some day."

"Why?"

"I lost a day because of the date-line coming out here eastward. I don't know any other way to get that day back."

"Did you know that a newly discovered Hebrew manuscript says that Adam had a daughter named Noaba?"

"Is that a fact? Well, did you know that Australian aborigines descended from a pre-Adam progenitor who was unaffected by Original Sin? That's what Foigny's *Utopia* says. And C.S. Lewis, who is a good sound Christian, thinks that the inhabitants of other planets may be in a different category from us. They weren't saved by Jesus and they don't need to be saved."

"You Westerners—always worrying about Original Sin and being saved."

"It's not easy facing the world day after day."

"You ought to do what a porter in England did. He went to bed in 1928 and stayed there thirty years. That's one way to avoid seeing the world."

"There's another way that J.K. Huysmans tried. He got so disgusted with the world that he had his eyelids sewn together."

"Chacun a son gout."

"Six is the Satanic number. Just as the darkest hour immediately precedes the dawn, so the number immediately preceding the complete seven is worst of all."

"But three is very important. Freud stresses the id, the ego, and the super-ego—all three of them."

"Jung says four is more significant. There are four elements and four basic psychological functions."

"Albert Schweitzer says happiness is nothing more than good health and a bad memory."

"Master, Master."

A bell rang melodiously and the conversations stopped. Mauvais announced, "The guru is ready. Shall we all go in?"

About sixty men and women, most of them sitting on the floor, filled the large room. I sat on a lounge chair in a corner, with Moss perched on the armrest. We all faced the east wall. In front of it, on a plain white mat, sat the guru.

In Western clothes, walking through the streets of Colombo, he would have looked like a brown-skinned, slim, clean-shaven, middle-aged doctor or businessman. But sitting cross-legged on the floor, wearing a long white sarong, looking intently at the audience, he had a special dignity. He spoke in English, with the precise intonation of the Oriental intellectual who has lived in England many years.

"What I am going to say tonight will not be new to those twenty-three of you who have been studying the Gurdjieff method for two years. You know that the method cannot be learned only by reading or by listening. A teacher is necessary. The exercises become more and more difficult, the lessons more and more complex. No one can summarize the method for you, or explain it to you by words alone, for more than the intellect is involved. There are many things in life that cannot be communicated by word alone. They must be experienced, and they can be experienced only after a prolonged, careful series of preparatory phases. People are willing to spend many hours of hard work learning to be good dancers or painters or cricket players. And yet they think that they can learn control of the infinitely more complex mystery of their souls in a few easy lessons. It cannot be done. Nothing that I tell you tonight will help you find the power and the knowledge that Gurdjieff and Ouspensky attained. All that I can do is to tell you that it is possible to attain them, and the method is what Ouspensky called The Fourth Way.

"Gurdjieff discovered the method, and for a quarter of a century his disciple Ouspensky tried to teach it to others. Now that Ouspensky is dead some of us who were his friends are carrying on the work. The method cannot be learned individually. It requires a teacher, a school, and a long period of time. There are several schools now operating in different parts of the world. It is only fair to tell you that most people find the method too difficult and give up quickly. Some of those who continue making the effort decide that they lack the intelligence or the strength to progress. They are wrong. All they lack is will power. But most human beings lack will power, and the surprising thing is not that so many fail but that even a few succeed.

"Ouspensky taught that there are three traditional ways to seek the miraculous. The first is the way of the fakir, who conquers pain. The second is the way of the monk, who relies on faith. The third is the way of the yogi, who transmutes the power of the subconscious. All of these ways require withdrawal from the world. But there is a fourth way, which can be followed under the ordinary conditions of life. It requires a normal sex life. It is based on knowledge rather than blind faith. It is consistent with the findings of modern biochemistry, physics, and psychology, but it transcends them by inter-relating them. The fourth way leads to something much more important than the surface of life. It permits man to change and to acquire new powers. There is, literally, only a limited amount of knowledge available in the world. If it were distributed evenly, no single person would get much. But because most people don't want it, those who do can get as much of it as they really want to.

"Man is a machine, an automaton, a marionette pulled by invisible strings. But in the right circumstances, and with the right effort, he can know that he is a machine and find ways to cease being a machine. Further evolution of man, according to laws of heredity and selection, is impossible. It can take place only in the form of evolution of certain *inner qualities*, which usually remain undeveloped and cannot develop without conscious effort. Man is incomplete. Nature develops him up to a certain point and then leaves him, either to develop further by his own efforts, or to live and die as he was born.

"Man has the possibility of four states of consciousness, in increasing order of development: sleep, waking state, self consciousness, and objective consciousness. Most men live only in the first two states and never progress beyond them. The higher emotional functions can appear only in a state of 'self-consciousness.' And the highest mental functions, sometimes called 'samadhi' or the 'ecstatic state' or 'illumination,' can appear only in a state of 'objective consciousness.'

"Man cannot develop to these higher inner states by himself. He needs a school to help him avoid the lies that fill our lives, especially the lie of assuming that we know things that we really don't know. Self observation, developed in our school, leads to recognition of man's harmful features—lying, imagination, expression of negative emotions such as violence or depression, and unnecessary talking. We all talk too much.

"Two harmful characteristics keep making man 'fall asleep' while he is awake. Ouspensky calls the first one 'identification.' That is, identification with everything—with what man says, feels, wants, doesn't want, what attracts, what repels. He substitutes these outside things for his inner qualities. The second harmful characteristic Ouspensky calls 'considering'—that is, the state of constantly worrying about what other people think of him. Freud would call these characteristics 'complexes,' but Ouspensky despises Freud and modern psychoanalysis.

"There are seven categories of men, ranging from the lowest, the purely Physical Man, through Man Number Two, Emotional Man, and Man Number Three, Intellectual Man, up to Man Number Seven, who has acquired a permanent identity, a complete individuality, and free will. Man Number Seven is immortal within the limits of the solar system.

"In learning to eliminate negative emotions, man must sacrifice his suffering. It is a fact that people hate to sacrifice their suffering. They are sometimes willing to sacrifice pleasures, because in a superstitious way they think they gain something by doing that. But they don't want to give up suffering because they think that God sends suffering as punishment or edification.

"The way to improvement begins by using a special method of developing consciousness. We concentrate the will on the 'intellectual center' of the body. I have no time here to explain the four 'centers' that control our ordinary actions—the intellectual, emotional, moving, and instructive centers. Nor can I here explain the nature and potentiality of these centers. But the chief point in working upon oneself is 'self remembering'—that is, being aware of yourself at the time you try to observe yourself. Most men are utterly incapable of doing this. For instance, if I told an ordinary man that he could win a million dollars by keeping the thought of a particular object—say a pencil—out of his mind for one minute, just one minute, he could not do it. Very few men in the world can.

"There are many truths about man and the universe that Gurdjieff discovered. I will mention only a few of them. Most men can bear themselves only because they do not know themselves or their relation to the universe. Organic life operates under certain influences from the planets. Unfortunately, on this earth, man lives in a very bad place in the universe, and many of the things that we regard as unfair, or that we try to fight against, are really the result of this opposition of organic life on earth. Planetary influences are responsible for wars, revolutions, and catastrophes of that kind. But an individual person is under planetary influences only to a slight extent because the part in him that could be affected by the planets is undeveloped. All our mechanicalness, for instance, depends on the moon. We are like marionettes moved by wires, but we can make ourselves more free of the moon or less free.

"Almost all art, drama, and fiction are an attempt to express negative emotions. It is imagination in the bad sense of the word—lying. In modern society a child of ten, because of seeing movies and reading, knows the whole scale of negative emotions and can identify with them as well as an adult. People have been unconsciously creating protective devices against genuine feeling for so long that there is practically no spontaneous feeling any more. Everyone has five or six kinds of emotions, appropriate for certain occasions. As a result, everyone knows beforehand what will happen. The repertoire of civilized emotions is very limited.

"Gurdjieff was asked how he could explain the great amount of suffering that exists in the world. He explained that, in organic life, man must be regarded as an experiment of the 'Great Laboratory.' In this laboratory all possible kinds of experiments are carried on, and they involve suffering as a means of bringing about a supra-physical fermentation. In some way suffering is necessary for all this, and one has the right to accept suffering for oneself. But one has no right to accept it for other people.

"The drama of Christ was not the drama of Christ alone. It was a drama with a great number of *dramatis personae* who played definite roles. All the characters in the Gospel drama are destined to play their parts eternally, to say the same words eternally, to do the same thing. For every single human being who ever lived goes through an infinite series of reincarnations, an eternal recurrence with some possibilities for change.

"In reference to the pattern of repetition on their lives, people fall into several types. In Group One are the people of absolute repetition, with everything transmitted from one life to the next. Group Two consists of people whose lives each time have the same beginning, but go on with slight variations, coming to approximately the same end. Group Three is unfortunate. The lives of its members display a clearly marked descending line, which gradually destroys all that is alive in them. In Group Four are the people whose lives show a definitely ascending tendency, becoming richer and stronger and more successful outwardly. It is from this group that millionaires, great statesmen, geniuses, and prodigies come. They succeed because they remember well from their previous lives and apply that knowledge to the present.

"Finally, there is Group Five. These are the fortunate people whose lives contain an inner ascending line which gradually leads them out of the circle of eternal repetition to a higher plane of being. Some of you in this room may be capable of achieving this state. Every one of you in this room should try to achieve it. But few of you will try. And very very few will attain it."

The guru stood up gracefully and glided out of the room. Mauvais turned on more lights. Moss, sitting next to me, looked thoughtful. Neither Dhanapala nor Miss Swanson was in the room.

We were near the end of the procession of cars streaming away from the rubber plantation. It was a long procession and as the night dragged on the distances between cars increased until finally we were alone on the road.

"You said this guru is the new leader," Moss said. "Did the old one die?"

George paused a moment. "No, the old one didn't die. Actually, it's a little embarrassing. The previous leader knew both Gurdjieff and Ouspensky and spent thirty years lecturing and writing about their work. But last year he published a new book, announcing his own system, which he claims supersedes Gurdjieff. So we had to choose a new leader."

We rode silently for a while, then Moss said, "I never did meet the dunning psychoanalyst or the crooked lawyer."

"It doesn't matter," George said. "You didn't miss anything."

The only sound was the chattering of monkeys, a shrill, incessant jabber, and again it seemed to me that they sounded noisier than I had ever heard them.

Eleven

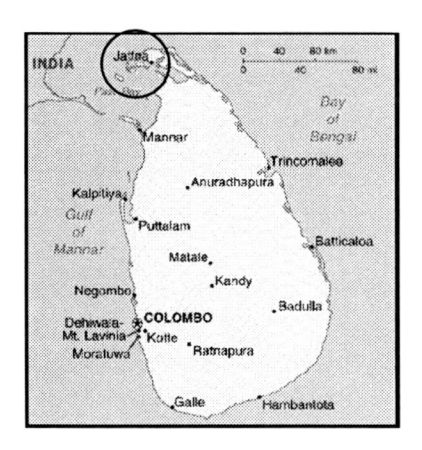

A month later I received a long letter from Moss, postmarked in Jaffna, the city at the northern tip of the island.

    Dear Westerling,

    I've been in this Tamil city a week now, supposedly waiting to attend a wedding that has been delayed, but actually delighted to be Ramanathan's guest. You know how much I admire his serene wisdom, his complete control of emotions. I find that here among his fellow Hindus he is respected even more than in Sinhalese Ceylon, and strangers greet me politely, knowing that I'm his guest. Often in recent weeks when I was depressed I wished I could talk to Ramanathan and try to learn how he has managed to accept life so calmly, to be the only genuinely tranquil man I knew. But I never got a chance to visit him, until he invited me to the wedding of his niece.

    The wedding has been delayed for reasons that seem ridiculous to me, but are apparently not unusual here. For one thing, the bride-to-be has had bad luck with this sort of thing before. Mala is an attractive and educated young woman, vivacious and charming, and three times in the past arrangements were made by her parents to have her marry eligible young Hindus.

But each time the astrologers claimed that the horoscopes did not match, and the arrangements had to be broken off immediately. I wonder whether this astrologer and marriage-broker racket is really a sensible device for discouraging what is likely to be an incompatible relationship by letting the position of the stars substitute for the voice of reason. They do have many fewer divorces than we do, but of course it's more difficult for a woman to get one.

This time they've found a young lawyer who meets the horoscope requirements, but now a dispute has arisen over the dowry. Mala's father, the brother of Ramanathan's dead wife, promised to give a dowry worth a hundred thousand rupees in land, jewelry, and cash. He's a lawyer and drew up the document himself. The dowry had been willed to Mala by her mother, long dead now, and her father remarried soon afterwards. But the bridegroom's father is also a lawyer, and he discovered when he examined the dowry that most of the jewelry has been sold, the land is mortgaged, and only half of the cash is actually available. Mala's father insists there's a misunderstanding, but Ramanathan told me that the old man used the money to finance a series of unsuccessful political campaigns, having been defeated as a candidate for mayor, councilman, and park commissioner. While the men wrangle, the original date of the wedding has already passed, but the women—there are dozens of them here—are feverishly baking, cooking, and sewing new clothes for the big event. They don't seem concerned in the least about the delay.

I asked Mala what kind of man her fiancé is. She says she doesn't know. She has only met him once, at the formal arranging of the wedding. I asked whether she is happy about the prospect of marrying a stranger. She looked at me, astonished. "Why should I complain?" she asked, with her charming British inflection. "He is a lawyer." Most devoted Hindu wives are completely unaware of their husbands' work and quite happy in their ignorance. Others share in, or dominate, their husbands' life almost as effectively as do American wives. There've been many changes in the old tradition since the time when a Hindu widow was expected to throw herself on her husband's funeral pyre and die with him. But Mala told me a pleasant anecdote about an ancestress of hers who refused, a century ago, to put her jewels on the funeral pyre. She didn't mind destroying herself, but she drew the line at wasting jewelry. Incidentally, a gold necklace called a tali and a wedding sari are all that the bridegroom is required to give. The bride's family has to provide everything else, including the expensive and elaborate wedding ceremony.

I met Mala's father the other day and found him a charming scamp. He talked to me very learnedly about Hindu emphasis on spiritual values and dissociation from any interest in physical possessions. He is well read and he made a number of caustic criticisms of American materialism and commercialism. He gave me a couple of pamphlets by a swami he knows who is supposed to perform some extraordinary feats—levitation, for one thing—and who explains how, by the practice of yoga and complete detachment from one's physical surroundings, one can attain the exquisite bliss of oneness with the Infinite. Mala's father told me he is a disciple of this swami and sometimes goes to his hut for periods of meditation. A little later, he told me gleefully how he had smuggled rupees out of the country on his last visit to India by having his wife and daughters come aboard ship to say goodbye and deposit in his cabin the rupees they had hidden in their saris. He's bitter about the government's high tax policy, and apparently sees no inconsistency at all in misappropriating his daughter's dowry while babbling about spiritual purity. He also told me, confidentially, that he is much more tolerant than his Brahmin friends, who can't stand the smell of meat-eating whites. He has learned to control his distaste, he says. He's a sanctimonious windbag. "You in the West," he told me pompously, "marry the woman you have learned to love. We learn to love the woman we've married."

The wrangling over dowries, I am told, is not unusual, although not always for the reasons in this case. Because of the frequent deaths of mothers in childbirth, due to lack of sanitation and primitive techniques, many widowers have second wives. As a result there are numerous stepbrothers and stepsisters, arguments over inheritance and dowry, and sometimes bitter intra-family feuds.

But I haven't told you about Jaffna itself and this part of the country. As you know, most of the people who live in northern and eastern Ceylon are Tamils, descendants of South Indians who originally raided the country, then stayed to live in it. Almost all of these people are Hindus, except for some Christians and a few Buddhists. They're very bitter about the discrimination of the majority Sinhalese, who have made Sinhalese the official language of the country and favor Sinhalese applicants in job appointments and civil service exams. Yesterday a mob of men was roaming around Jaffna tarring out the Sinhalese letters on auto licenses and buses. This is their way of protesting against mobs in central and southern Ceylon that have been tarring out Tamil nameplates and billboards. I'm afraid there'll be serious trouble between the races very soon. It's ironic that both Buddhists and Hindus, under British rule, had a centuries-old reputation for religious tolerance. But now that the country is independent both groups are being stirred by ambitious politicians to violence and brutality. Mark my words, there is trouble ahead in this Eden, and more than apples are going to be devoured.

To get to Jaffna I drove north through wide, dry plains, then along a road cut straight through the flatlands jungle. There were enormous ant hills along the side of the road, some more than six feet tall, shaped like miniature castles against the backdrop of jungle trees. Gray monkeys chattered along the roadside, and once I saw an elephant in the distance, but he had crossed the road and disappeared into the jungle by the time I drove past.

As you get closer to Jaffna the island narrows and water encroaches until there is only a slender stretch of land connecting Ceylon proper with the peninsula of Jaffna. This inlet is called Elephant Pass, and in the old days, when it was a shallow body of water, elephants are supposed to have crossed here regularly on their way to the succulent palmyra palms that dominate the Jaffna landscape. There are big salt flats here where men load the coarse salt on little boxcars that chug off to market. They sell the stuff, without any further refinement, to the consumer.

Jaffna itself is a tribute to the Dutchmen who two centuries ago built the colossal fort in the center of town. The massive coral stonewalls of the fort are as solid now as when the Dutch ruled these Eastern waters, long before Americans won their independence from England. Before that, in the seventeenth century, Jaffna was under Portuguese control.

The palmyra palm is famous, justifiably I have found, for a delicious, mellow, and potent toddy. The industrious natives also raise melons, sweet potatoes, and chilies, and they export mangoes, tobacco, turtles, and sea slugs. Tall fences surround almost every farm—the people here like their privacy far more than do their neighbors to the south.

After I'd been here a few days, Ramanathan took me in his car on a tour of the surrounding country. One of his servants drove. But we had some difficulty getting out of town. There was a loud roaring on the main street and a mob of people moving slowly. Then a large wooden chariot appeared, gaudily painted and elaborately carved. A dozen men pulled it, holding on tightly to the wooden poles protruding from the chariot and chanting as they walked. "It's a temple car," Ramanathan explained. "This is the end of a Hindu festival." Rolling on the ground behind the chariot were hundreds of men, all wearing short white dhotis. The leader was a fat elderly man and as he rolled puffing past us I saw that a pair of gold daggers pierced his cheeks.

"Those daggers were the weapons of Lord Subrahmayana," Ramanathan said quietly. "This man is the mayor of Jaffna. He is fulfilling a vow."

The men rolled on down the street. "Who are they?" I asked.

"Just people," he said. "They're trying to gain merit from the gods. They will roll to the temple, a quarter mile from here. It gives them pleasure to do it."

There was neither reverence nor sarcasm in his voice. He was simply stating a fact. We followed slowly behind the rollers until they reached the temple and went inside. I looked at the garish, incredibly ornate carvings on the frieze of the temple and turned to Ramanathan.

"What's the religious explanation of these erotic carvings?" I asked.

He looked placidly at the series of variations on the sexual act. In some a man and a woman copulated in different postures, some conventional, some strange. In others two men and a woman, and two women and a man, exhibited techniques of amour à trois. And through the open door of the temple, in the inner shrine, I saw an enormous rock lingam on a pedestal, the phallic symbol of the Hindu god Shiva, so profusely scattered all over the Orient.

"The explanation usually given tourists," Ramanathan said, "is that the erotic carvings remind the worshipper what he is to leave behind him when he enters a temple."

"There must be an easier way to stimulate forgetfulness," I suggested.

Ramanathan smiled. "There is. The more likely explanation is based on the essence of Hindu philosophy—the attainment of complete unity with God. Man's problem in the physical world is dualism—the constant conflict between the flesh and the spirit, lust and purity, desire and contentment. What Hinduism regards as the ultimate human fulfillment is mystic oneness with the Infinite. Now, can you think of a better symbol of dualism-uniting-in-oneness—with passion comparable to that of mystic intensity—than the sexual act?"

I couldn't. "Is that why the lingam is so popular in Hindu temples?" I asked.

Ramanathan laughed. "We were simply anticipating Freudian psychology. The psychoanalysts see sex symbols everywhere. We were rather restrained by comparison."

I laughed too. "Touché. But the number of women praying in front of the lingam is surprising."

He waggled his head. "They are praying for fertility. And yet it's surprising how many Hindus are unaware of the lingam's symbolism. It's just an object to them, its shape is irrelevant. And that blindness too is symbolic. Very few people see the truth."

"Will the major's cheeks bleed when the daggers are removed?"

"They shouldn't," Ramanathan said. "I've never suffered pain fulfilling a vow."

I don't know why I was surprised. "Have you done this?" I asked.

"I've done it," he said indifferently. "And I've walked the fire at Kataragama. There was no pain."

By now we were outside the town, turning off onto a country road. Here most of the carts were drawn not by bullocks but by white bulls with long sharp horns. I haven't seen these animals anywhere else on the island. Ramanathan says that races by these bull-drawn carts are popular. And bullfighting—in which one bull fights another—is illegal but can be seen in out-of-the-way places near Jaffna.

Along the roadside goats roamed, with long sticks tied across their chests to prevent their squeezing in between the fence-posts of neighbors' fields. Crows sat quietly on the backs of placid cows, ignoring the white buffalo head on a tall stick intended to serve as a scarecrow. In another field we saw a grotesquely dressed figure that was supposed to drive away evil spirits. It drooped forlornly in the afternoon heat.

We pulled off the road and walked to a large well. Boys using coconut shells for water wings were splashing around, learning to swim, while a young man at the edge gave them instructions. Ramanathan spoke to the man in Tamil and he smiled at us. "According to legend," Ramanathan said, "this is a bottomless pool. It was created when Rama, coming to Ceylon in his search for Sita—remember the pool near Adam's Peak?—wanted a drink. He shot an arrow into the ground to make a well, then traveled on. But the pool is still here, and no man has ever seen its bottom."

As we drove on down a narrow dirt road I saw a sign on a wooden board a foot or so above ground: "Cobra Gulch." Ramanathan saw my puzzled expression and smiled. "Some American engineers worked here a few years ago. They left a sample of their sense of humor."

We stopped next to what looked like a farm. The wooden shed was old but clean, and we walked to a small stone hut near it. "This is an ashram of the Rosarian Fathers," Ramanathan said. "I want you to meet Father Justinian, who is in charge."

We stepped into the windowless little stone hut and were greeted by a tiny brown man in the long white cassock of a Catholic priest. His black eyes twinkled pleasantly under his round spectacles, and his long white beard made me think of the seven dwarfs. He was very cordial, sat us down, showed us his books, medallions, and candles, and chattered fluently about the work the Fathers were doing. The Rosarians concentrate on work and prayer, he told me. All of the Fathers were out in the fields working, excepting two who were praying.

"What are they praying for?" I asked, saying it gently enough so that the priest wouldn't misunderstand.

"They are praying for all of mankind," he said gravely. "Twenty-four hours a day, no matter what happens, we have at least two Rosarian Fathers praying. If God decides to punish the Earth, it will not be because we have stopped entreating Him to forgive men's sins."

We talked a while longer, and the priest told me about the food they provided for poor people in the neighborhood. I gave him a large donation before we left, and he put it casually into the wooden box on his desk. The only other money in the box was a rupee.

The driver backed up the car, and eventually reached an asphalt highway again, then stopped by a large stone building. "This is a hospital operated by Protestant American Missionaries," Ramanathan said. He pointed to a field nearby. "Over there the great-grandmother of Foster Dulles is buried. She and her husband established a school here in 1824. It's still an excellent school."

In the entrance hallway there was a large painting of a young white man, and I stopped to read the plaque under the picture. The young man was an American doctor who had headed the hospital just before World War Two, and the picture had been sent by the Congregational Church in his hometown, Champaign, Illinois. I thought of you then, remembering that you had studied at Illinois. The doctor went down with a U.S. naval vessel during the war, refusing to abandon his patients. It was a strange place to find a tribute to an American and to be reminded that men are sometimes noble.

An American nurse appeared and greeted Ramanathan warmly. She thanked him for a recent contribution he had made to the hospital, then took us through the wards. One room was full of babies whose mothers had tuberculosis. On one of the cots a tiny wrinkled creature lay staring straight up at the ceiling. "She's four months old," the nurse said. "She isn't strong enough to turn."

From the next cot a miniature old man looked at us listlessly. "He's five months old," the nurse said. "His mother died yesterday."

I asked what would happen to these children. The nurse shrugged. "Their Hindu parents can't afford to raise them, but they refuse to release them for adoption in Christian homes. I don't know what will happen to them." She played peek-a-boo with the little boy for a few minutes, and the corners of his lips twitched tentatively. Then he closed his eyes and went to sleep.

On the way back to Jaffna we passed a pool near the side of the road. "We had quite a commotion here a few weeks ago," Ramanathan said, pointing in the direction of the pool. "As you know, Hindus have a predilection for calling themselves holy men. India is swarming with saddhus. Well, a saddhu showed up here two months ago. The local fakir, who felt his own prestige was threatened, challenged the newcomer to perform a miracle. 'I can live under water,' the new man said. 'Tomorrow evening let the people gather and I will show them.'

"Well, the following evening a big mob gathered and the saddhu made a long speech about his great powers, then jumped into the pool. He reached the bottom and stayed there, jerking and twisting wildly at first, then just standing straight up, his long hair streaming. The people marveled and shouted. When it got dark the saddhu was still down there so the people dispersed, talking about the miracle. The local fakir hid in his house and sulked, he was so ashamed.

"This went on for three days, and still the saddhu remained standing on the bottom of the pool. No one could go swimming, so after a while they called the police and a diver went down there and found that the saddhu was dead. He had caught his foot in the tangled roots when he jumped down there, and he tried to get free and couldn't, and he was just stuck there for the next three days. After they got him out the people went swimming again, and the local fakir came out of his hut and said he knew all the time that the other man was an imposter."

We were approaching Jaffna now, but again the driver turned off on a dirt road. "There is one more place I want you to see," Ramanathan said. "This is something new in our part of the country, a community center."

The center turned out to be a large, low, wooden structure with many windows and a large veranda. An energetic young man in a white shirt and sarong came bustling out to greet us. He held his palms together in front of his face when he greeted Ramanathan—the higher you hold your hands before you, I've learned, the more respect you are paying—and he thanked Ramanathan for a recent contribution to the center. I noticed an unusual vehicle standing in the driveway next to the building, a large multi-colored wooden cart with elaborate carvings and very detailed decorations.

The director saw me looking. "That's the cart used in wedding processions," he explained. "It's traditional in a Hindu wedding to have one of these built. But most of our people are very poor and have to borrow money for the rest of the wedding ceremony, apart from paying for a new cart. So we had the center build this one, and it's available to the whole community for a very nominal fee. We're very proud of this. On holidays, of course, it's used as a festival car and pulled through the streets by the people."

Inside, the center looked like its counterparts in the United States. There were desks and benches, a gymnasium section, and at one end a stage now hidden from us by a large curtain. On the bulletin board were announcements of forthcoming competitions in music, painting, drama, cloth design, and one subject I thought less likely to be found in an American community center: yoga exercises. I expressed the proper admiration and asked whether the center was open to everyone in the community.

"Oh yes," the director said earnestly. "There is no discrimination here at all—no caste, or color, or religion. We believe in complete equality. Here, let me show you."

He ran forward and pulled the rope, opening the stage curtain. On the back of the stage hung three large portraits, of exactly the same size. The one on the left was Jesus; the one in the center was Ghandi; and the one on the right was Karl Marx.

When we got back to Jaffna it was late in the afternoon and the streets were clogged with oxcarts, bullock carts, and men on bicycles. As our car crawled along, I saw a man with a small rectangular satchel stop a passerby and the two stepped to the side of the street. "That's a chiropodist," Ramanathan said. "He'll cut the man's corns right there, and for a few coins more he'll clean the man's ears. He carries all his equipment in that satchel. The town is full of these peripatetic foot-doctors."

At the next crossing the car stopped while a young man crossed languidly. As he swung his arms slowly I noticed suddenly that there were no fingers on his hands. Ramanathan saw it, too. "A leper," he said. "There's a hospital for them on an island near here. There is more leprosy here than people realize."

Two women, dressed in red and orange saris, strolled by. I asked about the marks in the center of their foreheads. Ramanathan smiled. "Originally a devout Hindu woman wore a saffron ash mark on her forehead as a symbol of Shiva's third eye. Later a black mark came to identify a married woman, a red mark a single one. But time and fashion march on, and today sophisticated Hindu women choose a color to match their saris. Even the shape of the mark has changed, from a simple circle to a shape that flatters the woman's beauty or pleases her aesthetic taste."

Our car had been standing still all this time, held up by a yelling mob with pails of tar. They were inspecting each car carefully and tarring out the license numbers on some of them.

"Don't be afraid," Ramanathan said. "They are only blacking out the new licenses, because they have Sinhalese lettering in them. Many of our Tamils feel that in this way they are defending the Tamil language, which is not used on car licenses. I myself don't think it's a wise procedure. In the rest of the island, Sinhalese are retaliating by tarring out Tamil names and letters. It will lead to bad trouble before it ends."

The mob milled around us but did not stop us. "I haven't bought a new car," Ramanathan said dryly, "because in Ceylon the license stays with the car instead of changing each year. And the older cars have only English lettering on their licenses."

He didn't say anything else on our way to his house, and I went to my room and rested until dinner.

I want to remind you again how much I admire Ramanathan, and how tremendously respected he is here in his hometown. I've never seen him angry or frightened or disturbed, and I decided to ask him how he attained this serenity.

We were sitting in the living room, resting comfortably after a pleasant chicken and curry dinner. The chicken was for me; Ramanathan never ate meat, but with his characteristic thoughtfulness he did not impose his beliefs on others. I didn't know what arrangements had been made about cooking meat in the house, because I had been advised before, by another Hindu friend, never to step into the kitchen. Ramanathan would not have objected, but the elderly woman who did his cooking would have insisted on a purification ceremony. There was a god in the kitchen, a squat wooden figure according to the houseboy, whose domain would have been profaned by my entry, and elaborate rituals would have been necessary to cleanse the kitchen and propitiate the god. So I stayed out.

The cooking of meat was not the only inconvenience my visit caused Ramanathan. Serving silverware was another problem. Ramanathan had had many distinguished guests—there were pictures on my bedroom wall of a governor general and three prime ministers who had slept in the house. But all of them had been Ceylonese and had eaten with their fingers. The business of serving me forks, spoons, and knives was a puzzling one to both the cook and the houseboy, and they had consulted the waiter at the Jaffna rest house before my arrival. Even then they were unsure, and I sometimes observed the kitchen staff watching surreptitiously as I manipulated the knife and fork with a dexterity that must have seemed as impressive to them as the skill of a Chinese with chopsticks seems to me. Ramanathan ate with his fingers.

I sat in the living room very much at ease, my feet resting on the extended footrest of the chair, which I had flipped out in front of me. There were only two pictures on the walls—one of a three-faced Hindu god with a tranquil expression on each of his faces, and the other of a handsome young man who I knew was Ramanathan's only son. He had drowned, someone in Colombo had told me, in a boating accident a few years before. The young man looked at the word out of frank, earnest dark eyes, and I was poignantly conscious of the exuberant vitality of his expression.

Ramanathan sat calmly in his chair, wearing traditional Indian clothing, as he always did. There was no hypocrisy about him, I thought, as I remembered some embarrassing experiences I had had when I unexpectedly visited some Ceylonese friends. In public they always wore Western clothing, and they sheepishly explained that they just happened to be wearing, at the particular time of my visit, the comfortable native sarongs and no shoes. Ramanathan doesn't put on an act for anyone.

A phonograph rested on a corner table, and I asked whether he liked music. He shook his head, and I noticed that there was a thick layer of dust on the phonograph. The rest of the room was very clean.

"I hope you'll forgive me," I said, "and I know how presumptuous it is to ask, but believe me it is out of respect and esteem for you that I ask: what do you believe in? What knowledge do you have that makes you so serene and kind and immune to ordinary human troubles?"

He looked at me for a long time, then shook his head, smiling. "I can't tell you that. Not because I don't want to—I would be happy to—but because I can't compress into a single statement what I believe. It would be oversimplifying. Life is not simple, and people are not simple, and the organization of the universe is incredibly complex. As your Hemingway says about the creative process, 'When you talk about it you lose it.'"

I nodded. "I understand that. But can you at least try to explain some Hindu beliefs that puzzle me?"

He smiled again, patiently, and I felt like a child addressing a tolerant father. "Do you believe in reincarnation?"

"Yes," he said. "But there is a difference between reincarnation and transmigration of souls, though some of your Western scholars fail to make the distinction. Reincarnation means the continuous upward movement of the soul through a series of human bodies, on its way to perfection. Transmigration, on the other hand, assumes either the random jumping about of souls from one human body to another, or even the retrogression from human bodies to animal bodies. I personally do not believe in transmigration."

"How can you prove that reincarnation exists?"

"I can't prove it in a laboratory experiment, but let's use the analogy to a law of physics: every action has a reaction. However, a murderer who has killed two people can only die once in this life. Correct? Reincarnation gives him another life in which he will have to pay for the second murder."

"That's sophomoric reasoning," I said.

He shrugged. "Then look at it this way. Some people are born wealthy, attractive, able. They live happy, comfortable lives and die with a minimum of sorrow. Others suffer, starve, work all day, lose loved ones, and die in pain and misery. If there is any order in the world, how can you explain this? Reincarnation explains it. The fortunate have earned this happiness in a previous existence. The unfortunate have earned their misery."

"How is reincarnation supposed to work?"

"I can only tell you what I believe," he said. "It may not be true. The soul is an entity that survives many deaths, but it is in a state of continuous flux. It shapes our lives in accordance with certain spiritual and physical laws, especially the law of karma. The goal of man is to lose all thought of 'I' or 'mine' and to achieve the everlasting happiness of union with God."

I squirmed a little. "It's a subtle philosophy," I said.

He chuckled. "My dear boy, of course it's subtle. You have only a child's notion of how subtle the speculations of some Hindu philosophers have been. Long before Western thinkers speculated on the subject, Hindus suggested that dreams may be reality, and that the whole physical world is a dream, a mirage, an illusion. Our philosophers have written that the mind takes the shape of each physical object it sees or remembers or imagines. Our philosophers have argued over whether reincarnation can move only upward, as I have suggested, or downward, too, to end as stone or metal."

I was trying to avoid abstractions so I said, "But how could philosophers as subtle as that accept the caste system?"

"Precisely because they are subtle. The caste system is a way of compensating, in the social order, for each man's behavior in a previous existence. Those who have lived well in earlier incarnations are rewarded by reincarnating now in a high caste. Those who had failed to develop in the past are sentenced temporarily to a low caste. It offers consolation and it offers hope."

I was shocked. "But surely you yourself don't believe in caste."

"How impetuous you are," he said quickly. "I believe in it in the same way you believe in it. Surely you admit that men are not born equal in intelligence, capability, physical inheritance, wealth, or environment. Surely you don't believe that the youngest child of a starving family in India has the same 'caste' as a wealthy American like yourself."

"But he has the same opportunities."

Ramanathan shook his head vigorously. "Not at all. The opportunities for one of ordinary ability in modern Ceylon—and modern India—are very limited. It's true, of course, that extraordinary people do rise from the lowest environment to the highest achievements. But that's exactly what we believe—the very strong can reshape their karma and forge their own destiny."

"It's true," I admitted, "that many great statesmen, reformers, and conquerors began at the bottom."

Ramanathan smiled tolerantly. "You miss the point, just as most Westerners miss the point. You're talking about controlling nations and institutions. But it's harder to gain control of your own self. Believe me, it is. I know men who run governments and great businesses, but they are unhappy and inadequate with their own families, and they lack confidence in themselves. It's easier to turn to outward activity and organizing—easier for some men, that is. It's also true that many men who achieve self-mastery would not make good administrators or executives. They may be too detached to care about social dislocation, or too naïve to suspect duplicity. Union with God is different from a seat on the Stock Exchange—and more expensive."

The houseboy brought tea and served it. We drank slowly. "Good intentions are not enough," Ramanathan said. "There was a wealthy American visiting Ceylon a few years ago. He saw a woman crying in a hotel—she was obviously an upper class, refined, middle-aged Hindu woman. He was kind-hearted and questioned her. It turned out that it was the tenth anniversary of her husband's death and Hindu religion required that she have an alms-giving ceremony on his behalf, so that his soul not be doomed to a lower level in his next incarnation. You see, Hinduism is too involved to be explained in a sentence, and I don't have time to tell you why alms giving by a widow can help a man's soul in his voyage to perfection. At any rate, the woman had no money and was weeping. The generous American gave her five hundred rupees, and she held the required ceremony. A year later she became insane."

I put down my teacup in surprise. "Why?"

"Because a Brahmin priest told her that by using a stranger's money she had unintentionally condemned her husband to a lower level in his next incarnation."

"Is the priest right?"

Ramanathan shrugged. "I don't know. Most Hindu priests disagree with him. But she believed him, and she couldn't take it. Don't look so glum. The soul is immortal and eternal. You need not grieve for her."

We talked of other things and I invited him to come to Colombo next month for the American Women's Club charity ball. He promised to be my guest. I felt immensely grateful to him for his hospitality, his conversation, and most of all for the living proof he offered that the spirit could conquer the flesh, that man could overcome ordinary emotions and be calm, serene, and tranquil—and beyond normal weakness. When we stood up to go to our bedrooms I paused by the picture of his son and said, "It's wonderful that your philosophy enables you to accept so calmly the death of your son."

He hesitated, just a moment, then motioned me quietly to leave the room ahead of him. "It isn't so bad now, thinking of my son's death," he said quietly. "It was much worse one thousand two hundred and twelve days ago."

Twelve

The cremation of the head priest was a festive event. Overnight, thousands of paper streamers and slivers of grass had been hung along Kandy road near his temple. At frequent intervals along this unbroken line dangled large pieces of paper showing a picture of the priest and listing his achievements. It was early afternoon, and the cremation was not scheduled until six o'clock, but already hundreds of people in their best white clothes were milling around the wooden tabernacle being constructed for the funeral pyre.

By the time I had picked up Moss at Queens Hotel and returned, the tabernacle was completed. We barely managed to find a parking place along the road as thousands of white-clad people converged on the locale. There wasn't a sad face in the crowd. If we had not been told that this was a funeral we might have thought that a merry festival was being celebrated by the cheerful adults and chattering children sauntering near the tabernacle.

At noon Piodasa had asked permission to take his wife to the dentist. She had a bad toothache, he told me, and I let him go. Now we met him, strolling happily in a white coat and long white sarong, his fat little wife and his youngest son pattering behind him. He beamed when he saw us and came over to chat, obviously glad to see us. I didn't have the heart to ask about his wife's toothache.

When we came closer to the tabernacle I saw a turbaned head and blond beard towering above the short Ceylonese. Shantinaha came over and greeted us. He had come up for the funeral because the dead priest had been a good friend of his, but he, also, showed no sign of grief.

The tabernacle had a large canopy and was covered with intricately carved paper decorations. It was so elaborate, Shantinaha explained, because the priest was an important man. An ordinary monk would be placed in a small structure, open at the sides. But this log building, about twenty by fifteen feet, was completely enclosed and cost 1,500 rupees. From the large white dome on the roof of the building a spire pointed towards the sky.

A black Plymouth cruised slowly along the road, trying to find a parking place, and a half an hour later George and Marian Burton pushed their way through the mob and joined us. George had his trick camera with him and took some pictures of the monks sitting on benches near the tabernacle. There must have been over a hundred of them sitting there in saffron robes, their shaven heads gleaming. A middle-aged woman passed a tray of fruits and pastries among them, and the monks nibbled placidly. Today their right shoulders were covered. A short monk with an aquiline nose came through the crowd and stood talking to some of the sitting monks. He was the same man Ramanathan had saved on Adam's Peak.

George looked around disdainfully. "These people will attend anything. Political rally, festival, funeral—any excuse will do."

Shantinaha said indulgently, "Their lives are pretty dull. Don't begrudge them a chance to enjoy themselves."

"If you say so, Swami," George said sarcastically. "While we're waiting, why don't you tell Moss about your cult?"

"I wouldn't call it my 'cult.' That word has a suggestion of the absurd about it, a group of naïve neurotics grasping desperately to a foolish illusion. A few people share some of my beliefs, but they owe me no allegiance and certainly they are not members of any organized institution. From time to time people speculating about the meaning of life have lived at my retreat in the jungle. They learn to do certain things there that previously they could not do. But they could learn some of those things from yogis, or hermits, or herpetologists."

"Are there women at your retreat?" Moss asked.

Shantinaha's eyes twinkled. "No. Women need a different religion from men. Not by nature, perhaps, but as a result of conditioning. Society prepares men for one kind of role, women for another. So the religion that may help men is not good for women."

"Is your—er, group—no different from any other 'mystic' retreat, then?" Moss asked.

Shantinaha smiled amiably. "It's different from all of them. For one thing, most mystics—whether Oriental or Western, Buddhist or Hindu or Christian—are convinced that they've found *the* Truth. I know that I do not have the Truth—only a number of small truths. Let me give you an example. Have you ever heard of Ramakrishna?"

Moss shook his head.

"Well," Shantinaha said, "Ramakrishna was a famous Indian sage who lived a century ago. He was searching for the Truth and he thought that when he found it he would achieve ecstasy. He followed the teachings of Hindu hermits for seven years and he achieved ecstasy. But he was a fair man, so he spent the next seven years following Buddhist teachings. Again he achieved ecstasy. Then he undertook the Christian road to mystic insight, and, after seven years, achieved it. Ramakrishna concluded from this experience that there is truth in all of the major religious and disciplines and that they all lead to God. But it seems to me more likely that men like Ramakrishna need ecstasy and can always manage to find it, one way or another. Or to persuade themselves that they found it."

"But why can't you believe that he did find it?" Moss asked.

"Because I don't believe anyone who tells me he has found *the* only Truth. Like Professor Whitehead, I think that reality is always changing. Nature is always changing, our bodies are constantly changing, our values are changing, God himself is in a perpetual state of change. Nothing in the world is permanent. Heraclitus knew this when he said, more than twenty-five hundred years ago, that no one ever steps into the same river twice. The person is different the second time—physically and psychologically—and the river is different. The water is not the same water that had flowed before, and the temperature and rate of flow are not quite the same."

"I know all that," Moss said, "But for all *practical* purposes we can assume a certain permanence and certain truths."

"Ah," Shantinaha said, "That's exactly it. Truths, not one Truth. There are many truths, and everyone has a piece of truth, but when a man assumes that the little piece he has is the whole Truth he is wrong. And most people do exactly that. The few who are strong say that the way they see things should be the universal way. And the many who are weak say that the way they happen to be imitating is the one everyone should imitate. Some are convinced of the truth of science, or of Christian revelation, or of Muhammad's vision, or Buddha's insight, or Karl Marx's, or Freud's, or Hitler's, or Dale Carnegie's. Now that's where my 'cult' is different. We claim no final knowledge. What we believe keeps changing, and we the believers keep changing. Only a fool is sure of anything."

"But a happy fool," George said.

"A happy fool," Shantinaha conceded. "I don't deny that certainty is psychologically healthy. Conviction relaxes a person and gives his life meaning. It lets him save his energy for specific practical jobs instead of speculating about the relativity of truths and values. I've never said that my belief brings happiness."

"What does it bring, then?" Moss asked.

Shantinaha smiled. "That I can't tell you glibly, standing on one leg. I don't have an epigram handy, like 'Love thy neighbor as thyself' or 'And this too shall pass away.' There is no shortcut. You would have to live with us and study and go through certain experiences. Then you would know what I have to offer, and whether it will help you."

A boy selling lottery tickets approached us, and Moss and George bought several. "Have you ever won?" Marian asked.

"No," Moss said. George didn't answer, but turned again to Shantinaha. "I agree that you can't summarize your whole system in a phrase. But you must admit that you start with one fundamental Truth."

"Absolutely not. Scientists have to know what they call objective truths to achieve objective results with physical things. But they keep discovering that those truths keep changing. You can't use a fifty-year-old physics or chemistry test today. And outside of science we live by subjective truths—beliefs that are often completely fallacious to everyone but ourselves. We need illusions to live by—the illusion that we are better liked than we are, or more capable than we are, or that we acted for nobler reasons than we really did. Nobody really wants to know the whole truth about himself. What everyone wants is an illusion he can accept without feeling foolish. Even science proves that we need illusions. Research by psychologists showed that people deprived of dreams during their sleep—they rigged up an electroencephalogram to control the experiment—became irritable and aggressive. Note that it was *dreams* they were deprived of, since they slept as much as ever.

"We absolutely need these illusions to give purpose to our lives. Bernard Shaw says he was shocked when a Christian clergyman told him that if he lost his faith in God, life would have no meaning. Shaw ridiculed what he called an illusion of the clergyman, but Shaw himself believed in something he called 'The Life Force,' which is as vulnerable an illusion to most people as was the idea of a personal God to Shaw."

"But surely," Moss said, "there are some truths outside of science."

Shantinaha nodded. "You play with words, my young friend. There are, as you say, many little truths, valid under limited conditions. But life is too complex, and you find very quickly that these simple truths come into conflict with each other. 'Thou shalt not kill,' you say is a truth. But you approve of killing in wars and in administering capital punishment. The other nine commandments are also true, up to a point, for each of us. The same holds true for all religions and all philosophies. They are true, up to a point. But as soon as you pass that point, they are no longer true. Socrates knew that very well, and it helped convict him. He noticed that people who were experts in one field assumed that their knowledge applied to all fields. But it never does. And scientists who try to apply rigid rules to morality and aesthetics and politics quickly learn their inadequacy."

"Let me try asking this another way," Moss said. "Aren't some things more important than others?"

Shantinaha shook his head. "I've found that many things important to me are completely unimportant to everyone else. They are not part of a planned overall pattern, in spite of our tremendous need to believe in such a pattern. I've met people and done things that are long gone and will not recur nor affect me one way or another. There are people whose paths have crossed mine, and faces I remember that I wish I had known better, but they are gone out of my life forever, and they have neither helped me nor hurt me."

A small dog kept twirling around, chasing his tail. Near the tabernacle the monk whom Ramanathan had saved was waving his arms angrily as he talked to another monk. In the distance a noise sounded, but we could not see what was going on.

Moss looked at Shantinaha sadly. "Haven't you found any insight into man's nature?"

"No," Shantinaha said, "no insight. Only insights. Only pieces of the truth. But at least I know they are only pieces and I don't try to build a whole philosophy out of them. Unlike Freud, I don't build a system on sexual intercourse. Unlike Marx, I don't erect a system on the stomach. Unlike millions of religious fanatics, I don't insist that my religion is the only true one. Unlike Menchen, I don't insist that all religions are false. Unlike the nationalists, I don't put country above individual. Unlike the racists, I don't put color above man. And unlike insecure English writers, I don't choose, of all the religions in the world, Anglo-Catholicism as my salvation. You see, it boils down to this: most men don't dare to live as they would like to live. They accept the conventions of their community—and even the conventional revolts of their community—but they never come to life as individuals."

George held cigarette smoke in his mouth and blew it out. "You're telling us a lot of things you don't believe in. But what do you believe?"

Shantinaha shook his head. "It's a long story, too long to tell here." The sound in the distance had been growing louder and now everyone was looking in that direction. A large float in the shape of a boat moved slowly down the street. On it lay a wooden coffin. Behind the float walked hundreds of white-clad men and women.

"The procession started at the temple and wound through many side streets, so the people could see it," Shantinaha told us.

In front of the float men were throwing a kind of silvery sand on the street. The float passed over it and turned toward the tabernacle. Four men in white sarongs took the coffin off the float, pushed it through a window of the tabernacle, then climbed inside and wedged the coffin in among the logs. Then the men climbed out.

Above us the loud speaker rumbled and a strong, confident voice orated in Sinhalese. "There'll be a lot of speeches before the cremation," Shantinaha said. "Priests and politicians and important people. That's the head priest of another temple talking now."

Moss walked off to get a look at the speaker, then came back and said, "I think that's Ranjini's new man."

Shantinaha nodded. "That isn't any secret. But it's not fair to the Buddhist clergy to think of this priest as typical. He's an ambitious man who happens to be in the clergy instead of in business or in the army. He is not really a religious man."

The voice rolled on, booming and self-assured. When it stopped we watched the tall, heavy-necked priest step away from the microphone. The monk from Adam's Peak joined him and they talked animatedly. In the meantime another priest stood behind the microphone and orated in a high, singsong voice. "They'll be singing praises for a long time," Shantinaha said.

George frowned. "Claptrap." He turned to Shantinaha. "What makes men do the things they do, Swami?"

Shantinaha spoke serenely. "Man is driven by three forces: physical passions, spiritual desires, social pressures. Each of these forces can be controlled, to a degree. The social pressures can be entirely eliminated by living away from society. What my status was in England, or yours in New York, is not important to the illiterate natives or animals in the jungle. The physical passions can be minimized by using a simple diet and removing temptation from your environment. The spiritual desires can be gratified by concentration and meditation, by exercises and rituals. I don't claim that my way leads to happiness. All I promise is the growth of your soul."

"But how about man's duty to society?" Moss said earnestly. "It seems to me immoral to turn away from our fellow men, to worry only about ourselves."

Shantinaha shook his head sadly. "You are still a child," he said gently. "Morality, immorality. You learned some words in Sunday school and you're still prattling them. What does nature have to do with morality? Is it unethical for the lion to kill the antelope or for the wolf to eat the rabbit? Nature has nothing to do with morality, only with physical survival. The mystic experience has nothing to do with morality, only with spiritual growth. The lion survives not because he is moral but because he is physically competent. The mystic achieves the transcendental experience not because he gives to charity or withholds his contribution, not because he indulges in sex or avoids it, but because he trains himself to do certain things that help attain a transcendental experience."

"No," Moss said stubbornly. "You're talking about the laws of the jungle. But civilization rejects those laws. In the jungle the sick are left to die; in civilized society we save them in hospitals. In the jungle the old are neglected; in society we provide for them. The survival of the fittest is an outdated argument. I can't get out of my mind seeing sore-covered children living in Hong Kong doorways, and women sleeping in newspapers on the streets of Calcutta. They haunt me. I feel futile and somehow responsible. It's precisely because we reject this law of nature that we're civilized human beings."

Shantinaha looked at him pityingly. "You really believe that?" he said.

"Yes," Moss said. "I do." George smiled, puffed on his cigarette, and blew out the smoke without inhaling. The loudspeaker blared on, another voice repeating in Sinhalese the virtues of the dead priest.

"Look at what you call the great civilized philosophies," Shantinaha said. "Buddhism teaches that to achieve happiness, man should stop being human—that is, he should gain freedom from pain by eliminating pleasure. Christianity teaches that to achieve happiness, man should stop being bad. But 'good' men, judging from Puritans and the Italians who burned Savanarola, have not been happy. So it's not simply a matter of ethics."

Moss was quiet.

"Is it ethical for you to be so rich when millions of Ceylonese people around you barely have enough to eat?" Shantinaha asked quietly.

Moss frowned. "I've thought about that," he said slowly. "My being rich has nothing to do with ethics."

Shantinaha smiled wryly. He looked out at the crowd and seemed to lose interest in the discussion. George took his camera off his shoulder and went with Moss to take pictures of the elaborate wood-and-paper house in which the priest's coffin lay. Another speaker, a bombastic politician, thundered over the loudspeaker, and the little dog that had been chasing his tail became frightened and slunk off. Marian said she was tired of standing and went to sit in the car.

The beak-nosed monk finished talking to Ranjini's priest and started to walk away, past us. Then he saw us and said something in Sinhalese. He seemed angry. Shantinaha spoke to him quietly, then the monk said something loudly and stomped off.

"What was that all about?" I asked.

Shantinaha was looking at the departing monk. "He said that when Sinhalese Buddhists take over the country there'll be no room for foreigners. We'll have to go or be killed. He says the prime minister promised the clergy that before election."

"Is he serious?"

"He's stupid but he means it. He told me that every man makes his own destiny and he will soon make his. I think he's dangerous."

When Moss and George returned, Moss looked at Shantinaha diffidently. "Nobody is more critical of the vulgarity and conformity of modern mechanical civilization than I am. Nevertheless, I really believe that the spread of scientific knowledge and education has improved society."

"But the most highly educated countries of the modern world—Germany in Europe, Japan in Asia—have been the most warlike, the most brutal, and the most immoral. How do you explain that?" Shantinaha said.

Moss didn't say anything. A thin voice was now chanting over the loud speaker, squeaking and mumbling and coughing. The microphone caught and amplified every sound he made.

Shantinaha smiled at Moss. "You can't explain it. The fact is that most adults are simply overgrown children. They have lost the spontaneous pleasure in play that they had as children, so they substitute provincial rules with which they play at living. If in the United States the rules require making money, that's what they earnestly try to do. If in Russia the rules require pretending altruistic devotion to the

State, that's what they earnestly try to do. If in Asia, the rules require pretending that physical comforts are unimportant, that's what they earnestly try to do—until they get a chance to revolt from capitalism in the United States, from communism in Russia, from murky mysticism in Asia. It isn't the particular society man resents, it's society itself."

"But man needs society," Moss objected.

"Weak men need society," Shantinaha said. "And most men, as I've just said, are overgrown children. Weak, sentimental, conformist. Many people in the West really need a strict morality to provide form and order in their lives and, perversely, to provide the pleasure of violating the accepted morality."

George lit another cigarette. "I suppose now you're going to give us a defense of Nietzsche's Superman."

"I am not going to give you a defense of anybody," Shantinaha said good-naturedly. "Nietzsche's Superman is proper for Nietzsche; he has been distorted by everyone else. Jesus's humanitarian is proper for Jesus; he has been distorted by everyone else. That's exactly what I'm telling you: Each man must make his own myth for himself. Otherwise it's second hand and cheap."

Moss shook his head. "You're anti-social. What you're recommending may lead to individual serenity, in an isolated situation, but it doesn't result in improvement of society."

Shantinaha nodded. "Right. I haven't the slightest interest in improving society. But since you've brought it up, I'll deny the popular charge that man is degenerating. As an individual, man hasn't changed much. The 'good old days' myth is nonsense, and the cynicism of post-war Europe is nonsense. Most people remain pretty much the same—interested primarily in themselves, their families, security, comfort, sex, and status. A few noisy existentialists don't change a generation, nor do a few nosy evangelists."

"Perhaps," Moss conceded, "but the average Westerner is more concerned about other people than Asians are. He is more moral."

Shantinaha looked at him commiseratingly and shook his head. "The avarice of Frenchmen is moral? The permanent sex-hunt of Italians? The callousness of the German? The brutality of the Russian?"

"Is the Ceylonese any better?"

"Of course not," Shantinaha said. "The average laborer or villager in Ceylon doesn't give a damn about anything except himself and his family. His Buddhism has no more effect on his daily behavior than Christianity does on Western laborers and provincials. He likes liquor and he drinks it whenever he can get it. He likes sex and enjoys it as often as he can, and he does it naturally and simply, without bourgeois qualms or neurotic guilt feelings. He has his superstitions and myths, and Westerners have their superstitions and myths. They're different in degree, but not in kind."

"In other words," George said, "there is no progress."

"There is progress in some respects. The lack of science in the Orient is not necessarily good; as far as health is concerned it's bad. The lack of education is not necessarily good. Mass art is almost always cheap and obvious and superficial. But civilization itself—if you think of institutions rather than individuals—is on a higher level than ever before."

"Well," George said, "I wouldn't say that. And I never expected to hear you say it."

Shantinaha smiled. "Individually, men are as selfish and materialistic and neurotic as they have ever been. But institutions have become better. For the first time, national and international organizations have at least made an effort to raise living standards, eliminate diseases, and provide a measure of freedom. In that sense the twentieth century is the most humane in history."

A new sound came over the loud speaker, the rhythmic chant of a praying monk. Men and women crowded around the tabernacle, throwing gifts inside. Then laborers nailed boards across all the windows except one, while the monk's chant was magnified and the crowd listened reverently. A priest threw a burning torch inside the little wooden house, waited until it caught, and ordered the last window boarded up. It was a moment before sunset.

A few minutes later the paper cupola was blazing brightly. Men selling food circulated through the crowd and children played and shrieked happily.

"How long before the body burns?" Moss asked.

"It'll take about eight hours," Shantinaha said. "I'm leaving now."

We walked towards our cars. "How long will the crowd stay?"

Shantinaha shrugged. "As long as they're having fun. I told you that life is dull for these people. This is a very festive occasion."

Thirteen

When we came home that evening Piodasa greeted us unperturbed. "How is your wife's toothache?" I asked.

"Huh? Oh, it get better. No hurt no more." He grinned cheerfully and went into the kitchen to serve dinner.

Moss shook his head in mock desperation. "He's either the most brazen man on the island, or the most stupid."

I told him that Piodasa was just stupid, and defending his stupidity wasn't always easy. Especially when Chitra Gunesena asked whether Piodasa had or had not sawn a limb off a tree while he was sitting on the part that he was sawing off. He had, and it was hard to make Chitra understand that Piodasa had intended to shift over to a safe part after he had done the preliminary sawing, but in his enthusiasm he forgot to stop sawing in time. He hadn't been hurt badly, and he seemed surprised that people kept making remarks about the incident.

"His looks are certainly against him," Moss said.

I agreed. Piodasa's appearance prejudiced people against him from the start. If I hadn't been desperate I probably wouldn't have hired him myself. But I had been in Ceylon only a month and had just lost my first cook and was stranded in a large house with a wood-burning kitchen stove.

"What happened to your first cook?" Moss asked. I had poured martinis and we were settled comfortably in the living room.

I told Moss about my first cook, Daha, whom I had inherited from Dr. Zeller, my American predecessor at the university. In Ceylon there was no nonsense about calling male cooks 'chefs.' They weren't chefs, and no one who had eaten their cooking would ever call them chefs. Dr. Zeller had written an enthusiastic recommendation in Daha's service book. I didn't know at the time that it was customary for Western employees of Ceylonese house-servants to write nothing but enthusiastic recommendations in the service books. Later, when I phoned an Englishman for whom Daha had once worked, he warned me fervently, "For heaven's sake, don't hire that rascal." I asked him why he himself had praised Daha fulsomely in the book, and he said, "Can't hurt the poor chap's feelings, you know."

Daha, a tall, slim, sharp-featured Sinhalese, was waiting in my bungalow when I arrived. The word "bungalow," I explained to Moss, is somewhat misleading. In Ceylon, it includes all dwellings more substantial than the thatch-roofed huts of the villagers and applies to one-room cottages as well as ambassadors' mansions. My bungalow was made of stone and concrete. It had three large bedrooms, an enormous living room, a study, a dining room, and three bathrooms. It also had, in a wing at the back of the house, a butler's pantry, two kitchens, rooms for the servants, bathrooms for the servants, and a two-car garage. Daha immediately told me that he needed two houseboys to help him take care of the bungalow, but I had been warned and said he could have only one. Daha promptly went to his room and returned with a handsome young man whom he introduced as Vasumal. "Him Tamil but him good houseboy," Daha told me. Again, I had been warned against mixing Sinhalese and Tamil servants, but since these two were friends I hired Vasumal. Daha told me to relax and let him take over, and, anticipating the pleasures of luxurious existence, I sat back and waited.

I waited a long time. Daha over-fried, over-boiled, and over-seasoned everything he made for dinner. At lunch he had less opportunity to make mistakes, for he served the same thing every day during the first week—canned soup, sliced Spam, sliced bread, and fresh fruit. Daha announced "sandwiches," but he clearly expected me to make the sandwiches myself. When Daha gave me the bill for the week's groceries, it proved to be higher than my food bill in the United States. Since the food in Ceylon was supposed to be one-fifth as expensive as in America, I was surprised. The meat that Daha served was stringy and tough, the eggs tiny, the cooked vegetables soggy, and the fresh vegetables so wilted that I couldn't eat them. I began to get a little suspicious.

According to the employment contract, Daha was supposed to stay in the bungalow at all times, except when shopping or on his day off. But from the first evening I couldn't find Daha in his quarters. Each time I went back there to call him I found only Vasumal, who smiled amiably and said, "Daha go temple." By the end of the week Daha had put in enough time at the temple to qualify for the priesthood, and even Vasumal giggled when he repeated the trite excuse.

But it was neither his atrocious cooking, nor his cheating on food money, nor his blatant absenteeism that finally forced me to fire Daha. It was his stealing. When American money disappeared from my locked drawer, I called Daha in and said, "There was a ten-dollar bill in my dresser yesterday."

"Yes, Master," he said, looking me straight in the eye.

"It is not there today," I said.

"Yes, Master."

"Do you know what happened to it?"

"No, Master."

"Do you have a key to the drawer?"

"No, Master."

"Daha, that money must be found, or something bad will happen."

He looked at me for a long time, then he said, "What ten-dollar bill look like?"

I took a bill out of my wallet and showed it to him. He looked at it carefully, turned it over and over, then returned it.

"So that how it look," he said thoughtfully. "I never see one before. I try find it."

"You do that," I told him, "because if that money is not found, there will be trouble."

The following afternoon, when I unlocked my drawer, I saw that the missing bill had been returned. But when, within the next few days, other small objects began to disappear, I decided to let Daha go. He did not seem surprised and offered no objections. He had only one request. When I reached for his servicebook, to write my evaluation of his work, Daha put out his hand for it. "No need write nothing, Master. No need bother." He walked briskly out of the house, his suitcase bulging.

The problem of keeping servants out of locked drawers is a standard joke in Ceylon. An English tea planter told me of an experience he had had. His wife was so strict about keeping the servants out of places where they didn't belong that every day she hid the keys to the liquor cabinet in a different place. One day Warren came home unexpectedly early and was told by the houseboy that Mrs. Warren was still at the golf club.

"Damn," Warren said. "I want a drink, but Lady has the keys."

"Master want drink bad?" the houseboy asked.

"I certainly do."

"Master have key to dresser?"

"Yes."

The houseboy smiled. "Today Lady hide key to liquor cabinet in third drawer, between handkerchiefs and shorts. I go bring ice, Master."

So I had fired Daha and was sitting dejectedly in the living room when I heard a knock on the door and Piodasa shuffled into my life.

I'll always remember my first impression of Piodasa. I saw a man with an extraordinary amount of wild, bushy black hair, his head held slightly to the right—a short man who was snarling at me through protruding, widely separated teeth and whose hands were trembling with rage. Later, when I got to know Piodasa better, I realized that he had a habit of resting his head on his right shoulder, that his stooping posture made him seem shorter than he was, that the snarl was intended as an ingratiating smile, and that he was trembling not with rage but with nervousness. I asked him to come in and he startled me by hissing loudly. I found out later that hissing was another nervous habit of his, and I grew so accustomed to it that I was hardly aware of it, except when guests suddenly turned in amazement and looked suspiciously at the man serving their dinner.

Moss laughed. "He does hiss a lot. I notice he has a livid scar near his right eye. Was that from falling off the tree?"

I told Moss the story of the scar. When Piodasa was the personal servant of an English major he accompanied his employer on a long drive at night. The major, who had been working since early morning, kept getting sleepier and sleepier at the wheel and finally dozed off. The car left the road and crashed into a tree, and both he and Piodasa required surgery before they left the hospital.

"Did you notice that the major was falling asleep?" I asked.

"Sure, I sit next to major. I see him go sleep."

"Then why on earth didn't you wake him?"

Piodasa looked shocked. "No, no," he said. "Very bad manners tell Master he fall asleep."

Piodasa's preposterous politeness didn't extend to women. One day my neighbor's wife came home with the hood and front bumper of her Austin badly damaged. She was furious because a driver with a "Learner" sign on his car had lost control and run into her. Piodasa was standing by the garage when she drove in. He looked at the smashed hood and said, "Lady, why you do that?"

A fly kept buzzing around Moss's face, and after he had made a couple of futile snatches at it, I called Piodasa. "We don't have a fly swatter," I explained. "Buddhists aren't supposed to kill anything, even an insect."

Piodasa came in and patiently waved at the fly until it flew out the window. Then Piodasa went back to the kitchen and in a little while the fly flew back in and buzzed around Moss. I told him that it sometimes took Piodasa a long time to catch hornets and wasps in his handkerchief, after which he released them outdoors. Since there were no screens on our windows, this method of disposal was not really very effective. But Piodasa told me that each of our souls had, at some stage in the long process of transmigration, inhabited insects and animals, and might again. He was taking no chances. By sparing the life of a particularly revolting rat snake, for instance, he was conceivably protecting a not-too-distant relative and building up good will for the future.

For cobras he felt, like most Buddhists, a special reverence. The Sinhalese are, according to two separate legends, the descendants of either lions (Sinha) or cobras. Since there are no lions in Ceylon, all of the available veneration for an eminent ancestor is directed toward the cobra, and the Sinhalese do everything possible to avoid killing the hooded snake. When I told Piodasa it was hard to see how both the lion and the cobra could be his ancestors, he said, "Not hard for Sinhalese to see."

He was so pleased with this rejoinder that he absentmindedly put a piece of betel leaf in his mouth and chewed it. In the house, he was expressly forbidden to use the smelly, mouth-reddening plant that is the Oriental substitute for chewing gum. It has a mildly narcotic effect, as does another herb, a white powder that he would surreptitiously pop into his mouth to "make toothache feel better." He apparently had a permanent toothache, as Daha had had a permanent call to temple, and after he had chewed the white stuff for a while his pupils would become dilated, his movements sluggish, and his reactions even slower than usual. At times like that I found it best to ignore him and his unexpected, loud giggles.

For a man who refused to kill snakes and insects, he found surprising compensation at the movies. At that time I thought his fascination for second-hand violence was quite funny. He loved American gangster and cowboy movies, and went whenever he could get away in the evening. When I asked, "How was the movie last night, Piodasa?" he replied either "Very good. Lots people killed, lots bungalows 'splode, lots fires," or "Hopeless. Nobody killed, no bungalows 'splode, no fires. Hopeless."

He found compensations in other ways too, I noticed. He and the dhoby sometimes teased the houseboy, Vasumal. The dhoby would return the clean laundry and leisurely gather the dirty clothes and stand around for hours, talking to Piodasa about the coming glory of Ceylon and the clear-cut superiority that Sinhalese Buddhists would enjoy at the expense of alien races. Vasumal, a Tamil Hindu, tried to avoid them on these occasions, and a couple of times I had to warn the men to stop harassing him. But like many Sinhalese, whom Buddhism had trained to repress strong emotions, when Piodasa exploded he exploded violently. Moss had seen him kick the dog on Adam's Peak. Once, while he was training Vasumal to serve dinner, Piodasa suddenly lost patience with the young man and began hitting him over the head with a plate. I pulled him off and warned him, but he didn't seem impressed until I remarked that he had no business using the university's dinnerware for banging people's heads. That line of reasoning seemed logical to him and he cooled down immediately.

There were sounds coming from the kitchen. I said, "Piodasa is making a big cake. Some of my students are coming in for tea tonight and Piodasa promised to bake a masterpiece. He usually bakes a pretty good cake."

But he didn't bake a good cake that day. The stove suddenly developed a leak, and the cake simply would not get done. At eight-thirty the students arrived and Vasumal served tea and cookies. Piodasa had not stepped out of the kitchen. He stood in front of the stove, glaring at it, throwing angry glances at the clock, then glaring at the stove again. When it was impossible to wait any longer, he took the cake out of the oven and put it on the dining room table. It was a sad-looking cake, bumpy, fallen, askew.

I was standing in the living room, talking to one of the students, when there was a whisper and a sudden hush. All eyes turned to the dining room. There stood Piodasa, ignoring guests, hosts, and everything except that wretched cake that had spoiled his reputation and which was now displayed where everyone could see it. Piodasa stared at the cake for a long time, his face slowly twitching into an expression of fierce hatred, and the cake knife in his hands slowly shifting to the position in which a matador holds his sword when he prepares to make the kill. We all held our breath—the students, Vasumal, Moss, and I—and Piodasa, oblivious of everything else, charged across the dining room and stabbed the cake.

A girl giggled hysterically, and Piodasa blinked his eyes and looked around. The knife was still in his hands. A quick-thinking student put an ashtray on his head and turned the giggling girl toward himself. Piodasa glowered at the group suspiciously, but everyone seemed to be fascinated by the silly boy, and finally Piodasa put the knife on the table and shuffled back into the kitchen. Moss remarked that the students left rather hurriedly, but I explained that they had their examinations to prepare for.

Fourteen

The American Women's Committee charity ball was delayed for two months, and Ramanathan never did get to attend it. Riots broke out between the Sinhalese and the Tamils, and before martial law finally restored order, hundreds of people had been killed; houses had been burned; and looters had run wild all over the island. The ball was the first big social event held after the riots, and the American women justified going ahead with the party on the grounds that the proceeds would be contributed to victims of the rioters. I had invited Sheila Dawson and Moss accompanied us. He had not been around much lately, and when I did see him he seemed thoughtful and absent minded.

The ball was not quite at the level of the British-sponsored events but it was important enough. The prime minister had been advertised as the patron of the affair and he was sitting at a table next to the dance floor, just in front of us. Having a patron was a carry-over from the colonial days, and the prominent patrons rarely bothered to attend the affairs whose ticket sales were presumably stimulated by association with a great name. It was the same kind of anachronism, Moss remarked, as the tendency of Ceylonese writers to include in their books a preface by some "Very Important Person" who recommended the book.

The prime minister had on the white high-necked coat and long white skirt-cloth that he had begun wearing during his campaign for office on a nationalistic platform. It was common gossip in Colombo that in the privacy of his home, and as soon as he went abroad, he reverted to the Western clothing that he had worn the first fifty years of his life.

He watched with good-natured superiority as six husky American males dressed as French chorus girls danced the can-can. The theme of the ball was The Gay Nineties, and the hotel dining room had been transformed into a gaudy caricature of nineteenth-century flamboyance. As the members of the chorus kicked their legs rambunctiously and shook their buttocks vigorously, the spectators roared with laughter and approval. The prime minister smiled, apparently in spite of himself, and I remembered that he had an ambition of his own: writing horror stories. Like poor Piodasa, I thought, the sophisticated and wealthy prime minister needed an outlet for violent instincts.

The can-can finished to loud applause and the dancers were called back for an encore. Then the room darkened and the spotlight focused on a lovely Ceylonese girl, about twenty years old, in a blue sari. She stood demurely for a moment, and as I looked at her Ceylonese features and costume and long hair I thought that she would sing a native song. I was wrong. What she sang was the current number one song on the American Hit Parade, a moronic piece popularized by the swinging hips of a popular American rock-and-roll singer. There was a puzzling stiffness about her pronunciation of the words, but Moss explained it. "She memorized the words by listening to the record," he whispered. "I've heard her sing it at the nightclub in town. It's her most popular number. She doesn't speak a word of English."

When she finished everyone applauded, and a fat politician at the prime minister's table kept clapping his hands after everyone had stopped. The prime minister looked at him, and the politician stopped, hands in mid-air, giggled embarrassedly, and looked away. The next singer was a young Sinhalese man who sang a lugubrious American song exactly as Frank Sinatra was singing it on a current recording. "This boy *does* speak English," Moss told me.

When the lights went back on, Mavis and Roger Chilton came to our table and Mavis took Sheila off to the powder room. Roger was about to sit down with us when the prime minister noticed him and motioned him to come to his table. Roger led Moss and me over; the prime minister ordered three more chairs, and we joined his party.

It was the first time I had seen the PM since the pirith and I observed him carefully. He was thinner and, I thought, more nervous as I watched his mobile face quickly register amusement, sadness, and superciliousness. His command of English was extraordinary—supple, witty, erudite—as he chatted with Chilton and occasionally made a friendly remark to us.

The American ambassador stopped by our table and we all stood up. The prime minister, his eyes twinkling merrily, introduced us to the ambassador and then paused, pretending that he could not remember the ambassador's name. The ambassador smiled. "Jones, Your Excellency," he said pleasantly. "The name is Jones."

"Of course," the prime minister exclaimed. "I can't imagine how it slipped my mind."

The ambassador moved on and we all smiled. Everyone at the table knew that when the ambassador had been questioned by a senatorial committee, in preparation for the Ceylon appointment, he confessed to not knowing the prime minister's name. The newspapers had made a big thing of this ignorance, and the PM was having a mild revenge.

"Actually," he said to us, "I'm very fond of your ambassador. He is doing a great deal of good for Ceylon, and his gaffe gave us more publicity in the world's newspapers than we had ever had. Also," the PM hesitated and smiled, "I suspect that most members of the senatorial committee that quizzed Mr. Jones didn't know my name either."

The prime minister talked on genially. He was a teetotaler, so there was no liquor on the table. Good-naturedly he admitted that he had hoped to impose prohibition on the country, but he had found the public adamant in its opposition. He had hoped to stop gambling too, he said, but the people weren't ready for that either. He chuckled wryly, "Not ready, did I say? On a per capita basis, Ceylonese bet more on horse races than any people in the world. I don't understand my people sometimes. Even when you try to do what is best for them, they refuse to obey. It's different on my own estates. There are hundreds of peons there, and they regard me as a father. I give them work, I feed them, I help them with their problems. When I give orders, they carry them out, whether they like it or not. They understand that I know better than they do what has to be done. Sometimes I wish the people of Ceylon were more like my peons. I could get a lot more done if they were."

The PM leaned back and puffed on an English cigarette. Moss cleared his throat. "I hope Your Excellency will forgive me," he said, "but some of the things that are happening in Ceylon disturb me. I realize that I'm a foreigner, and a guest has no right to criticize, especially when his hosts have been as hospitable as everyone has been to me. But it's because I've come to love Ceylon that I'm so concerned over what's happening."

The PM seemed puzzled. "I can't imagine what disturbs you," he said calmly. "We are going through a period of transition. But every newly independent nation has to do that. I'm very proud of the fact that our standard of living is among the highest in the Orient. We have a high rate of literacy, and it's constantly increasing because we've expanded the educational system. We're providing free medical care for everyone who can't afford it. I'm very proud of what Ceylon has achieved under my leadership. I am giving my people the best of both worlds—the political freedom of Western democracy and the economic security of Eastern socialism. We will combine the science of the West with the ancient wisdom of the East to create a new society superior to both."

Moss hesitated and looked at Chilton. Chilton stroked his waxed reddish mustache, patted the handkerchief immaculately protruding from his breast pocket, and said nothing. "Well," Moss murmured, "the strikes."

The prime minister frowned. "The strikers have been misled. As you know, the laws and contracts are written in English. Very few of the laborers can read English, so they have to rely on lawyer-politicians to lead them. These politicians are selfish, ambitious men who call strikes for their own benefit. When I can make the strikers understand this, they'll go along with the government."

"But in the meantime you have food shortages, ships leaving the harbor unloaded, transportation stoppages, near chaos."

"It's only a matter of explaining things to my people. When they understand, they'll behave and they'll sacrifice for the common good. They are really good people who have been misled."

Moss looked at me helplessly and I could see that he was appalled by the absurd statements the PM was making. Here was a highly intelligent, well meaning, humanitarian individual saying things that might make a high-school debater blush. Perhaps politics requires that kind of pretense, I thought. It's just a game he's playing and he knows better, but he feels the rules demand that he express all this claptrap.

"You oppose the use of violence?" Moss asked finally.

The PM folded his arms across his chest. "I am a Buddhist," he said simply. "Of course I oppose violence."

Moss looked frustrated. "But there's been official discrimination against minority groups."

"Has there now?" the PM said briskly. "Give me one example."

"Every year, in the civil service examinations, Tamils used to place a number of men among the top ten. In the three years since you've held office, not a single Tamil has been listed."

"Pure coincidence," the PM said. "Next."

"The Catholics wanted to put up a statue of a famous educator near his college in Colombo. When they had built the plinth, someone put a small Buddha on it at night. Since then, the building has stopped because no one dares to remove the Buddha. When the Catholics appealed to you for help, you had a canopy built over the Buddha 'to protect it from the weather.'"

"Mr. Moss," the PM said gently, "this is a Buddhist country. Minorities should not flaunt their differences."

Moss opened his mouth indignantly, closed it without saying anything, then blurted out, "Well, what about the race riots?"

A frown swept across the prime minister's face. "My dear chap," he said earnestly, "nothing has been more exaggerated than what the newspapers called 'riots.' There were a few minor incidents, a few unpleasant occurrences. But there was never any emergency, and there would have been no need to declare martial law if the press had not distorted the actual situation." The prime minister shook his finger playfully before Moss's face. "Mind you, the Sinhalese are lovable children. A little impulsive, but kind, gentle, and affectionate. Sometimes they blow off steam a little, but that's all there is to it."

Moss's face paled. "I saw men burning houses and looting stores. I saw them beating Tamils and demanding Sinhalese supremacy."

The PM shook his head sadly. "Most unfortunate," he said unctuously. "Most regrettable. A misunderstanding. Some of the people who campaigned for me took the platform literally. I didn't intend it literally. You have to promise people things to get elected. You know that, Mr. Moss. But many Buddhist monks are unhappy because I have not made Sinhala the official language. These things take time."

Moss bit his lip. The prime minister looked at him closely. "My dear chap, you really are disturbed, aren't you? And you think that I'm callous. Let me tell you something. Do you know what karma is?"

Moss nodded. The prime minister went on. "We believe that each man works out his own karma, his own destiny. Our actions, our thoughts, our intentions determine our fate. Well, I'm willing to rest on my record. I'm ready to let my actions determine my fate."

The women had returned to our table and we stood up. The prime minister shook hands with us, then said, "Mr. Moss, you seem skeptical about my government's achievements. Be at my office at noon tomorrow, and I promise you that the facts and figures I show you will convince you. My astrologer told me that today is an auspicious day for me."

Moss said he would be very happy to come, and the prime minister turned jovially to a group of admirers who approached his table. We danced for a while, then Sheila asked the Chiltons to join us. Mavis was, as always, exquisitely groomed and looked like a platinum mannequin. But dancing had made her flush a little, and the scar on her neck was more conspicuous than I had ever seen it. Chilton saw me looking at it and an annoyed twitch flickered momentarily over his face.

Moss still looked dazed. "That man amazes me. He has actually convinced himself that everything is all right. There were more than a hundred people killed in the riots. Trains have been derailed, buses burned, telephone lines cut. There's been arson, rape, looting, and beatings. And he calls it 'a few minor incidents.'"

Siri Banda came over to our table and stood behind Mavis's chair. He didn't say anything but she rose immediately, tucked her arm through his, and walked with him to the dance floor. He looked squat, powerful and sullen, and next to Mavis's accentuated blondeness seemed darker than he really was.

Chilton was on his feet, greeting a plump Ceylonese in formal Western clothes. He introduced Mr. Wardena, a cabinet minister, to us. Mr. Wardena shook hands, sat down, and lit a long American cigar.

"Nice party," he said. "Your American ladies manage things well. They get plenty of practice at managing, I understand." He winked amiably.

"Perhaps you ought to give your women more of a chance," Moss said.

Wardena laughed. "They're taking it. We've had more trouble with our one woman in the cabinet than with the rest of the country. Don't waste your sympathies on our women. They've gotten the Western message and they're beginning to take over. It's us poor men you ought to sympathize with."

He chuckled heartily, and it was clear that he didn't need much sympathy. He was enjoying his cigar; from his shape it was clear he enjoyed food; and he certainly seemed to be enjoying life. When a cigarette girl came by the table, he pinched her bottom playfully and she cheerfully brushed his hand away.

Moss said to him, "Do you agree with the prime minister that all of Ceylon's troubles are problems of transition?"

Wardena scratched his head and puffed happily on his cigar. "I suppose so."

"You don't sound as if you care," Moss said.

Wardena chuckled. "Of course I care. When I'm working I worry about it. But this is a party. That's the trouble with you Americans—you're too serious. Always planning, always reforming somebody or helping somebody or changing something. Relax, man. Have some fun."

Moss smiled, signaled the cigarette girl with the pinched bottom, and took a cigarette from her tray. "You're right," he said, "but some people claim that's one of Ceylon's biggest problems—that you people are too lazy and easy-going."

"That's what they say," Wardena agreed amiably, "but this is a tropical country and you can't expect people to be as energetic as in a temperate zone."

"True. But the Tamils and Moors live in the same country, and they work much harder."

"They have to. Minorities have to work harder to compensate for being minorities. That's the advantage of being Sinhalese. We're as lazy as we can afford to be. If it's necessary, we'll show as much energy as anybody else."

"Chauvinism, Mr. Wardena."

"Absolutely," Wardena agreed. "And a very good thing too. People need patriotism, even excessive patriotism, to give them a purpose in life. Tell me, what does our ordinary laborer or farmer have to be proud of? He is nothing much and too lazy to become much. But he has a country he can be proud of, a country twenty-five hundred years old. He has a race he can be proud of—Aryan, from the north of India, where the white men settled when they pushed west. He has a religion to be proud of—Buddhism—though not necessarily to take seriously. And he has a language to be proud of—Sinhala. It's the only one he knows. Hell, every country is built around nationalism, and you know it. The Russians learned it in a hurry in World War Two. It wasn't communism the Russians fought for, it was Russia. And it isn't communism or capitalism or any other ideology that our people want now."

"What do they want?" I asked.

"Nationalism and comfort," Wardena said, puffing on his cigar. "By comfort I mean economic security, free education, medical care, and all of that. If you want to call it socialism, go ahead. They also want individual freedom and the right to make as much money as they can and be superior to somebody. If you want to call that capitalism, go ahead. But everybody is really selfish and you know it. Everybody is out for himself and only himself. All this chitchat about Buddhism and spirituality and detachment is nonsense. If people want to talk about it, let them talk. But the only thing that counts is money—here, in the United States, in Russia, and everywhere else. I'd hate to tell you how much I had to spend to buy my election."

"Buy your election?"

Wardena looked at Moss pityingly. "Yes, buy my election. If you think that the right to vote means more than money to these villagers, you're more naïve than I thought you were. Look, Mr. Moss. Every political party has a symbol printed next to its name on the ballot. That's because many of the voters can't distinguish one group of words from another but they can remember a symbol they've been told to vote for, like a key, a star, an elephant, a wheel, a hand. Those were some of the symbols in the last election. I spent more than my opponent so I was elected."

"Was it worth it?" I asked.

Wardena seemed surprised. "Of course it was worth it. If I didn't think I'd make more than I spent, it would be a stupid investment. I'm not stupid."

Moss frowned. "But surely your society is changing for the better."

"It's changing all right," Wardena said. "Each family used to take care of its own—grandparents, cousins, distant relations—and the village used to take care of its own. Now the villages are disintegrating, and family relationships in the city are changing, and the cost of living is going up. When people are in trouble—serious illness, unemployment, old age—they can't depend on relatives or friends any more. They have only the state to turn to, and the state will have to provide, not by choice or affection but by law. It's an impersonal help, and it may lack the charm of other arrangements, but a hungry man isn't looking for charm and a sick man doesn't care about amenities."

"We haven't found it so in the United States," Moss said.

"We don't have the opportunities you have in the United States. There a mediocre person can do well. He can own his house and car, send his children to college, work a forty-hour week. But here a man needs extraordinary ability to achieve those things. It makes a big difference."

Moss sighed. "It looks as if you're going to end up opposing the United States and favoring Russia."

Wardena leaned forward. "I'll tell you the truth," he said earnestly, "we don't really give a good damn about the United States or Russia. The only country we're interested in is Ceylon."

"But if you had to take sides, which would you choose?"

Wardena smiled. "China."

"Why? What makes you think the Chinese are any better?"

"They're not. But they're 'colored' people, like ourselves. After four centuries of racial prejudice from Europeans we just don't take seriously white men's statements about equality."

"Are the Chinese more honest?"

Wardena grinned. "Of course not. They're just as hypocritical as the Russians and as shrewd as the English and as brutal as the Nazis. They're using Russia to learn from it. When they're ready, they'll break away and try to dominate the world."

"Do you think they'll succeed?"

Wardena grinned again. "They're pretty shrewd about it. I understand they've persuaded Chinese Christians to support the government by pointing out that Mary's husband was a good proletarian carpenter."

"You don't really believe in democracy, do you, Mr. Wardena?" Moss said.

Wardena chuckled. "When I was studying in London I got to know an English publisher. He told me that all biographies of Napoleon ever published made money, but almost no book with the word 'democracy' in the title is successful."

The French ambassador danced by with a pretty young Ceylonese in a pink sari, and Wardena said wistfully, "They say he has the most beautiful mistresses in France. Eh, Chilton?"

Chilton did not smile. "That's what we hear. I suppose he enjoys them."

Wardena looked startled. "Who wouldn't?"

Chilton didn't say anything, and after a pause Wardena said, "I don't understand this Anglo-Saxon reticence. Here everybody knows which prominent people are sleeping with whom, and every neighborhood knows who are the wives and who are the mistresses, and no one gets excited about it. I don't think we're any less moral than you people are. We're just less hypocritical about it."

Siri Banda brought Mavis back to the table and left. The waiters appeared and served dinner—seven courses of different fish, all caught off Ceylon shores. Ordinarily when Ceylonese cooks imitated Western cooking it was the English variety they duplicated, a regrettable counterfeit of an unworthy model. But for this party the women had hired a French chef and the food was delicious.

After dinner the people at our table changed. Siri Banda appeared and Mavis floated off toward him. I danced a few times with Sheila, then surrendered her to an embassy secretary. At the table when I returned Moss and Chilton were talking to a little bald man with a prominent nose. I recognized T.S. Wijesinghe, the editor whom I had met at Mauvais' house when the guru gave the lecture on Gurdjieff.

T.S.'s voice was less shrill tonight, and he seemed more relaxed. "I noticed that Wardena was sitting here before," he said. "The whole town's talking about his new Cadillac."

"What's special about his Cadillac?" Moss asked.

T.S. pursed his lips. "Only the fact that he suddenly acquired it a few days after he remarked in the American ambassador's hearing that Wardena's ministry might have to close down the Voice of America transmitter in Ceylon. It isn't hard to get favors from America. Even I've been approached."

"Oh," Moss said dubiously.

"I've just turned down an invitation from your state department to visit the U.S.," T.S. said. "It's not that I don't want to see the country I criticize so often." He smiled, and his face was transformed charmingly. "But it wouldn't be politic for me to accept now, when the editors of the two leading Ceylon newspapers have refused to go. Let's be frank about it. America just isn't very popular in Ceylon. Or in the Orient."

"But why?" Moss said. "I don't understand it. Our government gives billions of dollars to Asian countries. Individual Americans donate money and supplies to feed and clothe Asians. Thousands of American specialists are helping your people develop your industrial and agricultural capacities. And still you dislike us."

"Right," T.S. said. "We resent and distrust you."

Chilton spoke for the first time. "It's magazines like yours, T.S., that distort our image."

T.S. frowned. "You don't understand journalism, my dear fellow. People are interested only in criticism and in conflict. I give it to them."

Mavis and Siri Banda came to the table, and Mavis picked up her purse. "We're going now, Roger. Do you want to come along?"

Chilton hesitated a moment, then nodded. They said goodbye and left, and we sat down again. Moss looked after the departing trio.

"The poor bastard," Moss said softly. "There's no way to keep from being hurt by people, except by getting away from people."

"It is a bit rough on Roger," T.S. said, standing up. "A fine chap, really. My wife is signaling so I'd better be going. Cheerio."

After another drink and a few more dances, Moss, Sheila, and I left too. As we got into our car in front of the hotel I saw a man in monk's robes standing, silent and rigid, behind a hedge of bushes. It was the monk whom Ramanathan had rescued on Adam's Peak, and I wondered sleepily what he was doing outside an exclusive hotel at one o'clock in the morning.

Fifteen

Twenty minutes after we left the party, the prime minister was assassinated by the Buddhist monk in front of the hotel. The monk shot six bullets into the prime minister and continued to fire after his victim lay twitching on the ground. Then he turned and started walking away. He was immediately seized by men in the prime minister's party.

We heard the news on the radio in the morning, while the prime minister lay dying in the hospital. It was a beautiful day in Colombo. The sky was a lovely turquoise; palm trees providing a deep green shade, a tamarind across the street bloomed vividly, its yellow blossoms streaked with red. The bulletins on the prime minister's condition interrupted the regularly scheduled program, in this case a musical program sponsored by a manufacturer of patent medicine. In the understandable turmoil no one had thought of editing the program and the announcements of the prime minister's deteriorating condition were regularly followed by commercials extolling the miraculous healing qualities of the patent medicine. The final somber announcement, "The prime minister is dead," left thirty seconds during which the announcer urged confidently, "No matter how sick you are, don't give up until you try Horabana Magic Formula, guaranteed to cure all ills."

The next day Moss and I went to the prime minister's home to pay our respects. All the cars, taxis, and buses in the streets flew white mourning flags. On public and many private buildings the national flag of Ceylon featuring its handsome lion was flying at half-mast. We joined the two-mile-long line and stood under the scorching sun for three hours, waiting to file past the prime minister's coffin. Rumors flashed through the crowd, some later to be refuted. The assassin had worn an expensive new robe, the man in front of us excitedly told us. It had been sewn together by a woman named Ranjini because the monk wanted something special to wear when he killed the prime minister. Our informant listened intently to the Sinhalese chattering ahead of him, then turned and passed more gossip on to us. Ranjini was the mistress of a powerful Buddhist priest who hated the prime minister. She and the priest had fled the island on a plane. A half hour later, when we had progressed slowly toward the residence, the same man told us that the priest and his mistress had not fled the island at all. The priest was at that moment delivering a radio eulogy on the prime minister. The monk had been wearing an ordinary old robe when he was captured. It was Ranjini who was wearing an expensive new sari when she accompanied the priest to the radio station. There must have been some mistake made, our informant said regretfully.

A middle-aged Ceylonese woman behind us kept bursting out in tears. Her husband, a fat man in a Western suit, comforted her. To us he said, "India had Gandhi, Burma had Aung San. Now Ceylon also has a great leader who was assassinated." There was considerable pride in his voice when he said this.

A Ceylonese man on a bicycle, heading away from the prime minister's house, stopped to say hello to the man behind me. "A terrible thing," he said in English, "But wonderful for business. Just wonderful." He pedaled away and Moss asked the man what business his friend was in. "Florist," the man said wistfully. "Lucky chap."

The man in front of us turned excitedly with a new piece of gossip. The mail delivered to the prime minister's home that morning contained an anonymous letter warning him that an attempt to assassinate him would be made by the monk. The letter had been postmarked in Colombo a week ago and should have been delivered long before the assassination, but the mailman had sore feet and had stacked some of the mail in his house until he felt better. Today he had felt well enough to deliver it.

The sky had been darkening, and just before we reached the prime minister's house a cloudburst soaked all of us. No one left the line, and we filed soaking wet into the house. The prime minister lay in the coffin, facing the ceiling. His face was thin, calm, and relaxed. They had removed his glasses, and he looked a little different than he had two nights earlier.

"His astrologer told him yesterday would be a lucky day for him," I reminded Moss as we walked out of the house.

"Who knows?" Moss replied. "Perhaps it was."

By the time of the funeral four days later, many more rumors had flashed through the city. A minority held that the monk was a martyr who sincerely believed that Buddhism should become the national religion and Sinhala the national language. He had taken the prime minister's campaign promise seriously, had supported him vigorously, and then felt betrayed. He had gone to Adam's Peak to pray for Buddha's advice, and his rescue from death on the mountain convinced him that he was destined to kill the PM.

Other rumors contradicted this. The monk, it was said, was a fool. The head priest hated the prime minister for not awarding government contracts to a company the priest had subsidized. The priest cynically played on the monk's naïveté and provided the pistol and ammunition. When the monk lost his nerve at the last moment, Ranjini promised that she would be waiting in her bed naked when he returned.

"What can you believe?" Moss said disgustedly. "A monk whose religion forbids the destruction of ants kills the leader of his country. A priest, pledged to chastity, openly keeps a mistress in his temple and masterminds an assassination."

I pointed out that this had nothing to do with Buddhism. Every religion, I said, has members who violate its teachings. But Moss shook his head. "All institutions are rotten," he said. "The only way to keep from being contaminated is to get away from them."

The funeral took place on the prime minister's vast ancestral estate, a few miles outside of Colombo. We rode as far as we could, then left the car by the side of the road and joined the hundreds of thousands of people, all dressed in white, converging on the ceremonial grounds. It was before eleven o'clock, but already the estate was filled with people, and from a relatively high spot of land on the rolling grounds we looked down at the large lawn fenced off for VIPs. Word spread through the crowd that the family was at that moment providing alms for a thousand monks at the two nearest Buddhist temples.

Hundreds of people had been filing, in a carefully policed line, past the bier on which the coffin rested. But at noon the line was stopped, and the family and close personal friends gathered around the casket and kneeled. An old man in a ragged sarong wept loudly as he bent beneath the coffin, and a man in the crowd near me murmured that it was the prime minister's personal servant who had helped take care of him since the day of the PM's birth. There were so many floral tributes that an entire section of lawn near the house was covered with them. The skies were a delicate tranquil blue; the sun was a radiant ball of gold; and the trees and bushes were vibrant with life and color.

Now the speeches began. The new prime minister spoke first, in Sinhala, and a trousered young man near me whom I recognized as a student at the university was kind enough to give us a running translation. There had never been a day of mourning like this in Ceylon for twenty-five hundred years, the prime minister said. The dead leader had all the qualities of a bodhisattva, a human being just below the level of the Buddha himself. He had never said an unkind word against his enemies, nor had he ever borne ill will. We could all be certain that the late prime minister was now in the Ceylonese version of heaven and was looking down at us.

I noticed that there were very few Tamils or people wearing Hindu clothing in the crowd.

"Do you suppose the prime minister is looking down at the families of Tamils killed in the riots?" I whispered to Moss.

"I doubt it," he said. "That was only an unfortunate incident, nothing worth getting excited about."

Then five leading priests gave orations, crisply summarized by our student translator. The prime minister's death was a great loss to the nation, we were told. But the principles for which he lived would continue to be cherished by all. The prime minister was the reincarnation of a great Sinhalese king of the fourth century. He had been born to riches and could have spent his life as a prince in luxury, but he shunned this easy life to serve the people—and the Buddhist clergy. He was especially patient and kind to monks, and his respect for the clergy was a model of behavior that the nation would do well to follow. It was the saddest day in Ceylon in four hundred years, and the entire world would mourn his loss. In London, Washington, Moscow, and Beijing, everywhere the leaders of nations and millions of ordinary people were pausing today to pay tribute to the late prime minister and to find inspiration in his blessed career. Under his wise leadership, Ceylon had become again, as it had been in the days of the Kandy kings, the most beautiful and happy land on earth. The prime minister had been the avatar of the great king Parakramu, who ruled Ceylon in the eleventh century.

The casket was now covered by the Sinhalese lion flag, a wreath of red roses was placed upon it, and several men flanked by the six honorary pallbearers carried it toward the vault. As custom required, the men carried the casket around the vault three times before they placed it on the bier. Then the governor general, resplendent in his full ceremonial dress of blue and red, went up to the casket and saluted.

The man in front turned to us. "The casket was made to order," he said proudly. "In Ceylon it is bad luck to measure a man until he is dead, so they couldn't start making the casket until the prime minister died."

A high priest now officiated at the prescribed ceremony, and white cloth was distributed to monks. Thousands of voices around us cried, "Sadhu, sadhu," and Moss quietly repeated, "Praise be. Praise be." The prime minister's wife bent to touch the casket with her lips, and broke down weeping. The multitude watched, in hushed silence; jasmine flowers were thrown over the casket and it was put into the crypt. After a long silent moment, the family turned to walk back to the house, and we joined the dispersing mob. The barricades and temporary fencing had been knocked down by the surging crowds, and we stepped over the debris as we started the long walk back to the car.

The beauty of the countryside was overwhelming. On a quiet pool a huge lotus bloomed, larger than the water lily, its wide green leaf supporting an exquisite white flower in the center. Closer to the road a cashew-nut tree provided a bit of shade, and then a row of palm trees stretched languidly toward the west. We walked slowly, catching snatches of conversation as people passed.

A Ceylonese in a white Western suit was saying to the middle-aged woman with him, "The reverend priest was right. Ceylon is the most beautiful and the happiest country in the world."

They turned off and we walked around two houseboys arguing violently. Each claimed that he had been given the evening off in honor of the prime minister's funeral, and that it was the other who was supposed to return to work. One of them was angrily reaching for his knife when a constable pulled them apart and warned them.

Near our car a newsboy was selling the extra edition of the newspaper, featuring an account of the early activities at the funeral. He was about thirty years old and his eyes kept darting about the crowd suspiciously as he made change for us. His wife, accompanied by a rascally male cousin whom he didn't trust, had gotten separated from him hours ago and he couldn't find her. He had a pretty good idea of what she was up to, he angrily told the student who had walked with us and was buying a paper. When he caught her, they would have news for the newspapers, he vowed obscenely.

We finally reached the car and I eventually maneuvered it back into the Colombo-bound traffic.

"Too bad you missed the appointment with the prime minister," I said.

"It doesn't matter," Moss said distractedly. "I have a different appointment to keep."

Sixteen

When the race riots broke out again, I was visiting Moss in his Colombo apartment. The university was having its long vacation in late May and I had closed up my house on the campus and driven down to Colombo, giving Piodasa a ride to the edge of town. He had things to do in Colombo, he said vaguely.

The Burtons were giving a party that evening, and we were to meet Ramanathan at the station and bring him to the party. After high tea Moss looked at his watch and said, "The Jaffna train isn't due till six but maybe we ought to start now. With these mobs in the streets there's no telling how long it'll take us."

We felt the heat and the enveloping humidity as soon as we stepped out of the building. It was the worst of all times in Ceylon, sticky and enervating, and the wet heat hung over the steaming pavement with a malignancy that permeated everything. As we turned the corner we were stopped by a mob of yelling men—teenagers, young, middle-aged, a couple of dark skinned old men in short sarongs. Some of the men carried knives, some sticks or clubs. A big sweaty man peered at us suspiciously and muttered something in Sinhala. He was waving a large wooden club; dozens of phonograph needles had been imbedded into its head. Moss waved his arm authoritatively, and the man saw the white skin and stepped back grudgingly. But before we had gone ten steps we heard screams and turned around.

The thugs had stopped a passing car and were dragging out a terrified man, about forty years old. I couldn't tell whether the man was Tamil, but the leader of the mob was yelling something at the man. A young Sinhalese in white shirt and trousers walked past us and I called him.

"What are they doing?" I asked.

The young man listened to the argument, then translated. "The man says he's not Tamil. The thug is telling him to prove it by reciting a *gatha*—that's a Buddhist stanza in Pali."

The captive protested nervously and the man in the white trousers interpreted. "He says he doesn't know any *gathas*. He says he's a Sinhalese Christian."

A club suddenly rose above the prisoner's head and slugged him. More sticks and clubs shot up over his head, hit him, and he went down. The big man who had stopped us now smashed the needle-encrusted club down on the prostrate man and yelled. The gang raced, howling, down the street. We ran to the victim and Moss took his bloody head in his lap while I wiped his face. There was a needle sticking in his left eye. The top of his skull was smashed. He kept screaming shrilly. The man in the white trousers clapped his hands loudly and repeatedly until a cab stopped and we carried the broken man in and sped to the hospital. By the time we got there the man was dead.

We told the driver to wait, carried the body into the hospital, then took the cab to the station. It was late, but the train from Jaffna had not arrived yet. The railroad official wasn't sure when it would arrive, if at all. Not for another hour at the earliest, he told us.

We went out into the street again. A small band of rioters led by a man in monk's robes rushed by, yelling and cursing. "That may not be a Buddhist monk at all," Moss said. "The police say criminals have been shaving their heads and putting on saffron robes so they can loot more easily."

A group of men were holding a ladder at the top of which stood a grinning man in a loose dirty sarong. He had a bucket full of tar hanging over his left arm, and he tarred out the Tamil lettering on the board nailed to the wall. A boy in Western clothes yelled up to him, "Write the Sinhala letters instead."

The men near the boy translated the message into Sinhala and urged the tar-man to carry it out. He grinned happily, then climbed down and gave the bucket and brush to the boy. The boy climbed up the ladder and daubed in Sinhala letters. Moss shook his head. "This hoodlum is supposed to be fighting for the glory of his national language. He can't even write a letter of it."

A sharp scream sounded and we ran to the corner. Two dirt-stained men in short sarongs were holding a young woman by each arm while another hoodlum held up a Sinhalese newspaper before her face. The girl made moaning sounds, and the hoodlum was obviously ordering her to read from the paper. "That's another test to spot Tamils," Moss murmured, "but many educated Sinhalese would fail it. Even the prime minister couldn't read Sinhalese well."

The girl kept moaning, and the hoodlum shouted something to the men holding her. They tore off her sari and her underpants and stretched her out, shrieking, on the sidewalk. The leader lifted his sarong and mounted her, panting wildly. The girl twitched convulsively and screamed. Moss broke through the crowd and grabbed the man, and I followed, turning when I reached him to face the two other thugs. They stared at us, startled, then lifted their clubs and began to approach us. Suddenly a Buddhist monk appeared between us. He held up his hand calmly and said something to the men. They paused, grumbled sullenly, then backed off. The monk said something else, sharply. The men glowered, then bent and pulled the third man off the girl and dragged him down the street. The girl lay on the sidewalk, unconscious.

Again we waited for a cab, while the monk stood by us silently, cowering noisy passersby with his stolid gaze. When we had put the girl into the car, we put our palms together, in front of our faces, and bowed to the monk. He joined his hands before his chest and bowed slightly, first to Moss, and then to me.

The doctor told us that the girl would be all right. She had fainted. What her mental state would be he could not say. He was a Sinhalese and had been educated at Cambridge, he told us. He was working an emergency shift because people and corpses were being brought in from all over the city, and the evening had just begun. "I can't understand it," he said bitterly. "We Sinhalese aren't angels, but I never thought I'd see anything like this. They are animals—animals."

A nurse came, calling him urgently, and he went back into the operating room. It would be another half hour before Ramanathan's train arrived, and we decided to walk back to the station. A group of rioters pushed past us, following a tall, powerful man in monk's robes, accompanied by a beautiful woman in a white sari. The man had strong features, piercing eyes, and a bull neck. The woman stayed very close to him and Moss turned and looked at them.

"That's Ranjini," he said softly, "and her new lover, the militant priest. And look, she's rubbing her left breast with her palm, just as she always did before she made love."

The streets were even more crowded than before and we walked in petrified expectation of the next horror. It came quickly. A house halfway down the block was going up in flames. As we approached, the hoodlums massed outside jumped up and down, yelling gleefully. One of them lit a *chulu* light, a torch of dried coconut leaves, and tossed it through the window of the house next to the burning one. His companion, a familiar figure with wild black hair, howled with laughter, lit his *chulu* torch, and flung it through the same window. The light clearly showed the beaming foolish face of Piodasa. He has gotten tired of seeing violence in the movies, I thought sadly, as the torches flared inside and the house burst into flames. An old man and an old woman stumbled out, blinking their eyes stupidly. Piodasa approached them and said something, then looked embarrassed and turned to his gang. They all ran away down the street. We tried to talk to the old couple, but couldn't make ourselves understood. Finally a police constable on a bicycle appeared who spoke English. We told him what had happened. He talked to the old people and tried to comfort them.

"They are Sinhalese Buddhists," he told us. "It was a mistake to burn their house." He walked away with them, pushing his bicycle beside him. Moss shook his head. "Even on a job like this Piodasa makes a mistake."

In front of a Tamil jewelry store near the station two police constables were holding off a jeering mob. The thugs apparently wanted to pillage, and the constables had pistols in their hands and pointed them at the leaders. One of the thugs danced forward and backward, lifting his sarong shoulder-high to display his genitals to the police. They glared contemptuously but did not shoot. We walked on.

The train from Jaffna finally arrived and we closed in on Ramanathan protectively. Moss told him what was happening. "The safest thing is to take the next train back to Jaffna. We'll stay here in the station with you until it leaves."

Ramanathan looked at him thoughtfully. "It's kind of you, Anthony, to be so concerned. But do you really think that I am afraid? There is no death. There is only a sloughing of this particular body on the long road to union with God. Why should I run away?"

Moss shrugged helplessly and went out to get a cab. When I heard his whistle I escorted Ramanathan to the station entrance and hurried him into the cab, which the driver already had in gear. No one stopped us.

"I told the driver to take us straight to the Burtons," Moss said. "It's late, and we'll be safer there than in my neighborhood."

Ramanathan sat back and talked quietly. It was a very good year for mangoes, he said, and the Jaffna area was beautiful when he left. The wedding to which Moss was invited had finally taken place, and his niece seemed reasonably happy, though there was still some squabbling about the dowry. Ramanathan chuckled pleasantly as he described the bridegroom's bickering with his new father-in-law.

When we arrived at the Burtons', Ramanathan paused to admire the magnificent fan palm in front of the house. The trunk was smooth for about thirty feet, then the twenty-six evenly spaced branches flared out gracefully, topped by twenty six perfectly proportioned leaves, so that the tree looked like the exquisitely balanced fan of some gigantic deity.

Marian greeted us at the door and led us in. A little later George came out of the back bedroom. He seemed nervous and had a highball in his hand. "I was worried about you," he told Ramanathan. "You shouldn't have come."

"We tried to get him to take the train back to Jaffna," Moss told him, "but he refused. He's not afraid."

George's eyes flickered from Ramanathan to Moss. "Perhaps not," he said, gulping his drink. "But he took a chance coming here. The gangs have started raiding homes where Tamils are suspected to be staying."

Marian called us into the dining room and we had a quiet meal. Shortly afterwards the guests began to arrive. Mrs. Vitana came first, she too on vacation from the university and visiting her brother in Colombo. Roger and Mavis Chilton, formally dressed as always, arrived next, and finally Lakshman and Chitra Gunesena. Moss reminded us that he had met everyone except Mrs. Vitana on the climb to Adam's Peak, almost a year ago. It was a short of reunion, he said cheerfully. Ramanathan smiled but said nothing.

Chilton told us that he had lunched with a police superintendent and that the police were worried. "The administration refuses to take the riots seriously. They're supported by nationalists and they've ordered police not to shoot at the rioters. Driving here tonight we saw some hoodlums taunting the police. They were just standing there and taking it."

Mavis nodded vaguely. She seemed bored by the conversation and asked Marian where she had bought the blue shoes she was wearing. Lakshman showed more emotion than I had ever seen him display. "It's terrible," he said. "They're looting shops, beating up pedestrians, terrorizing the whole city. I never thought I would see Buddhists behave like that." Chitra wandered off with Mavis Chilton.

"What started the rioting?" I asked.

"It's been brewing a long time," Chilton said. "You know the Tamils in the northern province tarred out Sinhalese letters on licenses. Well, the Sinhalese retaliated by tarring out Tamil displays in Sinhalese communities. That led to arguments and beatings and all kinds of vicious rumors. Next the government tried to give some dispossessed Tamils farmland in a Sinhalese province. The local politicians, and some of the Buddhist priests, got the people all stirred up, so a mob stopped a train heading that way, pulled off all the Tamils and beat them up. The mob got out of hand and killed some of the Tamils. When word got back to the Tamil provinces, mobs there beat up Sinhalese and burned their homes. The new prime minister is afraid to admit that trouble exists. It would prove his government's inadequacy, so he pretends that nothing serious has happened and no special measures are required. I wish Ramanathan weren't here. No Tamil is safe in Colombo now."

We sat around for a while and had a drink, then Moss started pacing the room and looking out of the window. "I can't understand it," he said. "The Sinhalese Buddhists have a long history of peace and tolerance."

"That's sheer nonsense," George said testily. "You and I both like the Ceylonese, but let's not try to rewrite their history for them or their personality. The Kandyans represent the purest strain of Sinhalese blood. You know perfectly well that the Kandyan kings were cruel and brutal. You've seen the places in Kandy where men were punished by being crushed to death by elephants. You know that they maimed and tortured and murdered prisoners. The Ceylonese are no gentler than anyone else."

Lakshman frowned. "Yes, but everyone was brutal in those days. Look at the way the Portuguese behaved here—and the Dutch and the English. Now there's no need for it. We're independent. This is the twentieth century."

"It was the twentieth century in 1915 when Sinhalese mobs murdered Muslims. Of course, just before that, English soldiers had murdered Sinhalese," George said.

Moss shook his head. "I just don't understand it. Why?"

"For psychological reasons," George said, "and economic reasons, and chauvinistic reasons. They pretend that it's the language issue, whether Sinhala should replace English as the official language. But it's more than that. The language is just a symbol. After all, ninety percent of the people don't speak English. If this is their country, why shouldn't their native language be the language of the courts, the legislature, and the universities? And to the Sinhalese majority it's a clear indication of their raised status that Sinhala should be the official language."

"Don't the two million Tamils have a right to their own language?" Moss asked.

"A logical right, of course. But what chance does logic have against emotions? The anti-Tamil prejudice is actually based on economic, not linguistic, grounds. You know that since the war, Ceylon's population has increased enormously but the economy hasn't grown. There aren't enough jobs to go around, and thousands of Sinhalese have now been educated without getting good jobs. They're bitter, and they have to blame somebody, and the Tamils who hold good jobs are perfect scapegoats. There are a million Indian Tamils working on the tea and rubber plantations, and unemployed Sinhalese would like their jobs. There are thousands of Tamils in government and business, and unemployed Sinhalese would like their jobs."

"But Buddhism is supposed to be such a gentle religion." Moss spoke sadly.

"It is," George agreed. He was talking nervously, almost compulsively, and he was very pale. "But how many people really practice Buddhism? Christianity is a gentle religion too, but the history of Western Europe is hardly a peaceful one. Even the devout Sinhalese kings of the past were ferocious warriors, and the Sinhalese schoolboy grows up priding himself on the martial exploits of King Dutugemuna and King Parakrama far more than on the quiet resignation of Buddhist monks. The Sinhalese needs nationalism—or patriotism—to give him meaning in life as much as the Germans and Russians and we Americans do. It's very important, especially for a little country, to believe in your country's greatness. Look at the Colombo newspapers on an ordinary day—stabbings, suicides, violent deaths. It's not an accident that the most famous paintings in Ceylon, the Sigirya frescoes, were painted for a king who had murdered his own father. And it's ironic that even in those frescoes racial prejudice is clearly shown. All of the noblewomen are light skinned; all of their servant-maids are dark."

Moss stopped by the magazine rack and picked up a pamphlet. "Look at this," he said, waving a publication by a Ceylonese astrologer. "Forecasts of evil days, disturbances, violence. This time it looks as if he's right."

"When you make as many prophecies as the astrologers do, you're bound to be right sometimes." George picked up another pamphlet. "Here's an article by a Buddhist priest, claiming that the gods are sending all these calamities—floods and strife—because the people of Lanka don't honor the clergy enough. If the government makes Buddhism the state religion, all troubles will stop, he says."

Chilton turned to Ramanathan. "Do you have pierced ears?" he asked.

Ramanathan touched his lobes and smiled. "Yes, I do. I hadn't thought about it for a long time. It's traditional for Hindu parents to have boys' ears as well as girls' perforated. It was so long ago that I had quite forgotten. Why do you ask?"

Chilton made a wry face. "Because that's one of the tests the mobs are using to spot Tamils. Sinhalese males don't have pierced ears."

Ramanathan sighed softly. Chilton went on. "I saw both sides today. This morning we drove down from a tea plantation near Nuwara Eliya. On the road Tamils were stopping Sinhalese cars and stoning them. Here in Colombo the Sinhalese are killing Tamils. Buddhists against Hindus—two religions that teach non-violence and forbid the killing even of insects."

A loud noise sounded outside and suddenly everyone was quiet except Mavis Chilton. "Servants simply don't know their place," she whined. "Our houseboy wants thirty rupees a month or he'll quit. Now I ask you."

The noise outside was clearer now, an angry rumbling of voices. George was trembling, his face white, his hands shaking.

"Lock the door, man," Chilton ordered. George looked at him stupidly and didn't move. I started for the door but just before I got there it was pushed in from outside and a half a dozen men swarmed into the room. When they saw that there were white men present they stopped abruptly at one end of the living room. Our party had instinctively huddled together at the other end. The tableau was frozen for a moment, then more men pushed in through the open door and stood behind their leaders. Most of them were dark men, darker than the average Ceylonese, and they wore short sarongs and twitched their hands nervously.

A short, thin, middle-aged man with a cast in his right eye stepped forward and swept us with his eyes. "We are not looking for Europeans," he said, in a squeaky sing-song voice. "Not tonight. We were told there is a Tamil here. We want him."

I looked at George, but he was frozen with terror. Moss stepped forward. "There are no Tamils here," he said firmly. "Get out of here."

The short man glared at him, then said, "You don't live here. Who owns this house?"

George took a step, opened his mouth and gulped, but no words came out. His hands were shaking.

The short man looked at all of us, then stared at Ramanathan. The old Hindu looked at him calmly, a tiny smile raising the corners of his mouth.

"What is your name?" the short man said. "You, with the *verti* outside your cloth as the Hindus wear it."

Ramanathan stood, tranquil and silent. Lakshman spoke up, in a voice strident with tension. "His name is Gunesena. Now get out of here."

The short man bared his teeth and stepped toward George. "This is your house. If you lie to me we'll kill you. What is that man's name?"

"Ramanathan," George whispered. "He's a Tamil."

The tableau froze again. I could not bear to look at the terror on George's face. Ramanathan showed no emotion. The short man turned and said something in Sinhala to the men behind him, and they walked forward purposefully toward Ramanathan. We closed in before him and tried to fight them off. In the melee, before a club knocked me down, I had vivid flashes of Lakshman wrestling with two men, of Moss and Chilton punching at dark figures, of Mrs. Vitana clawing at a husky man who threw her against the wall and advanced on Ramanathan. I scrambled up and jumped on the man and then something hit me from behind and I lost consciousness.

When I opened my eyes all of the people in our party, except Ramanathan, were crowded together at the front window, looking out. I stumbled to the door but it was locked, and I could hear a yelling mob blocking the entrance. I went back to the windows and looked outside, over Marian's head. There was a solid line of sarong-clad men guarding the window.

"Oh God," Marian whimpered. On the lawn in front of the house, below the fan palm, two men were putting someone into a sack and tying it. Another man brought a large gasoline can and poured a liquid over the upright sack. The acrid smell of gasoline quickly penetrated the room. The man with the can stepped back, and the short man took a chulu torch from one of the men near him, lit it with a cigarette lighter, and touched the sack. Ramanathan broke out in flames.

Outside the men howled and jumped. In the room, women sobbed. Moss stared, bent forward, as if he could not believe what he saw. He was biting his lower lip so hard that it was bleeding, but he wasn't aware of it. George sat on the floor, his back against the wall, looking out of glazed eyes at nothing.

Not a sound came from the burning man. He stood there silently while the flames flared and lit up the beautiful palm and sharply delineated the twenty-six evenly spaced branches that formed a perfect fan. Then the burning figure collapsed and a bitter odor wafted gently through the air and into the room.

Seventeen

And that was what it all came to. Amid the idyllic beauty, under the brilliant tropical stars, near the symmetrical fan palm. A century earlier, I remembered, Bishop Heber had written of Ceylon, "Every prospect pleases, and only man is vile." The bishop's statement was still true.

I stayed on in Ceylon for another year to finish my contract. Moss disappeared the day after Ramanathan's murder and I assumed that he had left the island. I had regarded Moss's naïveté with amused superiority, but now it turned out that my own understanding of the Ceylonese was as superficial as his. I didn't really know them at all. I had seen them from the outside only, associating with the intellectuals and inspecting the customs and activities of the people with a dilettante's detachment and shallowness. What had seemed to me "exotic" or "quaint" was as much part of their culture as those characteristics that happened to resemble Western manners and consequently seemed "normal" to me. But what right had I to make such a judgment and to assume arrogantly that our ways of doing things were necessarily the right ways? Might not American neon signs, country music, and political conventions seem "quaint" and "exotic" to a visiting foreigner?

Abashed, I realized that I didn't really understand the people even of my own country. The glimpses I had had of prejudice in southern states, provincialism in midwestern towns, insularity in New York City, had made no deeper impression on me than books I had read or movies I had seen. They didn't really mean anything to me, these things. I had looked at them from the outside like a tourist racing through a city on a quick trip. I was shocked by the Ceylon riots, but they were not very different from American lynchings. I had been smug about Ceylonese sexual immorality, but it was not very different from conditions in the United States. I had been an amused, condescending observer at home, just as I had been in Ceylon.

I should have known better. I should never have swallowed the generalizations of scholars and editorial writers and self-appointed pundits. It was ridiculous to have accepted statements about a national stereotype, as if all Ceylonese were the same. There were malicious and aggressive and shrewd Ceylonese. There were gentle and kind and meek Ceylonese. Who makes up these "nations" the experts so glibly talk about? The successful, the rich, the mediocre, the frustrated, the hard working, the lazy, the idealists? And who were these experts whose pontifications I had indiscriminatingly believed? They may have been experts in one small field, but like most experts they assumed that by analogy they understood everything else. They were wrong. We were all dilettantes, all pretending to know more than we did. But I didn't have to do it any more and I wouldn't, I decided.

In the university building I looked up at the masks hanging in the hallway, and I understood that these grotesque faces were not just insignificant baubles. They were part of the Ceylonese heritage, inextricably woven into the nation's culture. We all keep carrying the dead ideas of our fathers, Ibsen said. It was as true for the playful Ceylonese as for the dour Norwegians. And it was true for most Americans, weighed down forever with the adopted guilt of Puritan and Judaic sins. The masks had been used in devil dances, and most Ceylonese believed in devils, just as most Americans believed in angels and demons. These masks were more visually obvious, perhaps, but they were nurtured from the same sources. I remembered walking into an obscure little Buddhist temple near the campus, and finding Vandenburg, the marxist historian, sprawled out flat before an image of Buddha. I backed out quickly to avoid embarrassing him. He wasn't being hypocritical, I knew. He was just carrying the dead ideas of his fathers, as I carried mine. I felt a strong surge of sympathy for him and for his predicament.

It was all part of the complex tapestry of Ceylon: breath-taking beauty and unbearable squalor; surface and undercurrent; rich colors of flowers and the frightening impenetrable jungle; gaiety and viciousness; charm and morbidity; fire walking and superstition and astrology and rituals and the perpetual desperate struggle for survival; snakes and elephants and charmers—it was all part of the appalling, inescapable burden of being human.

Eighteen

A week before I was to return to the United States, a servant delivered a letter to me at my Colombo hotel. It was from Moss. He knew, he said, that I would be leaving shortly and he wanted to see me before I went. For reasons that he would explain when he saw me, he could not come. If I would be good enough to follow the instructions he enclosed and drive down the dirt road off the Uva highway that he described, a boy would be waiting to lead me to him.

I made the trip the following day. The road ended at the edge of the jungle, and I stopped my car in the shade of a large jak tree and got out. A Sinhalese boy in a white sarong was standing there waiting for me, as Moss had written he would be. He was about twelve, dark skinned, with small delicate features and large brown eyes. He put his palms together lightly, then turned, and I followed him down a small footpath into the jungle.

It was four o'clock in the afternoon, but already the shadows were long as we walked past banyan trees, plantains, breadfruits, and Ceylon oaks. It was not the trees themselves so much as the climbing plants that thickened the green jungle into a nearly impenetrable web. Ferns, vines, rattans, and thorn bushes wound themselves around trees and between them, choking off the undergrowth and all the available space, hanging from branches and between limbs, cluttering the ground and the trunks and the skyline. Many of these climbers were parasites that would eventually kill the trees around which they now sprawled, getting their sustenance from the trees and straddling them with fantastic strength and irresistible purpose. Across the footpath lay thick strands of climbing thorn, knobby and covered with needle-sharp thorns. The boy moved quickly and gracefully while I stumbled behind him, more and more aware of the pleasant, pervasive fragrance of cinnamon.

After a ten-minute walk we came to a clearing. There was a stone bungalow in the middle, a bamboo structure about forty feet away from it, and a thatch-roofed hut at the back of the clearing. Two white men in white sarongs, one medium-sized and slim, the other a big man with a white turban and a long blond beard, were sitting on the steps of the stone bungalow. The slim man stood up and walked towards me in his bare feet. I recognized Moss.

His face was more gaunt than when I had last seen him, his cheekbones more prominent, and his chest and arms thinner. But his handshake was firm, his voice pleasantly low, and the expression on his face tranquil. He shook hands cordially and led me to the steps, where the bearded man had risen. "You know Swami Shantinaha," he said.

Shantinaha touched his palms together and inclined his large head a little. His beard was neatly trimmed and his pale blue eyes looked at me calmly. I noticed again the small brown mole on his left temple. Suddenly I stiffened and stared fixedly at his neck, where a thick cord seemed to be bunched under his beard. He looked down, smiled, and said gently, "Of course. So sorry." Casually but firmly he unwound a cobra from around his neck and put it on the ground. The cobra undulated lazily and slithered away into the grass. I started to move forward and then stopped, one foot in mid-air. There was another cobra on the steps. Moss walked over, picked it up, carried it a few steps away, and then put it down in the grass. I followed him and Shantinaha into the house.

The central hallway had openings to four rooms. There were no doors, only pieces of cotton cloth hanging over the entranceways. We went into one of the rooms and Shantinaha motioned to me to sit down. There was no furniture in the room, and I hesitated a moment until I saw him sit on a mat, cross-legged, apparently completely comfortable. I sat down more slowly, leaning my back against the wall and stretching my feet out on the floor. Moss slid down and crossed his legs. We looked at each other silently for a moment. A large steamer trunk full of books stood in the corner, and a clean white sarong hung drying over a beam. There was nothing else in the room.

Shantinaha said something in an Oriental language, and Moss smiled. Then Shantinaha turned to me. "Forgive me," he said. "I was reminding Anthony of a famous woman, an Indian swami many centuries ago. She was once criticized for sitting with her feet pointing toward the temple, a violation of proper ritual."

"Are my feet pointing toward the temple?" I asked.

He smiled. "Yes," he said, "but the woman's reply can serve as your excuse also. She said, 'If you look long enough, you will find a temple in every direction.'"

"Thank you," I said, and drew up my knees. "Have you lived in this place long?"

"Ten or twelve years," he said. "I don't keep track of time as carefully as I used to." I noticed that neither he nor Moss had a wristwatch, and there was no clock in the room.

"So you're going back to America," Shantinaha said.

I said that after three years' absence I was very eager to get back. He waggled his head absent-mindedly, just as the Ceylonese did to express agreement. "I visited England a few years ago. Quite pleasant—for two weeks."

We were quiet for a few minutes. Shantinaha smiled genially. "I'm sure you two have many things you want to talk about. I'll see you before you go."

He was standing suddenly, effortlessly, although I had barely seen him move. Then he glided past the cloth at the entrance of the room. From the window I saw him walk into the jungle. Then I looked at Moss.

"He was a major in the British army during the war," he said. "The headquarters of the Allied Command was in Ceylon. His parents are wealthy and they keep writing, asking him to come back to England."

"Will he go?"

"I don't think so. What he wants, the outside world can't give him. There is no reason for him to go."

I stretched my legs, cramped from the unaccustomed position on the floor. "He's one man who is exercising his free will," I said, "I haven't met many. He simply decided the contemplative life was preferable and became a swami?"

Moss paused before he spoke. "Well, no, not really. I thought so, too, at first, but I was wrong. Right after the war the army kept him in Ceylon, and he brought his young bride out here to join him. She got food poisoning six months later and died. That's when he decided to leave society."

"And you?"

Moss stood up, moving easily though not quite as gracefully as the swami, and looked out of the window. "I've found an enormous amount of satisfaction here," he said. "I've found something I've been looking for all my life: myself."

"Did you have to go into the jungle to do it?" I asked gently.

"I had to go somewhere where I had real privacy. It was enormously important for me to learn what I really was, to get an insight, even if it were only for a moment, into my own personality. I wanted to recapture the freshness, the spontaneous joy in life that one has briefly as a child. It isn't naïve to feel that there can be pure joy in life, moments of exquisite delight beyond the dull and rigid routine of life."

I didn't say anything. Moss was still looking out of the window and he spoke with simple determination. "Thoreau said that a real philosopher is a man who lives his philosophy, not one who merely writes about it. There is a Hans Christian Andersen story about china-shop figures that come to life once a year. Well, most men and women never do. They're caught by society and they go through life, acting out the roles of salesmen or teachers or soldiers not because they want to but because some minor bureaucrat of a casting director assigned them the part. They wear the mask that their role requires until the mask obliterates what was once their real personality and they become mechanical men and women, forgetting that once they were buoyant, spontaneous human beings with an infinite capacity for growing. I once had a dog that growled at vacuum cleaners, movie cameras, air conditioners—all objects that made noise—because he thought they were live competitors for affection in the house. Many human beings go through life as suspicious and foolish as that dog. I found that only in solitude could I stop imitating the behavior of other individuals and do what I wanted to do."

My legs had become stiff and I rose awkwardly and stood by him at the window. The jungle surrounded the clearing, dark, perilous, and for me, impenetrable. I asked him whether it had been a long year.

"Long? Oh no. Already I can do things I never dreamed I could. Like handling the cobra, for instance. You might say there are more important things for intelligent adults to do than play with snakes. But the snakes are not the important thing. It's the power of control that's important. I've learned to do certain things with yoga—breath control, concentration, and indifference to pain. Again, these things themselves aren't important. It's the insights they help me attain, the clues to the mystery, the getting closer and closer to the deepest secrets. Nothing I had ever done gave me the kind of ecstasy—not just pleasure, but genuine ecstasy—as the slight successes I've had here."

He paused and looked at me intently, but I had the feeling that he was not seeing me. "Shantinaha walks barefoot in the jungle every day. He is not afraid, and no one bothers him. Animals, snakes, nothing. He can do many things."

"Does he perform miracles?" I asked. "The things that we keep hearing Indian yogi do, but which we never get to see?"

"I wouldn't call them miracles," Moss said. "They're not violations of natural law, only superior knowledge of it. I've seen him put a dagger through one cheek and out the other, without bleeding and without leaving a scar. I've seen him stand without moving for two days. Once I asked him about yogis who claim to perform levitation and asked whether it's possible. 'Oh yes,' he said. 'I can do it. But it takes too much out of me, and there's no reason to do it except vanity. And vanity is my biggest weakness.'"

"Can he cure?" I asked.

"Yes. He doesn't like to, but sometimes the villagers bring a sick child or an ailing old man. He touches them, and he talks a little, and usually they recover."

"There is always the chance that they might have recovered anyway."

"Of course," Moss said.

"And you?"

"I haven't been able to do any of those things, and it seems utterly unimportant. What I have already experienced is much more satisfying than anything I have ever done. It's as if I had never really been alive before. I was breathing, eating, touching, existing like an animal, without having the slightest hint of what a human being is capable of experiencing."

He spoke earnestly, but he seemed completely relaxed. "And what have you experienced?" I asked.

He shrugged, not with indifference but with futility. "It's the kind of thing you simply can't explain to someone who hasn't shared it. You're an intellectual type of person, and you're accustomed to communicating in words. But this is not an intellectual experience, and I can't begin to explain it with words. The old clichés are all I have, and they're totally inadequate. 'Ineffable bliss'? 'Intimations of immortality'? 'A glimpse beyond'? 'The peace that passeth all understanding'? These are just words. And words are only names, symbols, second-hand objects. But the experience is real, and it so far surpasses in sheer bliss ordinary physical pleasures that it's ridiculous to compare them. I haven't had 'it' often, and it's very hard to achieve. But after it everything else seems so ordinary, so gross, so limited, that none of the conventional things have much value any more."

He was wearing only a white sarong and he was barefoot. I noticed that the pale band on his wrist, where he had once worn a watch, had completely disappeared, and I remembered that there was no air-conditioned Mercedes-Benz parked at the end of the road.

"The peaks come rarely," he said slowly. "In between there is loneliness and boredom and dysentery and depression. This is not the royal road to romance."

I nodded but didn't say anything. After a while he went on.

"The Buddhist priest at the pirith was right when he told me I was playing at the surface of life. I always concerned myself with superficialities because I was afraid of life. My wealth protected me, and civilization protected me. My search for a happy land was a child's quest. Society never gave me one experience as satisfying as the knowledge that I can now control a poisonous snake. All psychoanalytic theories are less profound than the glimpses I now get of the abysmal and celestial depths of my own soul. For the first time I am personally facing life, with the dangers and the joys that entails. For the first time I am beginning to understand who I am."

I smiled, and he did too. "And this time you can't say to me, 'Who is asking you?' The answer is, *I* am asking, and no one has a greater right—or a greater need."

I looked around the room, at the box of books and the drying sarong. "Will this new knowledge of yours eventually make it easier for you to live with other people?" I asked.

"I doubt it very much," he said quietly. "It is knowledge I am getting, not character or sophistication. Living alone prepares one for living alone, not for living in society. If anything, it will probably be more difficult for me to get along with other people. Sociability requires compromise, artificiality, and respect for status. And I don't really care about any of that any more. I am trying to find out about my own life, and I just don't have the time or energy for anyone else's."

"Anyone else's?"

He nodded. "That's right. Shantinaha has been kind enough to teach me certain preliminary steps and to help me get started. But he told me at the start, and he told me again recently, that in a little while I will have to go out on my own. There are two reasons for that, he says. First, there is only one way to find the conflictless perfection I have been looking for, and that is to live alone. Secondly, Shantinaha has his own life to live, his date with destiny to keep, and he, too, wants to be alone. He has great powers, but he is short tempered and vain, and he doesn't really want anything but servants around in his personal universe. He told me that sooner or later all human relations become unsatisfactory. Selfishness or fear or boredom intrudes and spoils them. So he avoids them. Only the eternal matters to him. It does not change."

"You'll be a hermit?"

He looked out of the window, at the darkening jungle. "I'm going to try." Then he turned to face me. "I honestly don't know whether I'll make it. Perhaps I've had too much soft living already. Perhaps the air conditioning has conditioned my system forever. Perhaps it's too late. But I am going to try. I want to live alone not for the sake of eventually improving society, or hurting society, or having anything to do with society. The world is full of people who are trying to improve it. It can spare a few who want to mind their own business. I am doing this for myself. I've had enough of society. Whether I can isolate myself successfully, whether any civilized man can isolate himself, I don't know."

He paused and looked down at my shoes. "I realize," he said, "that the compensations of this life are very different from the comforts of yours. Even if this should turn out to be the best way for me, it would be a horrible way for most people. Though there are probably thousands of people in the U.S. whose temperament would make them happiest if they lived as monks, but their society discourages that solution. Most men can't face moral issues directly. It may be that I'm trying to solve the problem by running away from it. In solitude there are no moral issues. At least I won't have to be a hypocrite. In society, men face their 'inadequacies,' or what competitive society calls 'inadequacies,' in different ways. They become aggressive, or they withdraw, or they develop neuroses. But almost always they have to pretend, to themselves and to others. Here I don't have to pretend. For me, the ascetic life seems best. At least, now it seems best. It is not best for everyone. And, eventually, it may not even prove best for me. All I know is that I'm already developing certain powers; I'm already having certain insights that I had never dreamed possible."

The sound in the hall was so slight as to be almost inaudible. But I knew that Shantinaha had returned and we stepped outside to join him. He had a large dark bird in his hand, resting on his palm and looking at us placidly.

"I'll have to be going soon," I said.

Shantinaha put the bird down on the stoop. "Eat something with us before you go," he said, and called something softly toward the thatch-roofed hut. A tiny old Sinhalese woman came out and waggled her head once from side to side. She went back into the hut and I asked what the third building, the bamboo structure, was used for.

"It's a meditation hut," Shantinaha said and led us back into the room with the trunk. He and Moss sat down immediately and crossed their legs, but I waited a few minutes until the old woman came in. She gave each of us a large plantain leaf, then put a few handfuls of cooked brown rice on each leaf. We ate with our fingers.

"Nona here," Shantinaha said, pointing to the old woman, "sometimes wishes we were as devout as Myoren." I looked puzzled and Moss explained. "Myoren was a Japanese monk who had such powers that his begging bowl would go by itself collecting food while he performed his devotions."

The rice was bland but satisfying. Shantinaha licked his fingers, put the plantain leaf on the floor, and said, "Have you seen the Gunesenas lately?"

"Yes," I said. "Lakshman has started another orphan home, for girls this time. He raised a lot of money for it, and Chitra's helping run it."

"And the Burtons?"

"No one's heard from them since they left."

Shantinaha sighed. "George was always asking for a second chance. You saw what he did with it."

No one said anything for a while, then Moss asked, "Are the Chiltons still here?"

"They've gone back to England. Siri Banda has a new job in Colombo. Oh, this may surprise you. Mauvais has become a Catholic."

"It doesn't surprise me," Shantinaha said. "It was only a matter of time."

"And Piodasa?" Moss asked.

"Piodasa was tried for his part in the riots. He was found innocent. Most of the rioters were found innocent."

I stood up and left my leaf near Shantinaha's. They walked with me to the stoop where the bird was standing quietly. Shantinaha bent down and put it on his left palm.

"Do you remember the assassin-monk telling you that he was master of his own destiny?" I asked.

Shantinaha nodded.

"He was wrong," I said. "At the trial it was proved that the politician-priest persuaded him to kill the prime minister."

"Ranjini's priest?" Moss asked.

"Yes. They convinced him that he was destined to be the liberator of Ceylon and took him out for pistol practice several times before the assassination. They gave him a pill to take right after he killed the prime minister. The pill, they told him, would give him courage. Actually it was poison, but he got so excited he forgot to take it."

"I told you he was dangerous," Shantinaha said.

I stepped out into the clearing. "If Ramanathan hadn't saved his life—" I said.

Shantinaha shrugged. "If. Ramanathan saved the foolish monk. The foolish prime minister belittled the tragedy of the riots, and insisted that his deeds would bring their own rewards. The foolish monk killed the prime minister. And foolish mobs burned Ramanathan."

We paused at the edge of the clearing, and the boy who had brought me joined us. "There's one more bit of foolishness," I said. "Do you know who won the big lottery last year?"

They shook their heads. "Ramanathan's estate," I said. "Ramanathan had bought a ticket a few days before he died."

Darkness comes suddenly in Ceylon, and it came at that moment. I could see the houses in the clearing, but when I turned toward the path I saw only a dark mass. "For you it is a little late," Moss said. "Do you have a match?"

I found a box in my pocket and gave it to him. He picked up a large dry leaf from the ground and lit it. When the stalk caught fire he handed the leaf to the boy. Then he shook my hand. "The boy will lead you," he said. "Thanks for coming. Goodbye."

It took a little longer going back because the creepers and thorns in the footpath were hard to see. But I was strangely undisturbed by them, or by the unfamiliar sounds of the jungle, or by the dark. The burning stalk showed me the way, and when it burned out before we had reached the road, I did not try to light another leaf but walked on confidently.

The little car was standing at the end of the road, and the boy waited while I got into it. I switched on the lights, turned the car around, and waved goodbye. The boy was gone and I drove away, knowing that Moss's way was not my way. I was safe because I was conventional and prudent, and I had substituted the study of philosophy for the study of myself. There was no danger of my behaving as foolishly as Moss and no chance of ever learning the things he knew. I was safe, I told myself again as I drove slowly at first, then much faster, away from the black jungle toward civilization.

Pilgrims Process

BOOKS FOR READERS WHO THINK

Other books by Leonard Feinberg

The ET Visitor's Guide to the U.S.A. is an urbane, sardonic view of American culture told from the perspective of an extraterrestrial. Like Mark Twain's *A Connecticut Yankee in King Arthur's Court*, *The ET Visitor's Guide to the U.S.A.* casts a wry eye on the customs and habits of America.

Hypocrisy: Don't Leave Home Without It is an exposé of hypocrisy in all its various manifestations—educational, legal, religious, and athletic, to name just a few. According to the author, "We live in a world where it pays off for institutions and individuals to create images better than their actual condition justifies."

Where the Williwaw Blows is based on Feinberg's two-year stint (1944-45) as a naval officer on the island of Adak in the Aleutians. In this darkly humorous novel, Feinberg explores the foibles of military life while he memorializes the quiet heroism of some of the men who were stationed on one of the bleakest military outposts of World War II.

Read more about our "books for readers who think" by logging on to:

http://pilgrimsprocess.com